'Andy Robb knows what it feels like to be an awkward boy and what it means to be a man. Jamie - drunk, lovesick, lost - will win your heart, break it, and mend it all over again. I laughed, I cried. And I cried some more. This is hard to read, but ultimately punch the air redemptive. A story that will stay with me for a long time.'

Jo Nadin

For the Bid,
the Boy, the Bride
and the Bean.

Smashed is a uclanpublishing book

First published in Great Britain in 2021 by
uclanpublishing
University of Central Lancashire
Preston, PR1 2HE, UK

Text copyright © Andy Robb 2021
Cover image illustration © Shutterstock.com 2021

978-1-9129794-0-0

1 3 5 7 9 10 8 6 4 2

The right of Andy Robb is to be identified as the author of this
work respectively has been asserted in accordance with the
Copyright, Designs and Patents Act 1988.

All rights reserved. No part of this publication may be reproduced,
stored in a retrieval system, or transmitted in any form or by any means,
electronic, mechanical, photocopying, recording or otherwise,
without the prior permission of the publishers.

Set in 10/17pt Kingfisher by Toni Murtagh

A CIP catalogue record for this book is available from the British Library.

Printed and bound in Great Britain by Clays Ltd, Elcograf S.p.A.

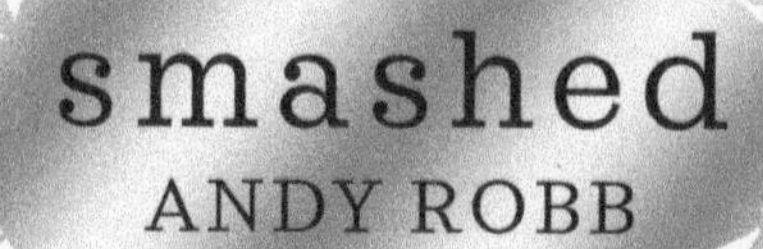

uclanpublishing

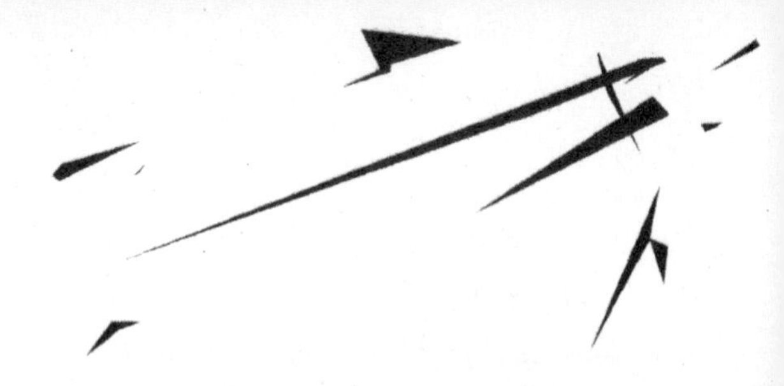

One

Even My Bacteria are Clean

Shower: I need a shower.

The fact that I showered last night is neither here nor there. When I get home after school, I'll probably have another one.

It's the bad days when I'm at my cleanest. To be honest, on those days, I'm surprised I've got any skin left. I think my record is five showers in one day.

That took some explaining.

The bad days are the days when I can't stop replaying things in my head. Things I'd really rather weren't there.

The noises from the night it all happened – The Night Everything

Went Weird. The ragged voices and the dull thud as mum hit the floor.

The next morning, the day of my mock-English exam, when I woke up to find her sobbing in a shuddering, crumpled heap on the end of my bed and dad crashed on the sofa.

The silence that swallowed everything, except for Bex's delight when she saw mum's black eye and thought it was make-up.

"Mummy, you've got a Rainbow Eye!" Her voice full of innocence and wonder and blissful, six-year-old ignorance.

The Rainbow Eye . . . Just thinking of Bex saying those words is enough for the recently installed radiator in my throat to get hot and my eyes to blur with the sting of salty tears.

Like a safe-cracker in danger of being discovered, I spin the dials on the shower, setting the exact temperature in milliseconds. The exact temperature is probably close to boiling. The fact that I'll feel like a newly cooked lobster for the next thirty minutes isn't important.

I must be the cleanest nearly-sixteen-year-old in the world. Two showers a day for the last three and a half weeks; even my bacteria are clean. I feel good in here: the shushing hiss of the water and the drum of a hundred peashooters against my skin dulls the sad chatter inside my head.

Usually, this works; I get ten minutes of shushing inside and out. Ten minutes of voluntary numbness.

Not today.

Today, just as I've finally put The Night Everything Went

Weird to one side for ten quiet minutes, Nadia decides to pay me a visit.

Not literally, not in the shower – although God knows how many times I've entertained that scenario and watched the fruits of my labours disappear down the plughole.

Don't get me wrong. If there's anyone on planet Earth who ought to be grateful they've got a girlfriend, it's me. And, for the first month of our courtship, I was *so* grateful. Prayers-of-thanks grateful. Let's be honest: beyond the obvious appendage, there's very little to recommend me as a man. There's not even the slightest hint of stubble, as though my face decided to spare me what my dad calls the Weight of Manhood. So the fact that Nadia even looked my way was something of a miracle. But something's changed between us and I don't know what it is.

For starters, Nadia is beautiful. I have absolutely no right to complain to management on that account. Hair the colour of midnight, eyes the colour of space and skin that smells like springtime, all year round.

Those things that once seemed cute and sexy like the way she laughs too long at my jokes; the flickering flames of my ego can only be fanned so much. No one's *that* funny. And the way she grabs my hand as soon as it's in grabbing distance? Two long months ago, it was like the touch of an angel. Now, it feels like some sort of restraining device.

Maybe it's me.

I've got to end it.

For the millionth time, rehearsals begin in the shower.

"Look, Nadia, I think we need to have a chat . . ."

"Hey, Nads, there's something I need to tell you . . ."

"It's not you, it's me . . ."

"Things between you and me; they're just not working . . ."

Part of me even wonders if I should tell her about what's going on between mum and dad.

No. I can't. I couldn't. That would involve tears. I don't do tears. Not with other people, anyway.

Plus, the timing's all wrong. With my birthday looming on Sunday, she's probably got me a present of some sort.

What kind of monster would I be to dump her just before my birthday?

It'll have to be next week. Monday. I'll do it Monday, after school. Honest.

Sigh. I know what I'm really doing. I'm putting it off because I haven't got the balls.

There's a bang-bang-bang on the bathroom door.

"Jay-ay-mee! Hurry up! I need the toilet!"

Becky.

For Christ's sake: can't I even plan how I'm going to ruin my life in peace?

Scrabbling at the shower controls, I reach for a towel, wrap it around my less-than-ripped waist and unbolt the door.

Even My Bacteria are Clean

My little sister runs in and, pulling her knickers down, climbs onto the toilet. She's a mass of brown curls and absent teeth, something like a cross between a piano and a poodle.

"Hello, Jamie!" she announces, bright as a button. "How are you?"

I blink twice, before smearing on the smile I rehearsed in the mirror.

"Oh, you know me, Becky," I nod. "I'm fine."

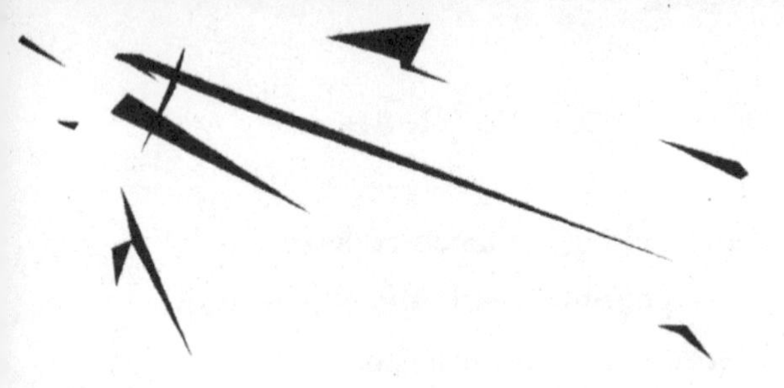

Two

Thank You, Arse.

"Toast's on the table!"

Mum does a reasonable job of making it sound as though nothing in our family, at no point, has gone mental in any way, shape or form. That everything's completely as it should be. That three and a half weeks ago, our father didn't hit her. That the pink, waxy skin around her left eye is as Nature intended it to be and that the fact that we're a man down at the breakfast table isn't anything to worry about. Becky appears to have bought into it, wholesale, smiling a sticky, strawberry smile at me. Mum boils the kettle with focussed nonchalance.

"Morning, love."

"Morning, mum. Good sleep?"

"Not too bad," she says, smiling a bit too brightly. "How about you? Were you up late? I thought I heard you."

"No," I lie, through a fake smile. "I was out like a light."

It's like me and mum are both wearing the exact same, gaily coloured masks, but we're both wearing them for the benefit of the same little person, no matter how uncomfortable. "And what about you, Bex? Did you sleep well?"

"She had a bad dream, didn't you, love?" Mum answers for her.

Becky nods forlornly; a huge, exaggerated nod, as if her neck is weakening with the strain of having to support her jam-encrusted head.

"Oh, dear," I reply, secretly envious that she's actually managed to get some sleep, even if it was plagued by nightmares. "Another one? What was it about?" I suddenly need to focus on something practical; something that'll stop me from being swamped by feelings. So, while I give Becky half my attention, I give the other half a mission: to spread the butter on my toast as carefully and as perfectly as I can. I leave half an inch around the perimeter, to prevent finger contact. My knife moves like it belongs to Van Gogh, spreading oils across a canvas.

Not the one that he cut his own ear off with. Although that might provide me with the level of distraction I need.

"Weeeelllll," she begins, obviously having told this story of woe to mum while I was busy boiling myself alive in the shower, "I had a bad dream that woke me up, but mummy was there and that made me go back to sleep."

"And what happened in the dream?" I ask, going for the jam.

"Weeeelllll, I had a dream that I was in a forest and it was very dark and I was scared, and I was shouting "Daddy, daddy!" but he wasn't there, but I could hear him, and he was far away, and he was trying to find me, but he couldn't, and it was scary, and I didn't like it."

I throw a look at mum. She catches it with a tight nod and springs into action as casually as she can.

"I explained to Becky that sometimes we dream about things that are worrying us and the best thing we can do is tell people who love us about those worries." There's an appeal in mum's voice; a call for back-up.

"That's right," I nod.

Judging by the look on her face, mum was expecting the cavalry at this point, I appear to have supplied her with little more than a pantomime horse. Smiling a quick apology, I try and dig out something more useful. Something a stand-in father figure would say.

"Are you worried about anything, Bex?"

Instead of looking at me, my little sister focusses on the toast she last took a bite from, her brow and mouth tightening a little bit.

"I miss daddy," she says, and two fat tears tumble down her soft cheeks.

Nice work, pantomime horse. That's everyone's morning ruined. What next?

Out of the corner of my eye, I see mum flinch. She puts her tea down and leaves the kitchen.

"Just going to the loo," she croaks, on her way out. I get up and go and sit on the bench, sister side, and put a clumsy arm around her: C3PO putting a leaden, metallic arm around R2D2. All it needs is an accompanying, metallic clang and the whole scenario would be complete. Just as I'm wishing I was better at this, my tone becomes thicker and clumsier, as three-week-old wounds threaten to open up.

"And daddy misses you, too."

"Mummy says he's got to do a lot of work."

So, that's the headline from today's issue of the *Family Times.* As an ace reporter for that very publication, I'm duty-bound to provide a supporting editorial piece.

"That's right and once he's finished all that work, we'll see him."

"But I wish he was here now." She buries her head in my armpit and shudders. Six years' worth of noisy, demanding child becomes suddenly small and mouse-like. I need to change this up; turn it into something else. Bring out the funnies.

A fart would be good right now. Farts are great levellers; you either snigger like you've never heard one before or you recoil in horror. I know which camp my sister belongs to and it's not the one my girlfriend's a member of.

As I quickly strain my ab-less abdomen for a residual pocket of gas, I wonder if this is the tactic I ought to employ to let Nadia go. Let her go by letting one go.

But I know my bowels like no one else; there's nothing worthy of release.

"Do you know what I worry about?" I manage, gritting my teeth for another pointless push.

Becky shakes her head in my armpit. I can feel her tears, hot through my shirt. A fart would be so very welcome.

Whatever I'm about to say next had better be as funny as anything my anus could come up with; it needs to be fart-worthy. My uneaten, pristinely painted breakfast catches my eye. I have an idea.

"Jam!" I announce.

Becky pulls herself out from under my arm and looks up, wet-eyed, but ready for a new idea.

"Jam? You worry about jam?" Her brow crinkles with confusion, but her mouth is beginning the upward journey towards a smile.

"All the time," I nod, enthusiastically, picking up a slice from my plate and ramming it into my mouth.

"But why?"

My answer is delayed as I crunch down the toast as fast as humanly possible and swill it down with gulps of trachea-torching tea.

"Watch a minute. Hang on."

Becky's head comes away from my armpit and she watches, fascinated, as I finish the first slice and then cram the second into my mouth, necking tea whenever breathing becomes unnecessary. Once the second one's gone, I pillage her plate for another slice and sluice it down with another painful glug. As my gastric geology changes, my stomach distends and the tea-sodden, tectonic plates of toast boil and roil together.

Something bubbles.

Something dark.

Something inhuman.

"Jam," I grunt, through another molten mouthful of tea, "makes you fart."

Becky laughs and then looks suspiciously at the remaining toast on her plate, as though she's just been handed a card by a magician and told it's 'completely ordinary'.

"No, it doesn't." She doesn't sound too sure.

"Oh, it does," I mutter, forcing a bubble of air that wanted to be born as a burp lower, into the more odorous recesses of my body. "Ready?"

"No!" Becky gasps, but there's a 'yes' fighting to get out.

"Get ready . . ." I concentrate my efforts into the downstairs region and feel another tentative bubble from within. Another swig of tea just might shift it.

"No!"

"Here it comes . . ."

Don't let me down, methane-filled organs.

My bowels release their gaseous payload in glorious bass tones, reverberating along the wooden bench with thunderous resonance. If you want to make your private pleasure a public joy, wood is the surface to aim for.

"There!" I announce, just in case anyone's in any doubt.

The scream of laughter that leaves Becky's lungs is almost enough to make my ear drums willingly self-detonate. It's good to hear, even if it's just to confirm that I have a gift for anal comedy – and there's not many who can make that claim.

As Becky's hysteria rises in volume, mum walks back in and I spot the tell-tale signs that she's been crying. She's trying to make it look like she wasn't.

"What are you two laughing at?" she asks, relief relaxing every line on her face.

"Nothing!" I fire a well-practiced, pointed look at my convulsing little sister.

"Jamie did a HUGE fart!" Becky howls.

"Did he?" It's hard to tell mum's fake-shock from her real-shock; by nature, I am not a casual trumper. The ones Nadia has been party to were entirely accidental.

However, in the right company and under the right circumstances, a quick toot on the trouser trumpet is a welcome addition to any emotionally charged conversation. Thank you, ladies and gentlemen, you've been a great crowd. My work is done here.

But not according to Becky.

"What are your bad dreams about?"

"Jam," I reply, scrabbling for a thread of logic to knit with. "Jam makes you fart and – you know – global warming. I have dreams where I melt ice caps with my bum. Terrible."

"What's this about jam?" Mum mock-frowns, joining the game and putting a newly brewed cuppa on the table. "Becky, you'll have to tell me all about this when Jamie's gone to school!" Her tone changes, hits Business Mode and I'm temporarily absolved from having to carry the Weight of Manhood. I'm demoted back to Teenage Son. "You'd better go, Jamie. You don't want to be late."

I glance at the clock. Yeah, I'm walking the line. If I walk it briskly, I might just pull it off.

"Give us a cuddle," mum smiles as I stand up.

We hug. There's an extra squeeze in there and a whispered 'thank you'.

I nod my understanding, grab my bag and put on my school jacket, giving the pocket a quick pat, just to be sure my phone's in there.

"See you later," I head for the door. "Try not to eat any jam, today!"

"Jam does NOT make you fart!" Becky shouts.

For once, I am blessed with a final, parting retort, which rings loud and proud in my wake.

Thank you, arse.

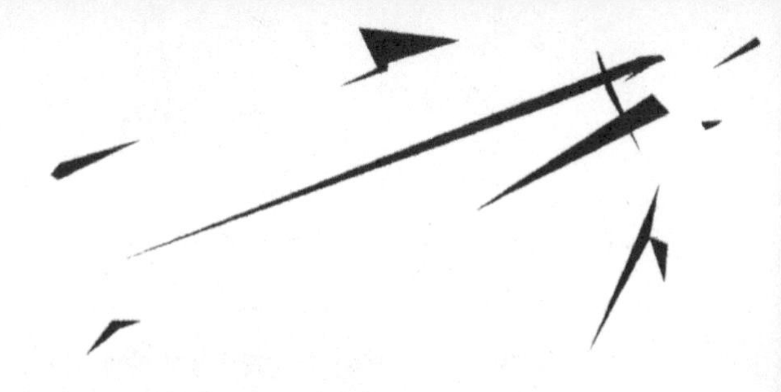

Three

Anthrax

Any relief I feel at leaving the turmoil of my home life behind me is cut short within seconds of stepping into the packed school corridor. An arm is suddenly thrust through mine, locking it tight.

"Hey!" Nadia.

"Hey, Nads." She hates being called that. Which is exactly why I call her it. However, today, rather than taking the bait and dumping me, she selfishly ignores it, smiling broadly.

"Isn't it somebody's birthday on Sunday?" she sing-songs. "Somebody's *special* birthday . . .?"

She's remembered. Of course she has. Maybe I should just call it quits, right here, right now; tell her that I'm just not ready for a relationship. Or that I need to focus on my coursework. Or that I think she could do so much better than me.

Even telling her that I'm suffering from a particularly infectious illness has a certain appeal.

I decide to go with something less likely to result in a public display of tears and leave me feeling like an abomination for the rest of my life.

"Oh, that." I shrug, half-heartedly. "Well . . . It's just a birthday, isn't it?" There's a certain, misguided hope in my voice. I'm praying there isn't a present involved. An actual present would make breaking up so much harder.

"But you know what you can do, when you're sixteen, don't you . . .?"

I am briefly caught off-guard.

"No. What can you do when you're sixteen?" What can you possibly do?

"You can play the Lottery, Jamie! You're legally allowed to gamble!"

The grip on my arm sends shooting pains into my shoulder, as her elbow grinds against mine.

I fabricate the rough approximation of a chuckle through gritted teeth.

"Good one," I nod.

"Did you think I meant something else?" I look at her. Oh my God, she actually did mean the Lottery.

"No, no of course not – "

"Got to go," Nadia is finally releasing her grip on my now

numb arm. "But I wanted to give you this."

She reaches into her book bag, pulls out an envelope and pushes it into my hands.

I stop walking.

"What is it?" I ask, dumbly.

"Open it on Sunday and you'll find out!"

I turn the envelope in my hands, experiencing similar levels of enjoyment you might expect from an arachnophobe who's just been handed a box marked 'Tarantula'. There's something in there, besides a card; I just know it. Probably something meaningful, like a hand-drawn voucher for one hundred free kisses. Or maybe a photograph of us together. What ever happened to good, old-fashioned cold and distant gifts, with no imagination or care involved? Like an Amazon Gift Card.

Or anthrax.

"Thanks."

"Happy Birthday for Sunday! Love you!"

With those two words and a parting kiss on the cheek, she reminds me what a complete and utter charlatan I am.

It's no good. Much as I might try and convince myself that this is all somehow her fault, it's not. I ought to be straight with her and just tell her what's going on at home and that's why I've been a bit weird lately. But I'm too much of a coward. I haven't got the balls. Much healthier to bottle everything up until it eventually manifests as a fatal heart attack and then I'm free of all responsibility.

As I watch her cluster with her classmates, she turns and throws me a look over her shoulder.

I can't wait for this day to be over and it hasn't even started.

Once the day ends, I've got to go back to a home that appears to have rejected any idea of normality.

What I really want is to be alone and far away from everything. Somewhere where I don't have to try and make other people happy or solve their problems. Somewhere where I don't have to pretend to be a father-figure or a boyfriend. Somewhere where I can just be me, James Chapman; nearly, but not yet sixteen.

Instead, I've got to go to physics.

Four

Adil

"Alright, Jim?"

I like Adil, because he's level. He seems to have got life sorted. Not the greatest, academically speaking, but he doesn't seem bothered. Not a star on the sports field, but so what? As long as he's got his iPhone and some new music, he seems perfectly content. Nothing seems to faze him.

"You know me," I nod, opening my physics textbook and flattening it on the desk, "just chugging on."

Adil never asks much further than that, which is part of what makes him such a good friend. Whether he suspects that there's something up or not, I don't think I'll ever know, because we only chat within our comfort zone which, in his case, is music or movies. Sliding his impossibly tall and unbelievably skinny frame into the chair next to mine, he plonks his bag in front of him and starts digging for his book.

"This bag . . . Ow!" he mutters, shaking his head and wincing as his fingers make contact with something sharp – probably a compass. "Bigger on the inside. Maybe it's a TARDIS. Maybe I could travel back in time and not take physics as a GCSE." With that, his eyes tighten up and a spasm of silent laughter travels up his spine and into his shoulders. Adil does that: he makes himself laugh at the smallest of things. Sometimes they're so small, I'm not even sure what they are but his muted mirth is always infectious.

"Maybe," I chuckle, "but maybe it'd be better to go forward into the future get the answers, come back and get an A."

"Yeah," Adil gurgles, "but, knowing my luck, I'd probably get all the answers for biology." Cue another round of wobbling laughter, causing him to stab himself with the unseen compass one more time. "Ow!" I reckon I could watch Adil all day and not get bored.

As we're respectively chuckling and wincing in pain, I notice something sticking out of the top of Adil's bag: a small, metal bar about three inches long, with what looks like the approximation of a metal hand on the end. What might be fingers are made from twisted wire; a steel zombie making a bid for freedom.

"Adil," I frown, "what's that?"

Adil looks towards the glistening claw.

"Oh, yeah," he shrugs, like he's just remembered something,

but it's not all that important. Then he gently pushes it back into his bag and zips it up, before pulling out a compass in the way you might handle a wasp.

I look at the bag and then back at him.

"Adil," I say, firmly. "What was that?"

"What was what?"

"That!" I over-enunciate the word slowly in the same way I do when I'm talking with my Nan who is a bit deaf. But only when she wants to be. At least, that's what dad says. Just to make sure I'm completely understood, I point my pen right, towards the bag and its mysterious, metallic contents.

"Oh. Just an armature."

As if that explains everything and a little bit more, Adil goes back to his bag-based excavations.

I very deliberately put my pen on my desk and stare at him. Staring at someone for about thirty seconds until they notice you does make you feel a little bit stupid, but I see it out. With the next piece of stationery that he puts in his desk, Adil eventually notices me and shrugs again.

"What?" This, of course, is followed with a shrug.

"Adil, what's an armature?"

"Oh," he replies, like he's just woken up. "Hang on."

He unzips his bag further and the adjoining sides part like a mouth.

"I don't want to take it out," he mutters. "It cost me a bit.

Some people wouldn't get it."

I peer over my desk, into this apparent treasure chest. The frame of what could be a miniature man shines back at me. It's completely metal, comprising ball and socket joints at the shoulders and hips, with odd-looking boxes around the elbows, knees, wrists and ankles. While this is a bit peculiar in itself, what really strikes me is that there's no head – just a metal bar, an elongation of the spine.

"OK," I frown, "but, what is it?" Just in case he tells me it's an armature again, I add, "what exactly is an armature?" You don't get much more specific than that. I like specific.

"Well, it's a frame. A posable frame."

"Yes, but what's it for?"

"Animation."

"CGI?"

"Stop-motion animation."

Dear God. Sometimes getting information out of Adil is like trying to push water uphill.

"Stop motion. As in *Wallace and Gromit*: that sort of thing?"

"Yeah."

"OK. So, we've established that the armature is a tool for creating pieces of stop-motion animation . . ."

"Yeah."

"So . . . why is there an armature for stop-motion animation in your bag?"

"I do stop-motion animation."

Adil and I have been friends for about two years, and I can't remember the words 'stop', 'motion' or 'animation' ever coming out of his mouth. Certainly not in the same sentence.

"What do you mean?"

"I make stop-motion animation films."

"As I suspected." It's becoming increasingly difficult to hide my levels of exasperation. "I didn't know that." I don't mean it to come out as accusingly as it does.

"No," Adil smiles, shrugging again. "It's just my thing."

We each turn to our respective pencil cases.

"Actually," Adil says suddenly, thoughtfully, "I was going to talk to you about that."

"About armatures?"

"Well, sort of." The inevitable shrug follows. "I'm entering a competition."

"A stop-motion animation competition?"

"Yeah. I need voices."

"I've certainly got one of those," I nod. "As well as the ones in my head."

The joke freefalls into an abyss, where all my other unfunny jokes gather to die in mirthless silence.

"OK."

"So, what are you thinking?"

"D'you want to come over to mine tomorrow afternoon and

do some recording? If we win, I could pay you."

"And if we don't win?"

"Well, it'll be a laugh, won't it? It'll take a bit of work. I've got six weeks to get it together and there's other stuff to do on it, if you're interested."

Saturday is normally the day that Nadia rings me up to hang out; go into town, do some homework and generally be as close to me as our atoms will allow. For six, glorious weeks, I'd have the perfect excuse not to see her. Play my cards right, and she might just save me the job of being the dumper and turn me into the dumpee! Suddenly, there is light at the end of the tunnel and, for once in my life, it doesn't appear to be a train coming straight at me.

"Yes," I say, quickly. "Yes. That'd be great. *Cool.*" Neither of us say 'cool', so I say it with as much irony as I can muster, just so that he knows I haven't started saying it in earnest. Which is cool.

Adil nods and arranges his books in a futile attempt that structuring them might further his understanding of the basic properties of matter and energy.

"OK, then. About three?"

"Three it is."

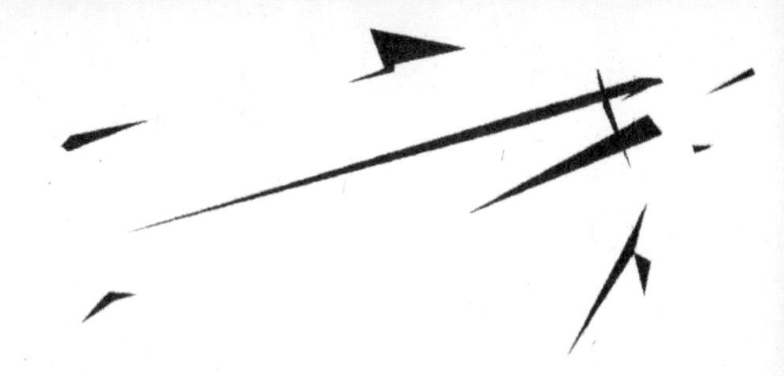

Five

Macbeth

Once upon a time, I used to enjoy English. I like writing stories and I like writing essays and, as it turns out, I also like Shakespeare – not that I fully get the language, but I get the gist of it. I even like Mrs Beattie and her fusty, old-fashioned approach to teaching.

English also happens to be the last lesson on a Friday afternoon, meaning that the weekend is mere minutes away.

It used to be my favourite lesson because, on top of all that, I could spend an entire, glorious hour sat next to Nadia.

Over the last three and a half weeks, that glorious hour has become three thousand, six hundred toe-curling seconds of sitting next to someone who I'm too cowardly to break it off with.

Smashed

I.

Count.

Every.

Single.

Second.

Today, as has been the practice for every Friday since the year started, she comes and sits next to me; always on my left and always jiggling her chair a few apparently precious millimetres closer to mine. It's as if she's trying to sit *inside* me, rather than next to me. This is swiftly followed by the blind, under-the-desk groping of her hand, as it looks for mine. Out of habit, and to prevent any oddness during the oncoming readthrough of Act Two, Scene Three of *Macbeth*, I drop my hand out of sight. I give hers the required squeeze, use my powers of necromancy to reanimate a long-dead smile, point it briefly at her and then return all appendages to the surface, ready to hold a pen or turn a page.

"Are you OK, Jamie?" Nadia murmurs, as Chris Lowe gives his Macduff, to Emily Holmes' drunken, slurring Porter.

"Yes, yes I'm fine," I rattle out a little too quickly. "Why?"

"You just sort of seem a bit distant lately."

"Do I?" I blink. I worry that I might be blinking a bit too much to appear genuine, so I try not to blink at all, which only results in my eyeballs drying out. This makes me blink more, so I pretend that I've got something in my right eye and start rubbing at the corner with my fingertip.

"Is everything OK with us?" Concern on her face, her hand fumbles once more for mine under the desk and finds it.

Talk about timing. Are we really going to do this now?

"Everything's fine," I mumble, giving her hand a brief but hopefully reassuring squeeze.

"Are you sure?" comes the forlorn reply.

"Chapman," Mrs Beattie intones, scowling slightly. "Shall we have your Thane of Cawdor?"

I nod vigorously, mentally thanking whichever god is digging me out of this particular hole.

"And as you can't seem to keep your hands off him, Miss Mahmood, perhaps you'd like to give us your Lady Macbeth."

This, of course, raises a snigger from the rest of the class and a flush of embarrassment from me. Nadia, completely unflustered, turns to the gigglers behind us and delivers a withering scowl. I am in awe of her self-possession, even more embarrassed by my lack of it and deeply irritated that Nadia's insecurities about our relationship have put me in this position, no matter how well-founded they might be.

"Chapman?"

"Yes, Miss," I cough, finding my place in the text. "Good morrow, both."

As we read, I become more and more conscious of how my voice sounds. It's not quite the sonorous velvet that I thought puberty might gift me with. The more 'thees' and 'thous' that pass my lips, the more I'm aware of quite how nasal I sound. Maybe my puberty ran out before it managed to fully transform my voice. Nadia, by comparison, sounds great. She's full of flint when the part requires it and manages to convey enough softness that when Lady M decides she's going to throw a sickie, it's utterly believable. I, however, sound like an elephant with its trunk trapped in a vice.

I get that feeling in my stomach I get when I'm somewhere high and look down.

By the time we get to the bit where Macbeth is about to ask whether everyone's ready to put on their manly readiness and hook up in the hall, my throat is impossibly dry and my heart is bumping against my ribs. I feel properly weird. My manly readiness is neither ready nor manly.

Chris Lowe sallies forth with a resolute "And so do I".

The rest of the class hits a unanimous, if slightly dispirited, "So all."

And then it's me.

I look at the page. There are a dozen words to get through.

My mouth tries. It shapes the first two, but nothing comes.

I blink madly, as the words in front of me go in and out of focus and a white noise crashes into my ears.

It all goes. Everything – the words, the classroom, Nadia – goes black and silent and I fall somewhere. As the world becomes midnight, my ears are filled with the sounds of hissing, hissing, hissing . . . "Chapman!"

"James!"

"Can you hear me?"

"Hallo? James?"

A blurry ring of faces is looking down at me. I make out Lennox, Macduff, Lady Macbeth and Mrs Beattie. Mrs Beattie's Scottish lilt cuts through the shash in my ears.

"Ah, there you are," she smiles, which is something I don't think I've ever seen before. "James, you appear to have fainted."

"Jamie?" Lady Macbeth's face is a study in concern.

Lennox appears to be giggling.

"Do you think you can sit up?" Mrs Beattie asks, reaching two arms towards me which, unfortunately affords me a glimpse of the pendulous milk tanks she keeps stuffed down her jumper. The urge to faint again isn't granted.

"Sorry," I hear myself saying. "I didn't mean to." I'm not sure whether I'm saying I didn't mean to faint or look down her top.

Hands go under my armpits and I'm hoisted into a sitting position.

"How are you feeling?" There's that touch of tartan again. Mrs Beattie.

"I think I'm OK," I mutter, seeing my feet hove into view.

"Jamie? Are you alright?" That'll be Nadia.

"I think James needs some space."

"You can say that again, Mrs Beattie. If everyone could just move back . . ."

I can feel the air clear around me as the circle of faces breaks up and previously blocked light breaks through.

"I'm OK," I say, pulling my legs towards me, ready to propel myself upright.

"Slowly, now," Mrs Beattie soothes.

The school bell shatters the burgeoning episode of *Casualty* that seems to be unfolding.

"No . . . No, I'm fine," I manage.

"I think you need to go to the school nurse."

"I'm fine, Miss," I affirm, breathing in a huge lungful of air and blowing it out.

Mrs Beattie's lips purse, probably weighing up her duties as a teacher versus her desire to get home.

"Does anyone walk your way?" she asks.

"I do!" Nadia's voice is possessed of the same level of intent you see on the news, when shoppers are trying to be the first to buy the new iPhone.

Mrs Beattie looks at us both, evaluating the situation.

"He's my boyfriend."

"OK. Off you go," Mrs Beattie mutters. "If he faints again, sit him down and call his parents." She leans forward. "Don't. Faint." I'm sure there's some humour in there somewhere, but I'm too intimidated to see it.

Nadia leads me out of the classroom, holding my arm as though a passing breeze might spirit me away.

We leave the school grounds, head through the park and make our way up Dinkley Hill. Although I'm terribly grateful for the company and the moral support, the constant questioning of whether I'm alright or not, every third step, is starting to wear thin.

"Yes!" I snap. "I'm fine." Then, realising what an ingrate I sound, I mutter the words again, this time with a bit less venom. "I'm fine."

"I'm just asking!"

"Yes, I know. I'm sorry."

Nadia loosens her grip on my arm, which is something of a relief.

"Jamie?"

"Yes?"

There's a pause. Loaded like one of those gins they use to play Russian Roulette.

"Are we OK?"

Oh, God. Here it comes. A scant twenty minutes from blessed unconsciousness and I'm being dragged into the courtroom to pass sentence on our relationship. The question is: have I got the balls to do it?

"What do you mean?"

"Well, it's just that . . . Well, lately, you've seemed a bit *distant.*

Do you know what I mean? Like you're holding me at arm's length? I might be reading things wrong, but . . ."

"No." The word bursts out of my mouth. Maybe it's the weird haze that's followed me since the faint or maybe I'm suddenly discovering my backbone. The smart money's on the haze. "Nadia . . ." I begin, suddenly feeling my heart rate go up again.

"Alright, Jim? Heard what happened in Mrs Beattie's."

By catching us up, halfway up the hill, Adil has sort of saved the day and sort of ruined it at the same time.

"Oh. Yeah," I shrug. "Just one of those things."

"Right," he shrugs back, pulling his earphones out. "Reckon you'll be good for tomorrow?"

"What's happening tomorrow?" Nadia asks.

"Jim's coming to mine to do some recording. I'm entering a competition. Stop-motion stuff."

We are nearing Handy's Sweetshop – the usual parting of the ways.

"In fact, thinking about it, I need a female voice," Adil continues, like he's solving a crossword clue. "What about you, Nadia? Would you be interested?"

Dear God! Has he lost his mind? My girlfriend-free Saturdays are now looking to be a thing of the past, before I've even got the first one under my belt! How in the name of Hell am I supposed to get anywhere near getting her to dump me without having to raise a finger, when he's inviting us both round to his place on the one night I'm supposed to be unavailable in my capacity as a boyfriend?

The way I'm feeling right now, if he wants a female voice that badly, I'd cheerfully invite him to punch me square in the balls and record whatever comes out.

"What?" I splutter.

They both turn to look at me.

"What . . ." I repeat, ". . . a great idea"

Nadia's face breaks into a smile that could redefine the word and her arm coils around my shoulders, feeling strangely like a boa constrictor.

"Yes!" she laughs, crushing me closer. "And then I could see you the day before your birthday!"

Oh God.

"Oh," Adil nods. "Your birthday's on Sunday?"

"Yes," I murmur. "On Sunday."

"OK, then. Happy Birthday. For Sunday. See you tomorrow night?"

"Reckon so," I manage from beneath Nadia's arm.

"This is going to be so much fun!" she exclaims, unaware that she's trapping the blood in mine and turning my hands into balloons.

"Nice one," Adil nods again, popping his earphones back in. "See you guys, tomorrow. About three."

He peels off down Rose Street, leaving me and Nadia staring at each other.

"Right, you," Nadia beams, suddenly yanking me in the direction of Handy's.

"Where are we going?"

"If you think I'm going to let you walk home on your own, without something to keep your strength up, then you've got another thing coming!"

I hate it when she does that mothering thing.

"Nadia: it's only five minutes from here!"

"Jamie!" she scolds me, raising an eyebrow, "you fainted in English. You could have low blood sugar. I am buying some chocolate."

"Nadia . . . really, there's no need . . ."

She will brook no argument. Opening the door and practically pushing me inside, she ups the humiliation by saying far too loudly and far too sternly, "Right! What do you want? Go on, you choose!"

Faces I dimly recognise from the school corridor turn to look at me, a row of judgemental grins. My face blooms.

"Jamie?" Nadia says again, "what do you want?"

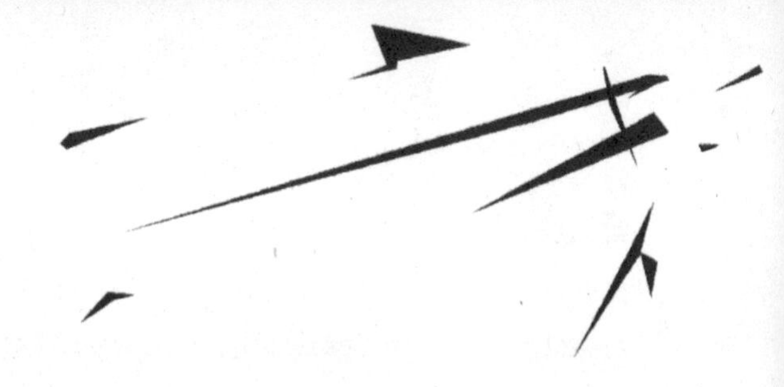

Six

Misery Mascara

It takes me a few moments to spot that something's wrong. Dad's car is on the drive, parked in front of the garage door. Not unusual in itself, but it's too early for him to be here. Ever since The Night Everything Went Weird, he's timed his daily return to coincide with everyone else going to bed. It's like being haunted by an overcautious poltergeist.

At this time of day, he should be at work, fixing boilers.

Odd.

The driver door is open and the engine's running, but there's no one sat inside.

Also odd.

The front door is also open.

The CSI investigator in my head has already joined a series of tenuous dots to create a scene worthy of the *Texas Chainsaw*

Massacre. This is then replaced with another idea: maybe there's a reconciliation in progress. Even now, my parents could be holding each other tightly, snuffling wet apologies into each other's ears.

My trudge becomes a trot and I virtually bound through the front door and into the hallway. A quick look to the left shows the lounge to be empty. No forgiving huddle; no weepy smiles.

What's going on?

"Hallo?"

Silence.

I try again.

"Hallo? Mum? Dad?"

I step into the lounge and look around. The only comfort is the lack of chalk outlines on the carpet.

"Jamie?" The kitchen door opens a crack and I see mum's face poking through.

"Mum?"

The door opens. Mum's there, wearing the now-customary shade of red around her eyes. She ought to trademark it: Misery Mascara.

"Jamie," she blurts, looking over my shoulder. "Did you see him?"

"See who? Dad?"

"Yes, your dad."

"No. I mean, his car's on the drive, but I didn't see him."

"It's Jamie!" Bex virtually runs through mum to hug my legs; an enviable beacon of ignorance. I gently rub her head while mum looks urgently at me.

"Good day, Bex?" I ask, dredging up something that might pass for a regular question.

"I got a star in English!" she chimes, looking up at me, while crushing my knees together.

"Clever girl!" I smile down at her and rub her head some more. It seems the right thing to do. Mum's face tightens and her voice follows suit, becoming urgent and fearful.

"Go and see him," she whispers. "See if he's alright."

Trepidation suddenly starts chewing at my ribs. So, I'm a Samaritan, now?

"Please?" she begs, without begging.

I nod, full of blinks and swallows.

"Just going to get my homework," I announce airily, gently pushing Bex behind the door which closes in front of my face.

I walk back through the lounge. Somewhere in the back of my head, I remember stories about people going through weird things and there's some sort of distance involved; it's like they're not really there or they're in a dream. I don't seem to have been afforded that luxury. Instead, I seem to have walked into a High Definition version of my life; an episode in which everything is much realer than it usually is.

"Dad?"

Calling up the stairs offers nothing but silence, so I go up and scour the bedrooms. I call out again as I go back downstairs. Still nothing.

Out on the drive. Dad's car chugs away, ready to go, but not going anywhere. I stop and try and think.

He's not in the road, or I would have noticed him and I'm pretty sure I would've spotted my own father, if he was sitting on the pavement. It's also highly unlikely that he's in a neighbour's house; round here, you could be living next door to Donald Trump for a decade and not know it. So, where could he be?

I turn and face the garage door and, grabbing the handle, open it. The door squeals and grinds as it opens and suddenly, I'm looking into dark space.

As my eyes adjust, I start to see the shapes I'm expecting. The makeshift workbench at the far end. Tools hanging from hooks. Handmade shelves. Toolboxes, open at the top, showing hammer handles and drill bits. A solitary lightbulb dangling from the ceiling, waiting to be lit.

The coppery tang of metal piping sticks two fingers up my nose.

Then I see it – what I'm looking for, but not expecting or wanting.

On the left-hand side of the garage, sitting on an old box, is my Dad, looking smaller than I've ever seen him. It's not that he's sat, head in hands, elbows on knees, facing the wall, in complete darkness in his garage. It's none of those things. He just looks small and, for the first time in my life, weak.

"Dad?"

In the dusty gloom, I just catch the shake of his head. I just hear the teary sniff and the shudder of breath. I've never heard that before.

"Dad?"

Without waiting for a reply, I step inside, my feet quietly crunching on forgotten screws and curls of metal and stand behind him.

"Dad?"

He shakes his head again, hunched in tight, quivering sobs.

I don't know what to do. It's too real. We've left HD and gone into some surreal form of VR where dads cry, but that's not what dads do – not in real life. They take it on the chin, shrug it off and keep going heroically forward. *That's* what dads do.

Isn't it?

My hands reach out and rest on his shoulders as I crouch behind him. I feel him flinch; not a recoil, but something similar. Something catches in his throat.

All I can do is keep my hands on him and feel his tremors run up my arms.

"I'm sorry." He whispers. "I'm so sorry."

"Dad?" I wish I had something else to offer.

"I'm sorry, Jamie," he judders, full of jagged sighs.

"What's going on, dad?"

"I tried." His voice constricts into a squeak.

"OK," I manage, feeling my own throat suddenly hot and sandblasted.

"She doesn't want me," he blurts. "She doesn't want me."

"OK."

"What am I going to do, Jamie? What am I going to do?" His hands scrape a path from his face, along the sides of his head, to the back of his neck and back again.

This is probably my cue to come out with something useful. My cue to assume my temporary position of Man of the House. To take on the Weight of Manhood. I don't feel qualified. I don't know what to do. But I've got to try something. Anything.

"What do you think you should do?"

"I don't know. I don't know."

I lean forward and wrap my insufficient arms around him. Whatever he's done, he's still my dad. So, I hold him, while he shakes and sobs and coughs and cries.

"Come on," I say, eventually, hooking him under his armpits. We both know he has to leave.

"I can't," he weeps. "I can't."

"Yes, you can," I say, softly, taking charge as gently as possible. "Come on."

His legs are unwilling at first, but find themselves and straighten.

"Don't look at me," he gasps. "Please, don't look at me."

I get it. If I didn't see it, we can both pretend it didn't happen. There weren't any tears. Not a drop.

"I won't." My words are so thick like cement.

I don't let him go. Instead, we walk towards the car like a forlorn pantomime horse, me playing the back end – forever cast as the asshole. As we approach the open door, his hands find my wrists and break my embrace. He steps away from me and climbs awkwardly into the driver seat.

"Don't look," is all I hear, before the door slams shut.

There's a moment of perfect stillness. Time freezes. Then, the car reverses out into the street, executes a three-point turn and disappears onto Duchess of Cambridge Drive.

I stand and stare, full of heat. Hot throat, hot eyes and hot blood, burning just beneath my hot skin.

Wiping my cheeks, I harrumph a few times, trying to restore factory settings. I need to look OK for mum and Bex. If there's no evidence of tears, then it never happened; that's how it works. No tears were spilt in the making of this divorce.

With clumsy fingers, I pull out my phone and turn on the camera. A quick flip of the screen and I can see the weakness written all over my face, in big, weepy letters. This isn't what men do. But I can feel the sorrow churning away inside, looking for a way out. Even my pores want to cry. So, I clamp my teeth together and hiss a breath until I can't breathe out any more.

Then a long, snotty sniff, followed by another hiss. I stretch my face and rub it with my hand, trying to erase anything that might give the game away. Swallowing hard, I cough and make a guttural growl, just to check that my voice isn't going to betray me. With a final wipe of my eyes, my face settles into place; a paper-thin mask to cover the boiling in my gut. Wallpaper over a volcano.

Once I'm sure the mask isn't going to fall off, I head into the house, shutting the front door behind me. The kitchen door is still closed. After a knock, it opens. Mum looks back at me.

"He's gone," I mutter.

"Jamie." Mum breathes whilst huggin me.

"Look, Jamie!" Bex beams as the door opens. "Here's my star!" It's gold and shiny and stuck to something that she wrote. I can't even see it. My vision starts to swim under a film of wet.

"I'm going for a shower," I rasp, already on my way to the stairs. "I need a shower."

Seven

Liquid Lullaby

While mum's upstairs reading Bex her bedtime story, I take the unusual move of sitting in the lounge. Ever since The Night Everything Went Weird, my usual routine has been to eat tea, do my homework, check mum's OK, see how Becky is and then, as soon as I hear dad click the front door, scurry, rat-like up to my room. How on Earth do you have a conversation, like nothing's happened?

"Hi, dad, how are you? Punch any relatives today?"

Tonight, the house feels different.

Instead of having the lights on, mum's lit the lounge lamps which leaves parts of the room in comforting shadow. But it's not that.

There's a peace in the house that I haven't felt for a long time. The reason – I hate to admit – is because of dad's decision not to come home, tonight. The fact that he's gone has lifted something. I like how it is, but I don't like the why behind it. I feel guilty about even noticing it.

The clock on the mantelpiece ticks like a metronome, measuring the size of my conscience, in seconds rather than inches. There's a sudden rush of anger through my chest and arms and for a split second, there's a real urge to pick it up and throw it across the room.

Mum pushes the lounge door open and sighs into the room. She's been sighing a lot lately.

"She's asleep," she says, but whether it's to me or herself, I'm not sure. Like a puppet whose strings have been cut, she just stands, gazing blankly into the space just a few inches in front of her nose.

"D'you want the telly on?" I ask, eventually.

"Not really," mum shrugs, suddenly coming to what's left of her senses. Her face changes and something is resolved. "I tell you what I do want though," she grins determinedly. "I fancy a drink."

Striding forward, she pulls open the drinks cabinet and roots around for a glass.

For a moment, a smell strokes my nose; the smell of wood that's been infused with alcohol, possibly from old spills or bottles being left open overnight. It's not unpleasant. In fact, it has a vague whiff of Christmas about it. Or good news.

Liquid Lullaby

The smell of better times.

There's the crystal-clear clink of glass on glass, then a squeaky pop as mum uncorks a bottle, followed by the tut-tut-tut of something being poured. Still standing, she takes a weighty sip, tops her glass back up and joins me on the sofa.

We both stare at the blank telly, watching it as intently as we would if there was something good on.

"What's going to happen, mum?"

Mum takes a deep breath.

"I think I want a divorce."

Her words sound strange, loud and out of place; alien words being spoken in my home.

My eyebrows knit together and break apart, as though my brain needs something to help it swallow this new, jagged thought.

"OK," I say, sounding vague and distant.

"I think it's . . ." She falters and takes another deep sip from her glass. "I think I need to think about it." There's another sip, a bit more grown-up – something between a sip and a swig. Her sip is followed by another bout of staring from both of us. We both gaze at the TV, as though it might have something intelligent to add.

"What d'you think, Jamie?" she asks, suddenly. "D'you think it's the right thing?"

My eyes meet hers and I can see she just wants someone to

tell her it's all going to be OK. She suddenly looks like Becky when she's trying to work out whether she's done something wrong and whether or not she's going to be told off.

"Are you unhappy?" I ask, not meaning to sound like a psychiatrist, but achieving it anyway.

Mum sits back in the sofa.

"Things haven't been good for a long time," she says.

"What d'you mean?"

"And this . . ." she continues, waving her hand in the general area of the Rainbow Eye ". . . it's not the first time . . ."

I look at her again, but she keeps her gaze fixed forward.

"What?"

There's another swip before she answers.

"That holiday last year. Remember?"

I do. My head presents me with a quick montage of edited highlights; dad wearing a comedy sombrero, men selling pineapple slices on the beach and Bex eating a giant ice-cream sundae. Lots of stray cats.

"Do you remember I was ill for a couple of days?"

I nod, sensing something on the horizon – something not good.

"It wasn't food poisoning, Jamie," she murmurs. "That was the first time he hit me."

Despite what they say, twenty-twenty hindsight isn't that wonderful. Suddenly, some things that I'd sort of swept under the carpet make sense; the icy atmosphere, not being able to see mum during those two days in case I caught her illness, the fact that she was wearing sunglasses in every single photograph. My brain quickly puts all the pieces together and my mouth responds with an outraged "why?"

Mum looks at me, like it's the first time she's seen me in weeks.

"Jamie," she blinks. "Oh, God. What am I doing?"

"Why did he hit you, mum?" There's a horrible, angry pressure building up inside me.

Her hand goes to my knee and she squeezes it. Maybe there's a release cap there and I'll deflate.

"We don't need to talk about this, now," she smiles, sadly.

But I can't let it go.

"You've got to tell me what's been going on, mum."

"I will, Jamie. I will, but not tonight, eh? Let's talk about something else, can we?" Her mind seems to scrabble for any available subject and comes up with, "Would you like a drink?"

I look blankly back at her.

"You're sixteen in two days, Jamie. Why don't we have a drink together? Just you and me."

The angry questions whizzing around my head seem to have hijacked my mouth, so I just nod.

Mum goes over to the cabinet, pulls out another glass and half-fills it, topping up her own in the process.

"Sherry," she says, handing me my glass. "It's all there is. Nan's favourite. Cheers.

Smashed

We clink glasses. I look down into mine, watching the amber liquid slosh its way to stillness. I've had the odd shandy before, at family dos and I've tried the tin-can taste of unpolluted beer, but fermented grape juice is a new world to me. A sweet, mellow, caramelly smell hits my nose.

"Go on," mum laughs. "It won't hurt you."

I take a sip and swish it around my mouth like Listerine. Hidden among the syrupy flavour of raisin, honey and fudge, there's a slight burn; a boozy warmth that lights up my throat as I swallow and it flows lazily into my stomach.

As soon as it's travelled south, my mouth misses it, so I sip again.

"Go steady!" Mum laughs, surprised. "You don't want to get drunk!"

I swallow, feeling the sherry warm my insides. There's the faint tickle of giddiness at the back of my head. My shoulders slowly relax. There's something else too; even with all the new and unwanted information I've just been soaking up, and all the weird feelings of missing dad and being angry at him and wishing he was here, and being glad he isn't, I don't feel angry anymore. It's like the sherry has put it to sleep; a liquid lullaby.

I feel good.

I feel normal.

I feel better than normal.

I take another sip.

Eight

A Little Odd

Saturday slinks in with all the enthusiasm of a dog that's about to have its testicles cut off and knows what's coming.

If what films have taught me is to be believed, a hangover only results after drinking a bottle of hard liquor after being dumped by the love of your life, who you'll win back eventually, but only after some deep soul-searching, a sudden epiphany and falling into the wrong arms. The hangover usually results in an aversion to light, loud noises and a throbbing headache. Luckily, all these can be rectified fairly swiftly by drinking copious amounts of black coffee.

I'm not entirely sure that two and a bit glasses of sherry on the sofa with your mum qualifies one for the Hangover Experience. Having said that, I do feel a little odd; flatter than usual and perhaps a little more angsty. There's no headache, which is a good thing, as I can't stand the taste of coffee. It would also seem that I can't stand the taste of food. I skip breakfast which, given that I don't crawl from my bed until about ten-thirty, falls more into the 'elevenses' category, than actual breakfast. In fact, it takes about five thousand episodes of Peppa Pig with Becky before my stomach signals its need for some input.

Mum, by comparison, seems fine. In fact, she seems better than fine; there's an air of lightness about her that I haven't seen since long before The Night Everything Went Weird – almost as if our sherry-powered powwow was somehow therapeutic for her.

A very specific gurgle from my empty stomach tells me that nothing seems more appealing to it than a glass of water – the bigger, the better. As I lunge gracelessly from the sofa, I can almost see it: glitteringly clear and pure. If there was a way that I could persuade a tiara of condensation to form around the rim, that would be perfect. By contrast, the only food I can consider passing my lips would be a bacon sandwich, cooked almost to the point of cremation.

I practically kick the kitchen door open, pull a glass from the cupboard and thrust it under the tap, watching the water roil and froth as it fills. I glug at it, as though I've just stepped out of the Sahara, before turning, wild-eyed, to mum, who's putting a load into the washing machine.

"Have we got any bacon?" I pant, breathless from my impatient glugging. I've got to have bacon.

"In the fridge," she grunts, wrestling with a pair of my jeans.

I'm over to the fridge in a flash, raking through half-opened packets of ham and pawing at a carton of smoked salmon. Then, with a gasp of relief, I find it. The answer to all my problems.

Pulling out three slices, I slap them under the grill, turn it on and then turn my attentions to the bread bin.

"There's no bread!" I cry, suddenly filled with an amount of fear that's not really in perspective with the situation.

"Hang on," mum mutters, pressing some buttons on the washing machine. Once it starts to grind into life, she opens the freezer door and pulls out a frozen loaf.

"Here you go," she smiles, handing it to me.

I stare at it.

"Mum, it's frozen." Just in case I'm not making myself clear, I tap it against the counter. It sounds like a piece of rock.

"Come here, you." Mum does one of those scowls that's got a smile woven into it, shot through with some very bright threads of despair. She opens the bread, knocks it against the counter to free a couple of slices, puts them in the microwave and presses a sequence of buttons. The microwave starts to hum and my slices start to irradiate.

"Have you thought about tomorrow?" she asks, returning the rest of the frozen loaf to the freezer.

"What's happening tomorrow?"

"It's your birthday, Jamie! You're sixteen!"

I'd genuinely forgotten. What with everything that's been going on, it slipped my mind.

The microwave pings and mum goes into Mum Mode, pulling out a plate and dropping the steaming slices onto it. She then turns her attention to the cutlery draw, retrieving a knife, before opening the fridge and staring into it.

"Have you thought about seeing your dad?" she asks. "Tomato sauce?"

"Yes, please. No, I hadn't really thought about it. I just . . ." I think I'd assumed that dad would be here but, somehow, I don't think that's happening anymore.

Mum locates the tomato sauce and goes to the grill to turn the bacon over. Somehow, she seems to know when it's ready to turn; it's almost supernatural. I can see the browning fat on the edges and the way it's starting to crinkle and curl.

"Well, obviously, you're going to want to see him . . ."

I hear her trying to disguise a question as a statement.

"Well, I . . . I hadn't really . . . I — "

It's not something I've ever had to consider in the past; my parents have always been there on my birthday. Their combined presence has been part of the fabric of my existence. It's just how things are.

Were.

Judging by the way mum's looking at me, the only person with the answers to this one, is me. But my decision will be the centre of a spider's web of other questions.

Is mum going to be upset if I say I want to see dad?

Is dad going to be upset if I say I don't want to see him?

How's Becky going to feel if I see dad without her there?

Part of me just wants to call it off – forget about turning sixteen – but I know that everyone'll be upset if I did that. Mum'd be upset, dad'd be upset and Bex just wouldn't understand it.

"Should I call him?" mum asks. The music in her voice has changed from that familiar, motherly sing-song to the discord of panic. She needs an answer and she needs it now.

"Should I?" she repeats.

In an instant, everything shifts. I'm no longer the child in the room; I'm the adult. I'm the one in charge of making a very important decision and I don't feel as though I've read the relevant rulebook. I'm not even sure which game I'm supposed to be playing. *Call of Duty: Family Warfare*?

"Don't worry," I smile, faking sincerity as hard as I can. "It's not a problem. I'll give him a ring and sort something out. I'll meet him somewhere. It's fine."

"Are you sure?"

The more I see the tension leave her face and shoulders, the surer I am. On the outside, at least.

"Not a problem," I nod. "It's all OK." Dear God, I'm even using words on her that she uses on me, whenever I've got a problem. I'm such a fraud.

A sudden curtain of smoke interrupts our gaze, billowing upwards from the grill, followed by angry spit from the bacon.

"The bacon!" mum splutters, reaching for a tea towel and pulling my carbonised lunch out. She flaps the tea towel, while reaching for the kitchen window. All too late, a series of piercing beeps from the lounge lets us know that the smoke detector's still in full working order.

"Oh, I'm sorry, I'm sorry, I'm sorry," she chatters, opening the window and flapping the towel. "I need a broom to turn it off!"

As she disappears, I'm left, staring through the smoke at the blackened remains of my bacon.

I'll eat it, anyway. If I throw a little extra sauce at it, I can pretend it's as it should be.

Everything's better with sauce.

Nine

Nadia

Walking to Adil's takes me through town and, for ten glorious minutes, my life is perfectly fine and everything's alright. Until something unwelcome hauls its way along my synapses.

Nadia. What am I going to do about Nadia?

Shaking my head, I try and bury the sudden fizz of emotion under a deadweight of logic. I need to think this through.

The problem is Nadia and, at the same time, it isn't. She has this habit of dispensing advice, like an overenthusiastic vending machine. Sometimes to the point where I don't feel like I'm running my own life. It's caused the odd argument in the past and, sometimes, I've felt like walking away. Something's always stopped me. Love? Loyalty? An inability to deal with the emotional fallout? I don't know. All I do know is that right now, with the wreckage of my life burning all around me, I don't need her questions and answers rolling around my overstuffed head. I need to step up and take control; although, to be honest, all I really want to do is hide and melt into a pointless puddle of tears.

But that's not what men do.

So I've got to let her go.

Thanks, Logic. Thanks for helping me ruin my life.

I can't see any other way.

The next question is: when? Swiftly followed by: how?

My phone pings. Nadia. The inevitability of it makes me suddenly weary.

Hi Gorgeous. Might be late to Adil's so don't worry if I'm not there when you arrive. xxx

Oh, God. It's almost as if she knows when I'm thinking about her, like she's got inside my mind. Like one of those wasps that lays eggs inside an ant, before the larva eats its way out through the ant's head.

The mere thought of dumping Nadia fills me with the kind of dread that seems to cause my body temperature to physically drop. Everyone else is out in t-shirts, with patches of sweat darkening the material, while I feel like I could do with an extra layer and a hot water bottle. I wish someone else would make the decision for me; just take it off my hands.

I start rehearsing lines again, trying to find the best way to terminate Nadia, without sounding too clichéd or patronising. Life has other ideas. My phone rings.

It's dad.

I stop and stare at my phone, as though I've never seen one before.

Do I answer it? Is he going to do something stupid if I don't? He didn't look too together when I heaved him into his car yesterday. What's he going to say?

My natural fear of authority kicks in and I take the call.

"Hallo?" I don't know why I'm saying that. I know it's him.

"Jamie. It's dad." I don't know why he's saying that. He knows I know it's him.

"Hi dad. How's it going?" My face knots up. Could I ask anything more stupid?

"How's your mum?"

"She's . . ." I'm not sure what to say. Suddenly I'm on the back foot. For some reason, I don't really want to tell him how she is; he doesn't need to know. How she is, is up to her to tell him. Not me. But he wants an answer of some sort.

"She's out." I lie, but it's a deflective lie. It's a lie that shields what's left of my family. I am the last line of defence: a laughable Luke Skywalker.

"Where's she gone?"

Again, I don't want him to know. I feel bad for lying to my

dad, but I feel a sudden, overwhelming need to make sure that mum's OK. To protect her. I need to say something else; something . . . just something else.

"I'm just off to Adil's." It's all I've got and my face twists up once more.

"OK." Never have two letters sounded so disappointed. "Well . . . look . . . tomorrow's your birthday . . ."

"Yes. Yes, it is."

". . . and I'd love to see you . . ."

Oh God. I pray there's a 'but' attached to his next sentence.

". . . but . . ."

I clench my fist in a fist-pump. I don't do fist-pumps, so it's not fully realised. I look like I'm a kid in nursery, pretending to be a train driver.

". . . given the way things are, I think it might be a good idea if I wasn't around tomorrow . . ."

"OK."

"But you know I'd love to see you, don't you? You know I'd be there if I could?"

The desperation in his voice hits my stomach like a heat-seeking missile and quietly detonates.

"Sure," I manage, "but I think you're right." Suddenly I'm taking charge again; making decisions for the people who – if I remember the small print in the Parent Contract – are supposed to be making them for me.

"Yeah," dad mutters and I can hear the bitterness that he doesn't even try to disguise. "But," he continues, "I was thinking . . . Look, I thought I might see you on Monday, give you your present and that."

"Sure," I say, nodding as if he can see me. "OK."

"I also think I need to talk to your mum."

"Riiiiiight . . ."

"I need a chance, Jamie. I know I've got a lot of explaining to do, but phones just don't work for this sort of thing. I need to see her face-to-face."

"Dad, I'm not sure she wants to see you like that." There it is again: role reversal.

"I know, I know . . . But, maybe if you could be there?" The question hangs like a corpse.

Logic. I call upon the Powers of Logic to help me now.

"I'll be at school." There's logic for you.

"Maybe you could pull a sickie? I could write you a note? Our family has got to be more important than French or whatever you've got on a Monday afternoon . . .?"

I don't know what to say and nothing comes out of my mouth,

"Think about it, eh? See what your mum thinks and get back to me. Message me or something."

"OK," I swallow. "I'll see what mum thinks."

"Thanks, Jamie. This means a lot, son, it really does."

"OK."

"Drop me a line tomorrow, OK?"

"OK."

"And Happy Birthday, son. Happy Birthday for tomorrow."

"Thanks." I mumble. "Thanks, dad."

"OK. Well, then. 'Bye. Love you."

"Love you, too." The words fall out of my mouth and I hate myself for the way they sound so hollow.

"Bye."

"Bye."

The phone goes back in my pocket and I stand for a moment or two, inert and unmoving. I'm another lamppost in the town centre, just another obstacle for people to get around. All I need is for a passing dog to pee up my leg and I might as well accept the job and stay here for the rest of my life.

I am, at least, spared that indignity and, without any conscious thought about where I'm going, my legs start to do what legs are supposed to and I start heading in the direction of Adil's house.

I don't really feel like I'm here; I don't really feel like I'm anywhere. Even though there are people all around me, going about their business, I don't feel part of the landscape. I feel entirely disconnected from everything and everyone, as if it's all part of a film I'm watching. Or I'm in the film and everyone else is watching. Either way, this movie's short on laughs.

It takes me a further fifteen minutes to get to Adil's place. It ought to have taken me less than ten, but I seem to have been walking through a fog that only I can see. A quick shake of the head to try and clear it and I knock on the front door.

His mum answers, with her customary smile.

"Oh, hello, James. How are you?"

"I'm fine, thanks, Mrs Khan." My face returns the smile with an even bigger version. The bigger the smile, the less people are inclined to interrogate. "Adil said I could come 'round. I'm helping him with his film thing."

"Of course, of course," Mrs Khan nods. "Would you like a drink? A cup of tea? A cold drink?"

"I'd love a cold drink, please, Mrs Khan."

"I'll just get it."

As Adil's mum goes to the kitchen, I'm struck by the sounds of his house. It sounds like a home. There's the sloop of water from the tap, probably diluting Ribena. There's the sound of the TV from the front room, blurred by the idle chatter of the radio in the kitchen. There's the sound of that creaking floorboard in the hallway as Mrs Khan returns, bearing a glass of pale, pink liquid. And I know that, in a minute, there'll be the sound of Mr Khan, calling from the lounge.

"Alright, Jamie?" Right on cue.

"Yes, thanks, Mr Khan!"

"You know you can call me Sid!"

"Yes, Mr Khan!"

We've been doing this little routine for at least two years. I think he likes it. He treats me like an equal but I tip my hat, without having to wear one. It's a respect thing. There's a tinkling giggle from Mrs Khan; giggling at our stupid man-talk. I wish my house sounded like this one. It used to.

"Jamie?" I think I must've disappeared into my thoughts but Mrs Khan's voice brings me back. "Here you are." She hands me the drink. "Up you go. They're waiting for you."

"Thanks, Mrs Khan."

As I near the landing, a delayed response gnaws its way from my ears to my distracted brain. 'They're' waiting for me – that's what Mrs Khan said. That can only mean one thing: Nadia's here ahead of me. My pace slows.

I turn right at the top and walk along the landing to Adil's room. As I get closer, I can hear the unmistakeable trill of Nadia's laughter, just audible over the bass thumps of whatever music Adil's playing. That cold thing happens to my body again and my heart rate doubles.

It's no good; I've got to do it today.

I knock on the door and walk in. Two smiling faces look back at me.

"Hey, Jim," Adil grins, drawing himself up to his full height and chuckling for no reason at all. "Ready to make a movie?"

"This is going to be so exciting!" Nadia laughs, perched on the end of his bed.

"Yes," I swallow. "Yes, it is. What are you doing here? I thought you were going to be late."

"Well don't sound too pleased to see me!" she replies, in mock-outrage. "I was running behind time but mum gave me a lift."

"Great," I nod, unenthusiastically. "That's . . . great."

"It means we can spend more time together!" Nadia announces, leaping up, grabbing my hands and planting a kiss on my cheek. A kiss that burns like fire and might signal the implantation of skull-shattering larvae.

Unconsciously, I rub my forehead.

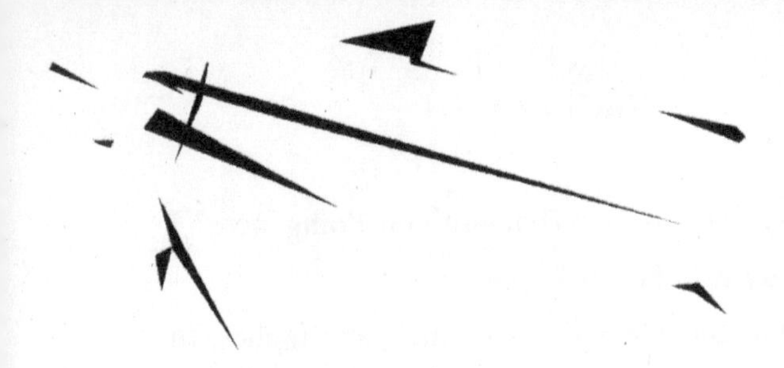

Ten

Falling Apart

". . . and this is Craig: your character."

I'm looking at the set, which Adil has built. It really is quite incredible. Perched on top of a small table, it's a miniature reconstruction of the front room in someone's house. There's a window, a sofa, a telly, a cabinet, carpet and even little framed pictures on the wall. Two figures stand, lifeless, staring at us through the missing fourth wall, facing Adil's tripod-mounted camera. He's even created lighting, using a well-aimed desk lamp and torches.

"This is amazing," I murmur, slightly awestruck at my friend's hidden abilities.

Adil shrugs automatically, but the crinkle around his eyes suggests that he's pleased at my reaction.

"Can I touch them?" I ask, looking at the figurines.

"Yeah, sure," he answers, shrugging again. "You've got to be a bit careful with the hands and face, though. It's only plasticine. Took me forever to get them right." His hand closes gently around Craig's body and he hands him carefully to me.

"It's heavy," I say, gently weighing Craig.

"That's the armature," Adil nods. "That metal thing you saw in my bag. That's what's under all the plasticine and fabric."

It really is quite brilliant. I'm holding a blonde boy wearing glasses and dressed in blue jeans and a white shirt. The features – rendered in modelling clay – are quite cartoony but packed with detail; the colour of his eyes to the mass of thin, plasticine sausages that make his hair.

"He's even got shoelaces!"

"My mum helped with the clothes," Adil shrugs.

"Can I see mine?" Nadia asks.

With a deftness that seems out of place with his size and huge hands, Adil reaches over to the set, plucks up the other figure and delivers it to Nadia, with a level of tenderness usually reserved for newborn babies.

"That's Eesha," he adds, Nadia delicately turn the figure in her hands. It's a girl and – judging by the name and the fact that he's used brown plasticine for her skin – I'm assuming an Asian girl, wearing jeans, trainers and a t-shirt. Much as I don't want to get too close to Nadia, I find myself craning over her shoulder, just to get a closer look at these modelling-clay marvels.

Nadia throws me a quick, coy look and I splutter a smile, before sitting back down on the end of Adil's bed.

"So let me get this right," I babble, trying to pretend I hadn't noticed Nadia's flashing eyes, "Eesha – played by Nadia – has created a chemical solution that can bring people back from the dead."

"And Craig – played by you – drinks it, just before he's hit by a car," Adil nods.

"As long as we're working within the realms of credibility."

"Oh, Jamie," Nadia groans, rolling her eyes back in her head so hard I'm surprised she doesn't put her back out, "why d'you have to be so negative?"

"I'm not! It was a joke!"

"Well it wasn't funny! Look at all the work Adil's put into this!"

I might be onto something here. Maybe a run of caustic negativity might finally drive her to the end of her tether, but I don't want to run Adil's project into the ground for my own nefarious doings, so I apologise.

"It's cool," Adil grins. "Wait 'til you hear what happens next!"

"What happens?" Nadia asks, all goggle-eyed enthusiasm.

"So, Craig's drunk the potion and Eesha tries to tell him about it, but Craig doesn't want to listen to her because he hates her."

"Why does he hate her?" Could it be because she's injecting her larva into his head?

"Because he's a racist."

"What? So I'm a racist, now?"

"No, Jim, Craig is. He's a racist, but he works out that he needs Eesha's help to find an antidote to the potion he's drunk."

"But doesn't that mean he'll die? Does he want to?" I have sudden sympathy for my plasticine alter ego's potentially suicidal tendencies.

"No," Adil laughs, "the potion only works for a week. His body still decomposes, so he starts to fall apart and Eesha tries to find a way of reversing the process and making him live."

"So I'm a racist zombie?"

Adil laughs again.

"The thing is, Craig's got to hang out with Eesha to find the cure and while he's hanging out with her, he learns about her and she learns about him and they sort of understand more about each other before he dies. The competition set the theme, which is 'peeling away the layers', so I thought . . ."

"So, I do die?"

"Yeah, but not until right at the end. You see, Eesha's in love with another boy . . ."

"Aw," Nadia interrupts, "can't she be in love with Craig?" Just to hammer the point home, much like Van Helsing hammered stakes into helpless vampires, she turns and theatrically flutters her eyelashes at me.

"Sorry," Adil shrugs, "but the thing is, right at the end,

Craig saves Eesha's boyfriend from a burning building, even though he knows it'll kill him. So, he dies a hero and he's learned that you can't judge people by their race or culture. It's a sort of happy ending. It's supposed to be an analogy; the more he learns about Eesha, the more his layers are stripped away, until the good guy inside him is revealed. Peeling away the layers."

"I think it's brilliant," Nadia breathes. "Well done you!"

"That's easy for you to say," I grumble, "you're not playing a rotting Nazi."

"But it's not you, is it?" Adil shrugs. "It's what Craig says. I just thought your voice would sound good."

"But don't you want something a bit more thuggy? I sound like I'm talking through a hosepipe."

"I like your voice," Nadia frowns.

"What I don't want," Adil says slowly, thinking it through, "is something too obvious. You know that kid in Mr James' class, that psycho kid – what's his name?"

"Nathan something," Nadia chips in.

"Douglas." I've made something of a career out of staying out of his way.

"Nathan Douglas," Adil nods. "Well, he sounds like a thug, the way he talks, and it'd be way too obvious. I don't think everyone would get it; they'd think that it's only about 'thug' thugs, if you know what I mean? But there's more to racism than thugs; it's everywhere and sometimes you get it from the people that you really don't expect it from. So, that's what I want: a voice that you wouldn't necessarily associate with racist things."

Suddenly, both sets of eyes are on me, waiting for me to make my decision.

"OK," I sigh. "I'll be your putrefying bigot." Not a sentence I've ever said before and one, I suspect, I'm unlikely to ever say again.

"Yay!" Nadia claps her hands together above her head, like she's suddenly become part of a gospel choir.

"Thanks, mate," Adil beams. "I knew you would. I mean I'd do it myself, but I sound too Asian." Then, just for good measure, he finishes the sentence with "innit?" before dissolving into muted giggles. "OK," he says, when he finally stops shaking, "I think the best thing is if we read it through, just to hear it out loud and I can maybe give you some pointers on how I want it to sound."

He hands us some printed sides of A4, neatly stapled at one corner. I read the title.

"Falling Apart," I say out loud,

"Yeah, Do, you like it?"

I read the two words again.

"Makes sense to me."

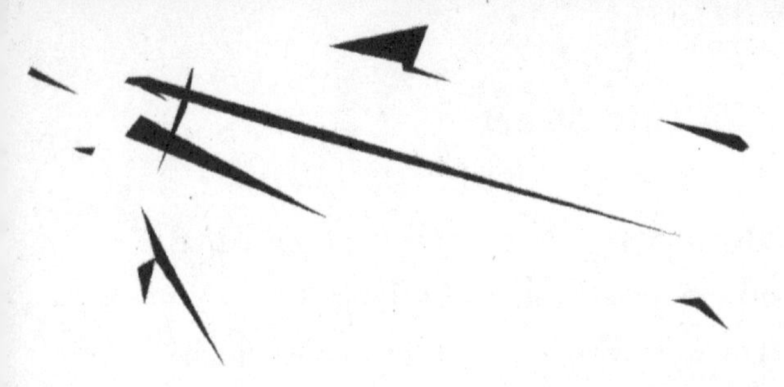

Eleven

Bleeding the Truth

"That was a-MAY-zing!" Nadia squeals when we're a safe enough distance from Adil's house that she can unleash her inner firework display. "I mean, look at the time!" she gasps, pulling out her phone. "Four and a half hours we were there! Four and a half hours! That didn't feel like four and a half hours to me! Did it to you?"

"No," I mumble, feeling quietly horrendous about the fact that we appear to be walking arm-in-arm. "No, it didn't." The urge to say that it felt more like four and a half years is almost primal.

"It's brilliant – what he's written! Just brilliant! SO funny! I couldn't stop laughing at that bit where Craig's nose falls off!"

"Yes," I nod, weakly. "It's very . . . witty."

"And that bit where Eesha has to make him a false arm! That was HIL-arious! That bit where his intestines fall out – ewww!" As if there's too much energy inside her for her body to deal with, she suddenly breaks away from me, in some sort of huge skip, turning to face me and walking backwards, a manic, fevered look on her face.

"And the end!" she declares, her arms flinging themselves apart. "Oh, the end! How sad is that? But it's beautiful too! I had no idea Adil could come up with stuff like that! The models! The set! It's incredible!"

"Mm," I blink. "He's very talented."

The excitement quickly drains from Nadia's face, no doubt prompted by my apparent lack of enthusiasm. Continuing to walk backwards, she puts her hands on my shoulders, looking at me, dead in the eyes; almost as if she's searching for something – probably answers. Answers that I really don't want to give.

"You were brilliant, too," she says, really quite intensely. "Really good. Just the way you said some of those lines was fantastic. It just wouldn't work if it wasn't you playing Craig. You're really good." As she says 'really' her hands give my shoulders a squeeze. For a second, I see an image of a hawk ripping a mouse from the ground, clutching the doomed rodent in its powerful talons.

"Thank you," I manage.

The hands leave my shoulders and one sits square on my chest. Nadia stops and the laws of physics dictate that I have to do the same.

"OK, Jamie," she frowns. "What's going on? Why are you being so weird?"

Oh, God. Is this really going to happen? Here? In the middle of town?

"I'm not being weird," I protest, but I can feel the atmosphere between us change, the way you can feel the air get heavy just before a storm. Everything's the same but seems that tiny bit different.

"Oh, come on, Jamie! I know you better than that! You've been acting weird for the last few weeks!"

"No, I haven't!" I'm desperately trying to steer away from the direction in which this conversation is going. I haven't got the guts. She gave me a present. She's a good person. She's nice. I'm not. I'm the Destroyer of Dreams, the Breaker of Hearts, the Slayer of Hope.

I'm an arsehole.

"Jamie." Nadia's voice drops, her tone all business and no messing. "It's like you're not really here half the time. We don't talk about anything anymore. You just seem – I don't know – unhappy. Even at Adil's you didn't seem like you were enjoying yourself. You don't even seem to want to be near me, these days. You don't hold my hand. You don't want to walk with me.

You don't want a cuddle. How long is it since we actually kissed? I'm not stupid, Jamie. Something's going on and it's time you told me what it is."

She drops her hand from my chest and stares at me. Unable to meet the flint in her eyes, mine drop to the pavement, drawn to the cracks in the slabs. I wouldn't say they're endlessly fascinating, but they're far easier to look at.

"Jamie."

I can't answer her. Although I know what it is I've got to do, the thought of doing it makes me feel faint.

"Jamie." Her voice is insistent now, stained with frustration.

My eyes are locked on the cracks in the pavement, almost as if they're my escape route; the portal to a world where you don't dump your girlfriend because Everything Went Weird at home.

"It's . . ." The sound of my mouth forming vowels and consonants surprises me and I cut it short. My eyes close .

"It's what, Jamie? What is it?" The frustration has gone, now replaced with the cool, killing comfort of concern.

My eyes remain closed and I shake my head. I can't do this. I need to make something up and put this to bed. Or into a coma. I take a deep breath.

"It's . . ." The same word again. It's all my mouth will manage. Sagging slightly, I give up. If I have to spend the whole night standing here with my eyes shut, I'll do it. Hopefully she'll get tired and go home long before I manage to finish the rest of the sentence.

"What's wrong, Jamie?" Suddenly, her hands are on my cheeks, cupping my face. I open my eyes and look into hers. They're searching me, trying to seek out whatever it is that ails me. "You know you can tell me, don't you? Whatever it is, I'll be there for you. I'll help. I love you, remember?" Her eyes soften and her lids start to close. Her lips part, ever so slightly, and pucker, just a touch. Her hands gently pull my head towards hers.

"I think we should finish."

Nadia reels back, as though she's been punched. Her hands drop from my face, to clench and unclench at waist level. Those eyes which, seconds ago, were dewy with love and care, are now wet with confusion, pain and anger.

"What?" Nadia gasps. "What do you mean?"

"I think we should finish."

There's a fragile silence, so I break it with a series of dictionary definitions.

"Split up. Unfriend. Stop seeing each other. Consciously uncouple."

"Why?" Her voice is barely more than a whisper.

Unfortunately for both of us, this is the one part of this conversation I hadn't rehearsed. All those hours in the shower, slowly poaching myself to death, only took me as far as annulling our relationship. The reasons I would inevitably have to give were never fully investigated.

"Because you're so happy," I blurt.

"What? What d'you mean I'm happy?"

"Wrong word," I scowl, trying to give my head precious seconds to come up with something worth saying. "Optimistic. Naïve. That's the word: naïve. You're so naïve." I pause, before saying it again, with a swear word involved, just make it seem more credible. "You're so bloody naïve!"

"About what, exactly?"

The fingerholds on this particular conversational cliff face are starting to crumble.

"About everything!" I yell, not meaning to, but doing it anyway. "Just . . . everything! Everything's fine for you! You just go around in this happy cloud, like you've just walked out of a Disney film or something!"

"And what's wrong with that? What's wrong with being happy?"

Oh God. There are tears running down her cheeks. Only two; I count them. Two more nails in the coffin I'm apparently building for myself.

"It's just weird!" I retort. "It doesn't make sense! Life isn't always happy! Life's really bad sometimes!"

"What is it, Jamie? What's wrong? Something's wrong! I know it is!"

This isn't going well. Somewhere, my mouth is blending the truth with lies. If I'm not careful, she'll ask the right question and I'll become a ruined, blubbering wreck. I can't afford to do that. If I fall apart, I don't think there'll be any chance of being put back together again. Mum needs me to be OK. Becky needs me to be OK. Dad needs me to be OK. I need to be a man about this. It has to be ended swiftly and, for her sake, without mercy.

"It's like I'm going out with a limpet!" I splutter, madly. "You always want to be near me, you always want to be touching me! I feel like I can't breathe without you wanting to share the same air! I feel like I can't hang out with anyone else because you'll want to be there! We're not boyfriend and girlfriend, Nadia! We're more like conjoined twins!"

We each retreat into our own, private, sponsored silences. I pant and Nadia blinks.

Finally, she nods. A sort of broken nod – jagged and staccato.

"Fuck you, Jamie Chapman."

"What?"

"You heard me: FUCK. YOU. If you want to break up with me, that's fine: break up with me. But — " She steps forwards, close – kissing-distance close and jabs a taut finger in my face. "DON'T. Ever. Lie to me." She steps back, suddenly afire with hurt and anger. Her mouth trembles as she speaks and her arms shudder with rage. "You've forgotten one thing, Jamie Chapman, one thing!" She's back again, jabbing that finger.

"I know you! I KNOW you! And I know when you're lying! And, you know what? Right now, I don't care what it is!" A bitter laugh bursts out of her as she steps back again. "I don't! I don't care!" Then, she's back in my face all over again. "But let me tell you this, if it's worth our relationship, if it's worth three months of our lives together – three months! – then good, because I don't want to be with you either!"

Her arms suddenly wrap around her shoulders as she turns her back on me and walks determinedly in the opposite direction.

I did it.

There's no feeling of triumph or joy or celebration, just emptiness and self-loathing.

I don't know what's wrong or right anymore. All I know is that I've dumped my first – and probably only – girlfriend. As the full weight of this realisation drops into my brain, my legs go weak and a rush of blood makes me giddy.

Suddenly, I'm leaning over someone's garden wall, purple pieces of my Ribena-stained bacon sandwich splattering onto their roses.

I need to go home.

Home is where the heartache is.

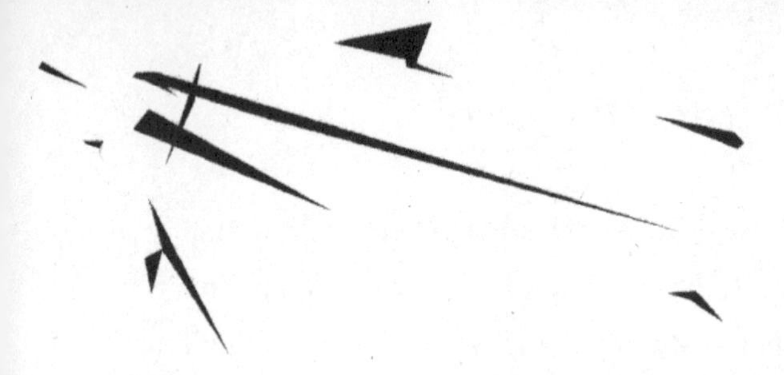

Twelve

Just the One

"Are you alright, love? You look like a ghost!"

"Oh, yes," I lie, blithely, sitting next to mum, on the sofa. "Fantastic. All good here. Where's Becky?"

"In bed. She was tired and got a bit teary."

"What about?"

"Nothing, really. She just got all worked up about doing her spellings. I think it's probably everything that's going on. She needed a good cry."

Mum's tone tightens as she speaks, and she reaches over the arm of her side of the sofa and retrieves a glass. It's a wine glass.

Something happens in my head, as I see her take a sip. Something very subtle, so subtle, in fact, that I barely notice it. A message travels to a major centre in my brain. The message is faint, but insistent and it takes a moment or two before it's decoded into a fully-formed thought.

I want a glass of that wine.

Just one. Just something to blunt the jagged edges of guilt that scrape at my conscience. Just something to fill the Nadia-shaped hole, no matter how temporarily. Something to repair the cracks.

I want a glass of wine.

I think – after last night's sherry-shenanigans – that particular avenue will remain corked. I'll have to live with the ghost of Nadia's hurt and the spectre of dad's request rolling around the space inside my head. At this moment in time, it seems like a very small, tight space indeed.

I don't want to tell mum about Nadia – she doesn't need to worry about that on top of everything else – but what am I going to tell dad if I don't tell mum about the conversation I had with him? He's going to expect an answer.

"Actually, there was something. Something did happen that I need to talk to you about."

"What is it, Jamie?"

I seem to be hearing that question a lot lately.

"It's a bit . . . difficult," I mumble. Already I feel as though I'm about to add that final strand of straw to a camel that's suffering from emotional osteoporosis.

"Well? What is it?" Her tone drops suddenly as the realisation of what it probably is takes root. "Is it your dad?"

So far, I'm not doing a very good job of protecting her,

just like I didn't The Night Everything Went Weird. Unlike then, right now, I'm wide awake and I need to step it up, and accept the full Weight of Manhood. The guy who was supposed to be doing it has dropped the ball.

"Yeah, it's dad. He rang me today, while I was in town."

"OK . . ."

"Yeah. He's not coming round tomorrow. On my birthday."

Suddenly mum shifts closer to me, an arm around my shoulders, pulling me against her. I can smell the wine on her breath. I really want a glass of wine now.

"Oh, sweetheart," she says gently. "Are you OK with that? Is that OK?"

"Of course I am," I say. "It's fine. Absolutely fine."

Mum's eyes lock on mine, full of sadness. Just like Nadia's were. To batten down the hatches on any genuine emotions that might seep out, I put on a smile. This one's diluted, weak and watery. It's not meant to be, but I seem to have run out of anything more concentrated.

"It's fine," I say, again.

Mum squeezes my shoulder before standing up, clutching her glass of wine to her chest and pacing backwards and forwards in front of me. Behind her, I can see the closed doors of the drinks cabinet.

"Oh, Jamie," mum breathes. "I'm so sorry about this. About all of it."

"Well, it's not as if it's your fault, is it?" I frown. "It's not as if you punched yourself."

At the word 'punched', she blinks hard and the glass in her hand goes to her lips. With one large swip, she half-drains it.

"Oh, God," she half-whispers and goes to the cabinet and opens the door.

"Do you want one, Jamie?" she asks over the tut-tut-tutting of red wine being poured.

I have never wanted anything more at any point in my existence.

"Yeah, why not?" It's a good reply – nonchalant and airy – but just to try and justify it to her a little bit more, I add, "It is my birthday tomorrow."

Another glass is retrieved, and the tut-tut-tutting happens all over again. It's a beautiful, comforting noise, promising that relief from reality is just seconds away.

"Just the one," mum says, handing me my glass which, I notice, isn't quite as full as the ones she poured me last night. "Don't want it turning into a habit."

"God, no," I agree, before taking a sip. This isn't a habit. This is medicinal. This is like first aid for the soul.

"Was there anything else? Did he say anything else?" Asking the same question twice in one sentence is mum's way of trying – but failing – to hide her worry.

"Yes," I say, gently, before taking a bolstering swip from my glass. Whatever we're drinking isn't sweet like the sherry was. By comparison, I can almost feel it absorbing all the moisture in my mouth, soaking up any leftover saliva, to blend it with something that tastes a bit like old cherries left to sit in tea. It's like cranberry juice with attitude. Somewhere in the distance, I can already feel the alcohol nuzzling at the back of my mind, gently massaging out all the knots. I still know that the next bit of information is going to be the bit she doesn't want to hear. I inhale deeply and then push the words out as fast as I can.

"He wants to come here on Monday and talk to you."

"Oh God," she says again, sitting back beside me on the sofa. "Oh God."

I give her a moment.

"I just don't know," she breathes. "I just don't know if I can do it. I know we probably need to talk, but I just don't know if I can be in a room with him." Her face twists and her eyes are suddenly shining with tears that she doesn't want to allow. Her hand grasps mine. "I'm scared of him, Jamie. I know it's probably not something you want to hear about your dad but he scares me."

Mum's hand tightens, so I squeeze it back, just to let her know that I'm here; to let her know that I can help. I swip again and feel the wine do its work, gently removing me from reality, making me distant. Here in body but without any connection to whatever might pass for my soul.

"If I'm here, nothing's going to happen," I say, evenly, suddenly sure of myself. "I can make sure of that."

"D'you think so? Really?"

It's as if all the self-belief I've ever wanted to have is suddenly given an access-all-areas backstage pass. With my insecurities dulled by the magical properties of – according to the label – Cabernet Sauvignon, the dam of self-doubt breaks and my long-withheld reservoirs of confidence and incisive thought break free to rush through my veins.

I'm sixteen tomorrow, which practically makes me a man.

This is what men do; they look after their mums, make the decisions for them and drink wine.

Goodbye, Clark Kent.

Hello, Superman.

"It'll be fine." As the words leave my mouth, like hope-filled shooting stars, my hand reaches for the wine glass. Either these things don't carry as much as I thought they did or I've drunk what was in there a little faster than I intended. There's about two inches in there; barely a mouthful.

Luckily, fate and mum's bladder both join forces to make my life a little better.

"Thanks, Jamie," she sniffs. "I need a pee and to blow my nose." As she rises from the sofa, she gives a little sniff and a shaky laugh.

There is a fleeting moment of silence and inertia, in which

I briefly consider whether I'm going to do what I think I'm going to do and how I'll explain it if I'm caught.

However, thanks to my newfound Sauvignon Superpowers, those things don't seem to matter that much.

I dart to the drinks cabinet – glass in hand – silently unscrew the bottle and pour myself another. Tut-tut-tut. Back to the sofa.

Oh God. I've poured myself way too much. Mum'll surely notice the difference between 'nearly empty' and 'almost overflowing'. A swip just won't be enough, so I take a hefty glug, draining my glass to about halfway in one mouthful.

While the taste leaves a little to be desired, the effect is delicious. The distance between me and my feelings is now a glorious canyon.

The toilet flushes and I quickly check my glass: there's enough to convince anyone that I haven't touched a drop, other than what I was originally poured.

As the winey warmth sets my stomach aglow, I sink back into the sofa, an easy, contented smile spreading across my face, like ink across blotting paper.

"Jamie," mum says, coming back in, before taking an almighty pause.

"Mum?" Uh-oh. Did she hear my surreptitious pours from the loo?

"Thank you. I know I'm putting a lot on your shoulders and I don't mean to, but — "

"But nothing," I smile lazily, as if my mouth is made of honey. "I'm your son. Tomorrow I'll be sixteen and on Monday I'll be here to help you talk things through with dad. Whatever happens after that, I'm going to be there too. That's what sons do."

"Only the best ones." Mum sits, ruffles my hair and sniffs again, picking up her drink and taking a sip. Definitely a sip.

"Shall I top you up?" I say in a posh voice, like I'm a butler or something. "Would madam like a refill?"

She chuckles, sniffs, and sips again.

"Oh, go on, then," she mutters in mock-surrender.

I go to the cabinet and retrieve the bottle, which is slightly lower on ammunition that it ought to be.

"There's not a lot in there," I frown, unscrewing the cap for the second time.

"There's enough to fill me up," mum answers. "And whatever's left, you can have. A glass and a bit won't hurt."

"A good choice, madam," I trill, suddenly finding myself quite funny in my butler persona. "A good choice, indeed."

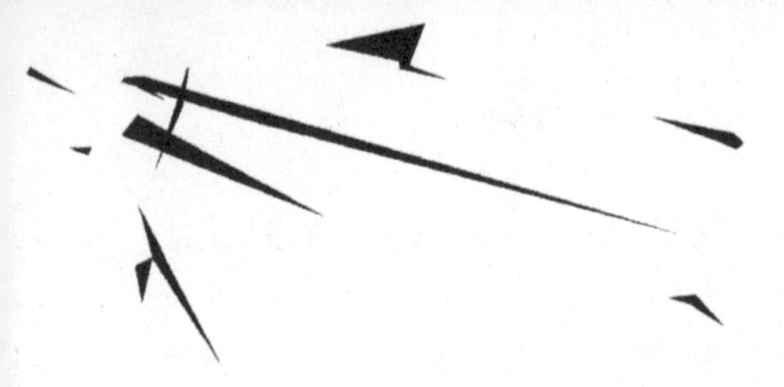

Thirteen

I am Sixteen

"Happy Birthday, Jamie!"

Becky's voice shocks me out of an unusually vivid dream about my teeth falling out. As I blink my way into bleary consciousness, my tongue does a quick dental roll call, feeling around to see that everyone's present and correct.

"Sorry, love." The blur that owns mum's voice comes into focus. She's stood, smiling at me apologetically. "I tried to keep her out, but you've been asleep so long and she's so excited . . ."

"What time is it?" I haul myself up into something between sitting and lying. Something doesn't feel right. My mouth is weirdly dry and I don't feel like I've been asleep at all. My eyes feel gritty and hot.

"Half ten."

I am Sixteen

Blimey. I have slept late. I don't usually tend to go much beyond nine o'clock at the weekend. Not unless I'm ill. Maybe I am. There's a slight heaviness in my head that could be an oncoming cold.

"Do you want your present?" Becky demands, half-laughing and throwing herself on the end of my bed.

What I'd really like at this moment in time is a glass of cold, clear water and a few more hours of sleep.

"Yes, please," I croak, through a ragged smile.

"Go on," mum says to her. "You can get it."

Becky's out of the room as quick as lightning, her footsteps thundering on the stairs. Mum stands at the end of the bed, trying to hide the sadness in her smile.

"Happy Birthday," she says, like she's a million miles away.

"You OK?"

"Mu-um! I can't reach it! Can you get it down?" Wow, it's as if my sister swallowed a megaphone at some point in her development.

"Coming!"

Before she goes, mum pauses in the doorway.

"I'm sorry it's not much, but – you know. What I said last night."

What she said last night? The urge to call after her as she heads downstairs and ask her what she said last night isn't as strong as the urge to try and hide the fact that I can't seem to remember it.

Last night.

What did she say last night?

We drank wine and watched something on Netflix. I let her choose in case I chose the wrong thing – something upsetting.

Stranger Things. We watched *Stranger Things.* I think she liked the eighties-ness of it all.

What was after that?

Now I think about it, I don't remember *Stranger Things* that clearly. I could give you a rough idea of what happened, but the details are sketchy.

We talked. After *Stranger Things*, we talked. What did we talk about?

Dad. We talked about dad. Mum was saying that I shouldn't feel divided between him and her; that I shouldn't take sides. Somewhere deep in my gut, I know I already have.

But there was something else . . .

My memory suddenly finds itself and replays the entire evening in a matter of seconds. It's like watching the director's cut of a film you know really well; there are unfamiliar scenes that suddenly stand out and don't seem to quite belong there.

Money. Mum was talking about money. She was saying how dad had frozen their joint account and how she couldn't withdraw any. She said that she couldn't get me much for my birthday. She was sad. She got teary. I said it didn't matter. She got more teary. She said that she thought this was dad's way of trying to get her to come back to him. "Trying to starve us out" was the phrase she used.

What on Earth am I doing, facilitating a meeting between mum and dad? This isn't right. You don't do what he did and then go for the purse strings. That can't be right.

That's not the man I thought I knew.

Doubt mixes with the anger to create something subtler. Confusion has a pain all of its own.

Dad must know that what he's done isn't right. If that's true, then this is the action of a man clutching at straws. That must be why he wants me to facilitate the meeting tomorrow. So that he can face facts, say sorry and go back to being my dad, Becky's dad and mum's husband. That's why I'm doing it. It's the right thing to do. That's it. Easy. It'll all be fine.

The drumming of my little sister's feet on the stairs and the slower plod of mum's behind her brings me back to the here and now.

"Happy Birthday!" Becky yells, charging forwards, holding a wrapped present in her outstretched hands. She stuffs it into mine, before climbing up onto the bed and staring at it expectantly, her fingers tying excited knots in each other. "Go on, then! Open it!"

I look up at mum, coming in through the door with a cup of tea that she puts on my bedside table. It's not clear and it's not cold, but it is liquid. I take a quick, tentative sip before turning my attentions to the gift. Under the ribbon, there's an envelope, so I open that first.

It's a card with a cartoon of a spider, sitting proudly on his web. From his smiling mouth, a speech bubble says, "I made it with my bum!" I flick a covert look up at Bex, who's mouth is starting to tremble into an uncontrollable smile. Knowing she's watching, I take the appropriate course of action.

"I made it with my BUM?" I roar in faux shock.

Bex collapses into laughter.

"With my BUM?" I roar again.

More laughter. Being six is so easy. Wait until you've got another decade on the clock, kid.

I open the card and the first thing I see is the twenty-pound note. Even as I pick it up and thank mum, it doesn't feel right. Not when things are "a bit tight", as mum put it last night. Not when we're being starved out.

Lifting the twenty from the card reveals the message inside:

Happy Birthday.

Love you. Mum and – in six-year-old scrawl – Becky.

There's a signature missing. It's funny how the little things like that can pack so much of a punch, but I find myself staring at the space where dad's name ought to be.

"Open your present!" Becky moans, getting bored. "Come on!"

"OK, OK," I mutter, sliding a finger under the wrapping paper, to break the sellotape seal. I'm not a ripper or a tearer; I like the paper to come away whole. I feel the same about the foil on a KitKat.

It's a wallet – a black, leather wallet – complete with sections for cards that I've yet to own and a space for paper money, which I have.

"Do you like it?" my little sister asks, anxiously.

"My first proper wallet!" I beam. "I love it. Thanks, guys." Knowing what I know about the state of mum's financial affairs, I really mean it. The usual guff – PS4 games, a new laptop, trainers – that doesn't matter. This wallet has cost money that mum doesn't have and yet, she still managed to get it for me. Of course I love it. "But I tell you what I'd love even more . . ."

"What?" Becky's eyes swell in their sockets.

I scoop her into my arms for a hug.

"I'd love it even more if you made me my birthday breakfast. Toast, please. Two slices."

"Ohh-kaayyy." Becky doesn't seem overly enamoured with the idea but trudges out of the room and back down the stairs. Like I said, being six is easy.

"Happy Birthday, love," mum says, fondly, turning to follow my little sister, her ears no doubt already working overtime for the telltale sounds of possible toaster-related electrocution from the kitchen.

"Mum."

"Yes?"

"Come here."

"What?"

"Come here."

Mum comes over to the bed and gives me a hug.

"What?" she says again.

I pick the twenty off the bed and push it into her hand.

"No," she protests. "That's for you! That's your birthday money!"

"I know, I know," I nod, gently. "It's also shopping and groceries and bills. Please take it back."

"No, Jamie. Thank you, but no."

"Please, mum. It doesn't feel right, not after what we talked about."

"Jamie," she says, sternly. "I can certainly afford to give my son twenty quid on his birthday! I only wish it was more."

"Well, I don't," I say, in as grown-up a tone as I can muster. "Just hang onto it for me, mum. Please? Hang onto it and if it needs to go on something else for the minute, then that'll make me feel better. Please?"

Mum sighs and sits on the bed, clapping her hands to her face.

"Mum, you're not allowed to cry on my birthday, OK?"

"OK."

"Please take the money and when everything's all sorted out, you can buy me whatever you like. Let's be sensible about this. I've got my wallet and that's all I need. Please, mum?"

A choked snuffle comes out from behind her hands. She wipes her eyes and sniffs, again.

"I'll look after it for you," she concedes. "Thank you. I love you."

"I love you too. Now go and make sure Bex doesn't blow the kitchen up."

Once she's left, I pull my phone from the bedside table. The screen is discomfortingly blank. No message from Nadia although it might be a bit rich to expect one.

Nothing from dad.

I guess I'll have to make the first move because that's what Real Men do.

I am sixteen, after all.

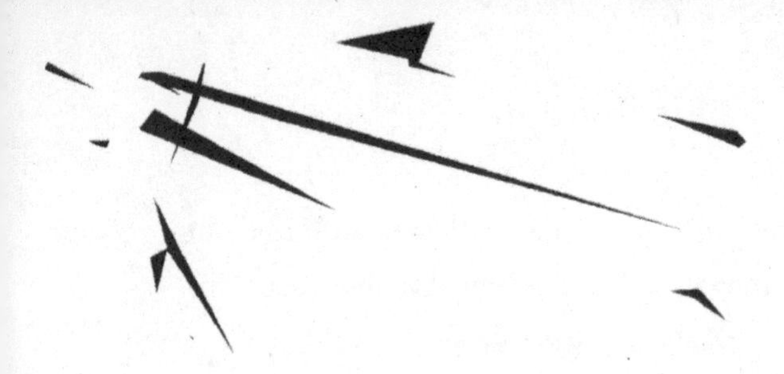

Fourteen

Happy Birthday

"Happy Birthday to you
Happy Birthday to you
Happy Birthday, Dear Jamie
Happy Birthday to yooouuu!"

Mum places a shop-bought chocolate cake on the table in front of me. Protruding from it at varying angles are sixteen miniature candles. The whole thing looks like a hedgehog that's suffered a massive stroke.

"You've got to blow them out!"

I do enjoy the six-year-old assumption that I've never had a birthday before and am therefore entirely ignorant of the accompanying rituals.

"Can I do it with you?"

"No, Becky, let Jamie do it. It's his birthday."

"It's OK, mum," I say, feeling a flood of warmth for my little sister. "I probably need some help, what with being sixteen and everything. Getting old and all that."

"Yay!"

"Alright, then," mum says, rolling her eyes. "On three. One . . ."

I breathe in and lock eyes with Becky.

"Two . . ."

I go cross-eyed and puff out my cheeks, just to see if it'll make her laugh. She disguises a tremor of giggles with a fierce scowl, like an angry puffer fish.

"Three!"

We both blow, waving our heads back and forth across the candles to ensure we get them all. One flame on Becky's side clings desperately to its wick, fluttering and flickering like a flag on a pole, before coming back brighter than ever.

"You missed one!"

Becky drags in another lungful and blasts the rogue candle with enough force that palm trees in Australia are probably bending. Needless to say, the candle gives up in the face of superior weaponry and winks out, leaving a solitary spaghetti string of smoke to unfurl.

"Well done!" Mum claps her hands together. Becky's not done, not yet.

"Now, you've got to make a wish!" she orders, with all the

flexibility of a Gestapo officer.

"OK," I nod. "What am I going to wish for?"

My mobile phone rings, vibrating its way towards the cake plate. The screen lights up.

Dad.

This wasn't the wish I was aiming for.

I look up, but no one's looking at me; they're all looking at my phone. Mum's face is frozen, giving nothing away. Becky's face is a portrait of delight.

"Can I talk to him?" she beams.

"Let Jamie answer it," mum blurts. "Dad probably wants to say Happy Birthday."

Becky responds with a pained whine.

"But you can talk to him after," she adds, throwing me a pleading look.

"I'll take this outside," I nod, grabbing it and getting up from the table. "The signal's better," I lie. I don't want mum feeling awkward with me talking to dad. I'm her son and that's what sons do. They look after everyone. I don't want Becky hearing anything she might not need to. That's what big brothers do. They bear the load for their little sisters.

This Weight of Manhood thing is fairly heavy though, and it seems to be getting heavier by the day. I wonder if there's a formula to calculate its actual weight? And I'm not talking about putting my willy on some scales. My life's bad enough as it is.

Within a couple of hurried strides, I answer dad's call, heading towards the door to the back garden.

"Jamie, It's dad. Happy Birthday, son."

"Thanks."

"Have you had a good day? Sorry I'm not . . . you know . . . there."

"It's been good." Just the sound of his voice floods my system with a level of anger that – until now – has been alien to me. For the sake of everyone else – especially Becky – I've got to keep a lid on it. I've got to play the game.

Dad doesn't answer. Maybe he's sensing what I'm trying to hide or maybe the signal's gone.

"Hallo?" I say suddenly, full of unforeseen panic.

"Yeah, I'm still here. You just sound . . . Is everything OK? You sound a bit . . ."

He doesn't finish his sentence and suddenly my feelings are in conflict. His voice is sad, distant and lonely. He's alone. I feel sorry for him, but angry at the same time. I don't know which feeling to pay attention to. So, I let both of them slug it out in the background while I carry on talking.

"I'm good." It's a stock answer, one that's seen me through innumerable unwanted questions. It can only be followed up with, "How are you?"

"Well, I've been better!" he laughs bitterly.

A thought strikes me; something obvious that I haven't asked and, for the sake of mum and Bex, something I really ought to know.

"Where are you, dad? Where've you been staying?"

"With your Aunty Hannah. She's putting me up in the spare room. It's not exactly the Ritz, but it's better . . ."

While dad goes all TripAdvisor on the standard of his current accommodation, my brain does a Google Maps and tries to work out roughly how far away he is. Aunty Hannah lives in a small town which, if my memories of innumerable, unwilling, childhood trips to go and see her are correct, is about half an hour away. In miles, that's probably about ten. That's a good enough distance to prevent him randomly turning up. His weekdays are going to be filled with work and Aunty Hannah, much as I've never really enjoyed her company, is probably going to be telling him to stay away until things calm down. Now that these details are resolved in my head, my ears go back online and I catch the end of what he's saying.

". . . but, anyway," he says, "none of that's important, right now. I've got a roof over my head and that's what counts."

Not the fact that mum hasn't got any money. Maybe now isn't the time to raise that one. I let him go on.

"So, you're having a good day." I know this tack. He's repeating what I've said earlier in the hope that I'll elaborate; give away a detail that he might be able to use. Or maybe he wants me to say that I miss him.

"Oh, you know," I sigh. "It's just another day really."

"That's how it is when you get older." There's a pause. "Have you . . .? Have you had a word with your mum about what we talked about? About meeting tomorrow?"

There's his desperation again, tapping at the fragile wall of emotional distance that I've managed to put up.

"Yeah. Yes, I have. She's up for it but, like you said, I think it'd be good if I was there. Just to . . . you know."

"Just to make sure I behave myself."

I take a deep breath.

"She's scared of you, dad."

"Well she doesn't need to be!" he snaps back, his voice jagged with corners. It's not exactly anger. It's more like embarrassment. Probably the shame of having to be carried, weeping, to his car.

"But she is." He needs to understand this isn't just about him.

"I'm sorry, Jamie," dad says, eventually, sounding tired and worn. "I'm sorry. Sorry about everything. Look, if your mum's OK with it and feels better with you around, that's fine by me. What time? Morning or afternoon?"

My mind quickly weighs up the possible outcomes. If it goes well and everyone's happy, then I can go to school afterwards and leave them to it. If it goes the other way, then I'll probably have to take the rest of the day off and sit with mum. Best to get it over with, however it pans out.

"Eleven o'clock?" I offer. "How does that sound?"

"Eleven o'clock," dad affirms. "I'll see you then."

"OK."

"Oh, and thanks, Jamie."

"No worries."

"OK, then. Well, have a great rest of your day and I'll see you tomorrow."

"OK."

"Love you."

"You, too. Oh, before you go, can Bex say hello?"

"Of course she can. Put her on."

"Hang on."

Covering the mouthpiece, I go back inside to the front room, where mum and my sister are staring at the cake.

"Bex," I mouth. "It's dad on the phone. Do you want to say hallo?"

"Can I?" Becky asks mum.

"Of course you can!" mum coos, putting on an Oscar-worthy act.

"The signal's better in the garden," I lie again, handing the phone over. Bex takes it, clamps it to her ear and wanders through the kitchen, shouting "Hallo? Daddy? Daddy? Can you hear me?" Then she's outside, her words fading with her.

Mum sighs and leans forward, her elbows on the table, her hands in her hair.

"You OK, mum?"

"Yes," she says smartly, sitting up straight. "Yes, I'm fine. It's my baby's birthday!"

"I've said eleven o'clock for tomorrow. Is that OK?"

Mum blinks quickly, trying to cover up her trepidation, but I can see the bits she missed. I think that's half my problem: I seem to be able to see what people want to hide. The other half is that I don't know what to do about it.

"Eleven o'clock is fine. I've got to go into town in the morning to go to the bank after I've taken Bex to school, but I can be back by eleven."

"OK. I'll take the morning off. I'll be here, just in case he turns up and you're out. If he does, I'll message you. That way, there's no surprises." That's me, organising other people's lives because they can't.

Mum tilts her head and smiles again sadly. Her hand reaches across the table and rests on mine.

"Thanks, love."

"I need a wee," I rasp. "Back in a minute."

Taking the stairs two at a time, I go up to the bathroom and look at myself in the mirror. My eyes are lined red and my lips are trembling, but there's no room for tears. Tears aren't going to help mum. Tears aren't going to help Becky. I suddenly wish I had a glass of wine or sherry to take away that roiling, boiling feeling of hurt in my stomach, but I haven't. Instead, I turn the cold tap on, full blast, and splash my face repeatedly, the cold slap startling my face out of doing anything I don't want it to. Like crying.

I've seen what tears do to men. They make them weak and they have to be carried out of garages. Tears aren't even an option. I've got to keep strong and strength requires energy and everything I'm feeling is an energy source. I'll hang onto those feelings and burn them up as fuel.

A few splashes later, I think I'm OK enough to go back down. Flushing the loo to complete the illusion, I'm out of the bathroom where I take a deep breath, just to be sure.

Out of the corner of my eye, I see my bedroom door open and my schoolbag lying on the floor, also open.

I see Nadia's card: a bright, white envelope against the tattered green, blues and oranges of my exercise books. Walking over, I reach in and pull it out.

Do I open it? Would that just be disrespectful to her? Looking at her heartfelt scribble, the day after I've just broken her heart?

"Jay-meee! I've got your pho-one!" Becky has said goodbye to dad and doesn't sound any the worse for it.

I look at the card, turning it over and over in my hands.

I'm not going to open it. I don't want to. It'd hurt too much.

Hating myself, I tear it in two and drop the pieces in the bin.

Fifteen

Doing the Voices

A few hours later and I'm stepping out of the shower. Wiping the steam off the mirror, I look in.

I look a bit better. My complexion has a tinge of colour to it. Maybe that's because I'm taking charge of things. I've organised a meeting between mum and dad, where things can't get out of hand because I'll be there. It plays out in my head, in soft focus and probably underscored by one of those dreadful, eighties power ballads. A few tearful apologies from dad and some generous forgiveness from mum, and everything goes back to the way it was. I can even see Becky being picked up by the two of them and falling happily into a family embrace. All the while, I'm watching over them, like some benevolent being, ready to go and fix someone else's life.

"Jay-meee!" There's a knock at the door, as if my sister

somehow thinks that trying to vibrate it off its hinges with her voice isn't enough.

"What? Hang on!"

After a quick spray of deodorant, I dress and unbolt the door. Becky looks up at me, wearing her pyjamas and her fluffy dressing gown. Her arms pop open, revealing a life-size glove puppet.

"Cuddle!" she demands.

"Is it bedtime?" I stoop for a hug.

She nods into my shoulder.

"Will you read me a story?" she pleads softly.

My heart sinks briefly. I'm sure there are other things I could be doing.

"Please?"

Then I remember, Sunday night is Dad's Story Night. I've been promoted again, from Brother to Stand-in Dad. Time to bear the load.

"Yes, I'll read you a story," I puff, scooping her up. "God, you're getting heavy!"

"Mu-um!" Becky shouts down the stairs, as I lug her to her bedroom, "Jamie's going to read me a story!"

"Is that OK, Jamie?" mum replies from somewhere below.

"Ye-es!" I yell, using Becky as a makeshift battering ram to open her bedroom door, before throwing her on the bed. "Go on, in you get. Snuggle down. What story d'you want?"

"Mr Gum!" she giggles, slapping the bedsheets in excitement. Mr Gum's her favourite. Never read it myself.

"OK," I smile, looking through her bookshelf, "but you get in that bed and get comfortable or I'm not reading you anything." I find a Mr Gum book, turn off her light, turn on her lamp and perch on the side of her bed.

"You ready?"

Becky nods back, in wide-eyed anticipation, so I start reading in my best let's-see-how-quickly-we-can-get-you-off-to-sleep voice.

"It all started late one afternoon in the peaceful little town of Lamonic Bibber . . ."

"We've done that bit."

"What?"

"Daddy's read that bit to me. We got to the part where Polly falls asleep."

"Which chapter was that?"

Becky shrugs.

"I think it was near the start because I fell asleep quickly, and daddy said the next day that I fell asleep when Polly did."

"OK," I mutter, riffling through the first few pages with my thumb. "OK. Did it finish with: 'The hot sun beat down and soon she was drifting, drifting away'?"

"I think so."

"OK, then. 'When Polly awoke, it was dusk and the afternoon

was fat with shadows . . .' Close your eyes, Bex, and just listen to the story."

Bex closes her eyes and I keep reading.

"'What strangery is this?' whispered Polly."

Becky's eyes flash open.

"That's not what she sounds like."

"What?"

"Polly doesn't sound like that. Daddy does a different voice."

A sudden flurry of irritation fills my bloodstream.

"What voice does he do?" I sigh tightly.

Bex shrugs again.

"Well, I'm going to need a little help here . . ." I offer through gritted teeth.

"I don't know!" Becky whines, "but not that one!"

"Well, if *you* don't know, how am *I* expected to do what he does?" My voice is louder than I expect it to be, catching us both by surprise.

"I don't know." Becky's voice is smaller than I expect it to be. A film of tears makes her eyes glisten.

Everything goes quiet. Becky rolls onto her side, her back toward me, and snuffles into her cuddly unicorn. I sit and look at her shuddering shoulders, suddenly feeling about the same age as she is.

"Becky . . .?"

She sobs.

"Bex? I'm sorry . . ."

"I wish daddy was here," she wails, sitting up and wrapping her arms around me. It's not a slight against my story-reading abilities; it's the sound of grief. My Adam's apple seems to inflate, until it feels too big for my throat.

"I know," I murmur, holding her close. "I know."

"Why are mummy and daddy fighting?" she keens, soaking my shirt with hot tears. "Why isn't he here?"

"It's OK," I croak, trying to soothe her. "It's OK." I stroke her hair and hold her until she stills. She needs someone to give her something to cling to. Gently, I lie her back down and pull the covers up to her chin.

"OK," I say, smiling as much as my face has the strength to, "it's like this . . ."

What is it like? This has never happened before, but there's a little, tear-streaked face looking back at me, like I've got all the answers. So, I'd better come up with some.

"It's like this. Sometimes people have arguments, and the people who really love each other have the biggest ones because they love each other."

I've no idea where this is going.

"Sometimes, those people who really love each other need some time apart, just so they can calm down and think whether what they were saying is right or wrong. When they've done that, they can sit down and talk about it properly."

"When's that going to be?"

"Well . . . mummy and daddy are going to meet tomorrow and have a chat. And that's a good thing."

"What if they shout at each other again?"

Here we go, deep breath, and jump.

"They won't. Do you know why?"

"Why?"

"Because I'm going to make sure they don't."

"Promise?"

"I promise I won't let them shout at each other." Because that's what Brothers-slash-Stand-in Dads-slash-Relationship-Counsellors-slash-Sons do. "I promise that they'll just sit and talk and we can get things sorted, OK?"

"OK."

"So, you shut your eyes and I'm going to read you the story. The voices won't be as good as daddy's, but I'll do my best. OK?"

"OK, but what if I can't get to sleep?"

"Then I'll read you the whole book if I have to, and if you're not asleep by then, I'll sit here until you are."

Because you're my little sister.

***

Once I finally creep out of Becky's room, I tiptoe into mine and check my phone. Nearly nine. The story-reading expedition took about three quarters of an hour and just over half the book, but it was worth it, just to see her swallowed up by sleep.

I just hope she stays there and doesn't have any nightmares.

Adil WhatsApped me half an hour ago.

happy birthday jim sorry its so late I forgot!

With the way today's been, I'd almost forgotten there was a world beyond the house.

No probs better late than never

Knowing Adil, the likelihood of an immediate answer is pretty remote, so I head downstairs and into the lounge. Mum's there, with the ironing board, wrestling with clothes.

"Did she go off alright?"

"Eventually."

"Thanks, love. I've done your uniform. You can take that upstairs."

Before I can moan that I've just come down, my phone pings.

nadia messgd me and reminded me! im useless!

My body temperature suddenly drops. Nadia reminded Adil? Why? Why would she do that after what I did to her?

"All alright?"

I look up. The iron is hovering over one of Becky's t-shirts.

Mum thinks it's dad messaging me.

"Yes. Yeah, it's just Adil saying Happy Birthday." My mouth is a saliva-free zone.

"Aw, that's nice." The iron is lowered, hissing mum's relief on her behalf.

"Yup," I mutter distractedly, replying

What did she say?

Should I send it? Should I? My finger slips and makes the decision for me.

"Have you heard from Nadia today?" Mum's focus is back on the ironing, her voice conversational and calm.

"Yep!" I lie smartly. "She rang me earlier and said Happy Birthday!" Mum doesn't need to know what's going on in my life; it would only give her something else to worry about.

"Aw, that's nice," she says again. "How is she?"

Possibly creating her first voodoo doll.

"Yeah, she's fine. She's good."

"Good."

My phone pings again.

she just sd its yr birthday y?

My eyes flick to the drinks cabinet, then back to the phone.

No reason. See you, tomorrow.

"You should get her round one night."

"Who?"

"Nadia."

"Oh. OK. I'll see what she's up to." Then, just in case mum suggests I do it now, I add, "I'll see her, tomorrow."

"That'll be nice. Uniform? Upstairs?"

The drinks cabinet is only two strides away, so near and yet so far.

"Yes." Pocketing my phone, I hunt out two shirts and two sets of trousers and run upstairs. Do something normal. Do something distracting. Put your clothes away.

As I hang things, fold things and force things onto overstuffed shelves, my eyes are drawn to the right, as if commanded to by some higher power. The bin. I'm looking at the bin. More specifically, I'm looking at the two halves of Nadia's birthday card, still in the bisected envelope.

I'm standing and looking and not doing anything. It's like when you see a spider, and you freeze and watch it, to see what it's going to do next.

I retrieve the pieces. As if the weight of them is too much for my legs, I find myself sitting on the end of the bed, holding them together, reading my name on the torn envelope.

Breathing hard, I stand up suddenly, staring at the card.

I feel angry, helpless, sad and confused all at once. Wine would cancel all of it out. Just a single, solitary glass of liquid numbness. Then my mind dredges up a memory from last night. Mum saying, "We don't want it turning into a habit."

With a resigned sigh, I carry the pieces of card to my bedside desk before putting them gently into the drawer.

Sixteen

My Top Five Things about You

It's two o'clock in the morning and I haven't slept yet. I'm turning on my bedside lamp and fumbling in the drawer beside my bed.

Of course I am. Because life's not hard enough.

With the two halves laid out on my knees, I drag my pillows up behind me, so I can sit up. The envelope lies ripped and ragged and no matter how much I edge the halves together, they won't knit together.

I turn them both over and gently extract the pieces of card. With them face down, all that's exposed is the glossy, white side. The side with 'Hallmark' written on it and that this card has been left blank for your message.

For Nadia's message. Written pre-her-boyfriend-revealing-himself-as-an-utter-twat.

Pieced together, the card shows a pug, wearing trainers, a baseball cap and headphones, looking forlornly into space. Beside it are the words, 'Bro! You Rock, Dude!" and '(Nice Kicks!)' with a little arrow from the brackets to dog's trainers. Unfunny as the card might be to anyone else, a smile flickers across my face and then the long-underused muscles in my abdomen spasm. I think it was meant to be a laugh or a chuckle, but the sound I make is neither. A cross between a moan and a wail involuntarily escapes my control, catching me off guard. The card blurs.

No tears. Not now. Store them up and use them as fuel.

A sniff and a deep breath later and I think I'm ready to open it. Not so much ready as resigned to the fact that it's going to have to happen. Probably the same way that people on the guillotine felt, staring into that final basket.

Holding the pieces together with one hand, I open the card.

Happy Birthday, Jamie!

I could make some lame jokes about sex or voting, but I'm not going to! What I am going to do is try and tell you how special you are. I know you don't like that sort of thing, but it's your birthday and I'm going to do it whether you like it or not. I also know you like structure, so I've put together my list of Top Five Things about You. Here they are:

My Top Five Things About You

You're very thoughtful. Remember that time I got upset about my cat dying and you sent me a packet of Kleenex in the post? It might not have meant a lot to you, but it did to me.

You're funny. Every time you make me laugh, my world gets a little bit brighter.

You listen to me and not a lot of people do. I know I talk a lot and sometimes about things that aren't important, but I always know you're listening.

You're very handsome. I know you don't think you are, but it's that that makes you even more attractive, so maybe I shouldn't be saying this!

You're strong. The type of strength you have doesn't come from going to a gym. Thank God – how dull would that be?! You're strong in that you take on more people's problems than you should – mine included! One day, if you'll let me, I'd like to take on some of yours, but only when you're ready.

There is a sixth:

I love you!

Happy Birthday!

Love,

Nads

Nads. She signed it Nads, even though she hates it when I call her that.

OH GOD I AM THE KING OF ALL DICKHEADS.

Of course I read it ten more times, before my eyes start to get heavy and sore and I have to turn the light off.

Of course I cry in the dark because there's no one else to hear it.

No one needs to know how weak I truly am.

Seventeen

Helium

Monday morning announces itself quicker and more noisily than I'd like. Mum hurricanes in at half-seven, all dressing gown and fluster.

"Jamie? Jamie!"

I groan some acknowledgement that I am, despite all outward appearances, still alive.

"Morning, mum."

She puts a cup of tea on my bedside desk and plonks herself on the end of my bed.

"Jamie, I know you're going to take the morning off, but could you sit with Bex while I take a shower? I won't be a minute."

"Oh God, mum," I moan.

"Please?"

"Alright, alright," I mutter. "Give me a minute to wake up."

Trying to wriggle out of this one isn't going to work, even though I am dedicating my morning to TRYING TO SAVE THE FAMILY.

"Thanks, love. She's downstairs, having her breakfast."

Mum bustles out of my room and I drag my body out of bed. Why do duvets always feel so much cosier in the morning? At least I don't have to bother with uniform for the moment. With a sigh, I pull on yesterday's jeans and a t-shirt, grab my tea and lumber downstairs.

Becky's playing with her breakfast, supporting her head with one hand and tapping out some sort of semaphore on the dish with a slice of jam-smeared toast.

"Morning, Bex," I mumble, as brightly as four and a half hours of sleep will let me.

Becky looks up and gives me a brief apology of a smile.

"What's up, kid?" I sit down, opposite her and take a tentative sip of tea.

There's a pause before she answers.

"Are they going to get a divorce?"

That one stops me. Are they? I don't know. All the signs seem to be pointing in that direction: arguments, the Rainbow Eye, sleeping on the sofa, frozen bank accounts . . . But a six year old doesn't need that kind of thing in her head. Not before she goes to school. But neither do I think that a round of raucous farting is going to give her the hope she needs to get her through the day.

"What do you notice about me?" I ask.

Becky looks me up and down, knotting her eyebrows together in concentration.

Her shrug is my answer.

"Come on," I cajole her, "look harder."

"What?" she snaps after a moment. "What is it?"

"I'm not wearing school uniform."

Becky sits up at that, dropping her toast and squinting at me suspiciously.

"Why aren't you?"

"Because I'm not going to school until the afternoon."

"But why?"

"Do you remember last night, when I told you that mummy and daddy were going to have a chat today?"

"Yes . . ." There's a glimmer of hope in her face.

"Well, they are, and I'm going to stay here and make sure they talk to each other properly."

Becky's eyes leave mine and dart about the room, as if she's tracking a particularly aerobatic fly. Just as quickly, they lock back on mine.

"Can I stay? Can I do it, too?"

"No," I say, as though I know what the hell I'm talking about. "It's better if I do it. It's no good us both taking time off school. Besides, you know what grown-ups are like. It'll be long and boring." In the midst of my impromptu improvisation, a thought lights up some dark corner of my brain. "Do you know what else you could do if you go to school? You could ask Evie if she wants to come and play on the weekend!" Bex hasn't had anyone round to play since Everything Went Weird. Mum didn't want anyone to see the Rainbow Eye and the general tension in the house wasn't going to be lulled by the sound of two little girls rampaging around.

"Can I?"

"I don't see why not!" I announce, as though I'm in COMPLETE CONTROL of the entire planet. "Ask mum on your way to school."

"Ask mum what?" Mum comes into the kitchen, rubbing her head vigorously with a towel.

"I'll let you guys sort it out. I need a shower." Chucking a wink at Becky, I head upstairs. I turn the shower up to the max and step in.

I'm nervous.

Actually, that's not entirely accurate. Scared is closer to the mark. I sit cross-legged beneath the scalding water and try and rationalise it.

Question: What am I scared of? After all, I'm only sitting down with my mother and father, both of whom I've known my entire life.

Answer: It could all go wrong, and I might not be able to keep them together. I'm not even sure that they should stay together, if I'm honest, but there's the horrible feeling that I might be the only person to give them that chance.

Question: Why should I be scared when I know my parents are meant to be rational and loving human beings?

Answer: I don't know that anymore, not for certain. I never thought dad would hit mum, but he has. I never thought mum might want a divorce, but she does. This is a bit like proving the existence of fairies. Suddenly, everything I have taken for granted can't be taken for granted ever again. Given his tears, I'm pretty sure that dad wouldn't do it again, but I can't be one hundred percent certain, which bothers me. I don't want to think of my dad in that way. I don't want all my memories of him to be tainted, but they already are and I feel guilty about it.

Question: Am I right in trying to mediate some sort of peace conference in our front room?

Answer: "Jamie! How long are you going to be in there? Becky needs to brush her teeth! We've got to go!"

Slipping and stumbling out of the shower, I grab the towel and start to dry my stinging body.

"Hang on!" I yell through the steam. "Just getting out!"

After a quick spray of the pits, I dress in record time and open the door, beaming like a crescent moon. No one's going to ask if I'm alright if I'm wearing a smile this big.

"Are you alright?" mum asks.

There's that theory blown.

"Yes. Of course I am. Why?"

"You've been in there an awfully long time."

"But don't I smell better for it?" I give her a hug.

"I suppose so." She sounds unconvinced but is, thankfully, distracted by Becky, who pushes her way between us and heads for the sink and her toothbrush

"Did she ask you about Evie?"

"Yes, but I'm not sure it's a good idea. Not with the way things are."

"Mum." I use my assertive voice which is usually reserved for telling Becky to get out of my room or to go to bed. "She needs to do something a bit normal. Having Evie round is normal. If needs be, I'll tell dad to stay away."

"I'll think about it," she nods, looking over my shoulder. "Come on, Becky! We need to get a move on!" mum's attention comes back to me. "Are you sure about this? Today? Are you sure? It's a big thing you're doing."

"It'll be fine." I squeeze her shoulders and give her another hug.

"Thank you." It's faint, but it couldn't be more heartfelt if she shouted it. "Right, Becky, rinse. We've got to go!"

I follow Bex and mum down to the front door.

"I'm going to try to get back about half ten," mum says, planting a kiss on my cheek as she steers my sister outside.

"I'll text you if he gets here before you do. Don't worry. It's all fine."

"Bye, Jamie!"

"Bye, Becky! See you later! Be good!"

"Thanks, love."

"Go on, mum, don't be late."

Another peck on the cheek and they're walking, hand in hand – silhouettes of Winnie the Pooh and Piglet – into the morning sunshine.

I shut the door and breathe.

I'm alone.

I can let it all go; the smiles, the being in control, the making stuff up to keep everyone happy and the endless façade of looking like I know what I'm doing.

The sofa seems like the best place to be right now, so I go there. This ought to be a moment of freedom and relaxation but, instead, I just feel sad. Not tears sad; somehow, it's beyond that. It's the kind of sadness that makes your head feel like it's being squashed. The kind of sadness that sucks all your energy away and leaves you feeling weary and empty – a hundred years older than you actually are.

Is this how my life's going to be? Forever looking after mum? Forever distrusting dad? Looking out for my sister because she's too young to do it for herself? Nipping relationships in the bud in case they get too close for comfort?

The last thought hits me like a cosh. That's what I've been doing with Nadia. All she's been doing is what partners are supposed to: looking out for me, checking I'm OK, loving me. If I'm honest, I've given her enough reasons to worry. I've been distant, moody and all-out weird. What was she supposed to do? Ignore it and pretend everything was OK? I've reframed everything she's done.

Care has become clinginess, worry has become nosiness and dedication I've cheerfully reinterpreted as possessiveness. Who am I trying to protect? Her or me? The answer's so obvious, I don't even want to look at it. All I know is that I'm probably going to live out the rest of my life in the foetal position.

There's a sudden rush of energy to my legs and suddenly, I'm standing. There's a noise like a roar. I don't know where it's coming from and then I realise, it's me. I'm shouting something that has no consonants; it's just a long, wretched vowel. The energy from my legs goes into my arms and my chest, and I am filled with hot, white rage.

I give the sofa a damn good thrashing.

Roughly three minutes later, I'm a puffing heap. That sofa's tougher than it looks but the anger's still there, bubbling away, fizzing in my veins. There's too much fuel for me to handle. I need to burn some off. I start pacing from one end of the lounge to the other.

As I walk, my fists clench and unclench, stretching out and balling up, in time with my steps and I'm breathing through my teeth. Twelve steps. Turn. Twelve steps. Turn.

I've no idea how long I do this for, this regimented marching up and down, but something happens, something that I don't notice until I stop. With each parade up and down, my path has been moving, inch by inch, to the left. My final step stops me beside the drinks cabinet.

Trying to ignore it, I look up at the clock above the sofa. Ten o'clock. An hour until lift off.

I know what I want but I know that I shouldn't, so I start pacing again. Twelve steps. Turn. Twelve steps. Turn.

Fifteen minutes later, I'm stood in exactly the same place, looking up at the clock again. The anger's gone, but it's been replaced with a hideous feeling that I'm going to ruin it for everyone.

Then, it's like I'm not me anymore. It's as if I'm disconnected from my body and watching my hands through a camera lens. On some sort of autopilot, I see them pull the door of the cabinet open, reach inside and pull out the nearest bottle. Baileys.

My hands unscrew the crusted cap and lift it to my nose, filling it with the smell of Christmas and cream. They lift the bottle to my lips and the mouth that doesn't seem to belong to me either takes a good swig.

It's like drinking melted ice cream, but there's a boozy tang to it that burns ever so gently as it coats my throat, makes my chest glow and tingles in my stomach. My hand gives me another glug and I can feel the Weight of Manhood getting lighter and lighter.

I look at the clock. Twenty minutes to go.

"One more. Just to even things out."

There's a delicious lightness in my head, as though it's full of helium and wants to float away, but there are some practicalities to take care of. I put the bottle back exactly where it was, then drift upstairs to brush my teeth, smiling fluffily at myself as I do it.

No one's going to know except me.

Even the sound of a key in the front door doesn't startle me or get me all jittery.

It doesn't matter if it's mum. It doesn't matter if it's dad.

I'm ready for anything.

Eighteen

Switzerland

"So . . . we should talk, shouldn't we?" Dad is taking control from his chair.

Me and mum are sat on the sofa; her on the far end closest to the door, where I told her to sit, me on the end closest to dad, a boozed-up bridge between the two of them. Mum doesn't say anything; she looks at the floor, not daring to make eye contact. She looks smaller than she's ever looked in her life. I have to try and stay neutral. I'm here as the mediator. I am Switzerland.

"Well, perhaps you could start the ball rolling." Calm and easy.

Dad shifts in his seat and looks at me and then to mum. I've just asserted myself as chairperson for the inaugural meeting of the Confused Parent Association. A distant detonation of anxiety goes off in my chest, but it's too far away for me to really hear it.

Dad looks at me.

"OK," he frowns. "The first thing I want to say is how sorry I am. I'm sorry, Lizzie. I really am. If I could take it back, I would, but . . ." His words trail away and he looks to mum for a reaction, but mum's still looking at the carpet.

There's a long silence.

"Mum?" I say. "Dad says he's sorry."

One of mum's arms crosses her stomach. Her other hand goes to her face, half-covering one of her eyes, unconsciously making contact with the ghost of the Rainbow Eye.

"You hit me," she says, quietly and simply.

"I know!" Dad's voice is pained, exasperated. "I know what I did, Liz! Christ, don't you think I feel terrible about it? I do! I feel awful! Dreadful! But I just lost it! Come on, after all those things you said?"

"What things?" She's suddenly upright, alert and bristling, like someone's just tapped her with a cattle prod.

"You basically called me a failure as a husband and a father!"

"That's not what I said!"

"That's what it sounded like!"

"But that's not what I said!"

"What did you say then?"

"I said that we hardly ever see you — "

"Because I'm out working, out earning money to keep this family!"

"I said that we ought to go on holiday and do something together. All of us –"

"Which we can't afford!"

"What about some time with your family?"

This is like watching a game of Olympic-standard ping-pong. My head turns right, then left, then right, then left, until my neck gives up and fixes straight ahead. Meanwhile, my eyes drift slyly towards the drinks cabinet.

Ransacking the rest of the Baileys, while extremely tempting, probably isn't the best idea right now.

"Guys, guys!" I cut in, breaking the rally. "This isn't exactly moving things forward, is it? Perhaps we ought to be looking at what happens next." I can't believe how adult I sound; how sharp and incisive my thoughts are. Without the usual curtain of anxiety and fear to get caught behind, I'm making more sense now than I probably ever have done. Who knew adulting could be this easy?

My parents fall silent again, each retreating into their own little worlds, but if things are going to move forward, they've got to communicate.

"What's the best thing we can do?" I ask.

"I think we should go and see a counsellor," mum says, eventually.

"A counsellor? What for?"

"To talk about our problems."

"Oh, I see where this is going!" dad snaps, his tone all acid. "To talk about *my* problems. That's what you're saying! Well, I don't need to talk about my problems with anyone."

"That's not what mum said," I say calmly. In the back of my woozy head, I'm controlling rowdy politicians on a talk show. "She did say *our* problems." Dad tries to say something, but I talk over him; something I don't think I've ever done before. Never dared. "Wouldn't it be *useful* to sit in a room – neutral territory– in a controlled environment, where you could both get your points across and really listen to each other?" I ought to be writing this down. I could probably end wars if I put my mind to it. I might even grow a beard and invest in some sandals.

"The only person I need to talk to is your mother. Come on, Liz, can't we just sort this out between us?"

"Does that work for you, mum?"

"No," she says, falling back into herself, quiet again.

"Then you're throwing this family away," dad counters, full of accusation.

"No, I'm not. I'm saying that there are things we need to talk about, but I'm not comfortable doing it like this."

"Why not?"

"You hit me."

Dad groans in his seat, as if to suggest that this is something mum should just get over. If my head wasn't seventy-five percent Baileys right now, I think I'd be angry at his tone, but because my head is seventy-five percent Baileys right now, I let it go. I won't forget it: that casual dismissal. That's not right. That's not the dad I know.

Knew.

"It's not been easy," mum continues. "It doesn't just fade with the bruise."

"D'you think it's been easy for me?" dad spits back. "Having to leave my family? Having to lie to people about why I'm not staying at home? Having to tell my own sister that my marriage is in tatters?"

"Did you tell her why?"

"It's none of her business! That's family stuff. Our family. I don't want the whole world knowing our ins and outs."

"No, I don't expect you do," mum mutters.

"And what's that supposed to mean?"

I've seen dad angry before. He's told me off when I was a kid. He's always been where the buck stops – The Final Word – but this is different. Maybe it's the Irish Cream goggles I seem to be looking through, but this anger seems twisty and snakier. It moves, changes direction, probes and pokes. It's loaded with venom. I don't like it. I don't want him to be like this. I want him to calm down and be who I think he is.

Thought he was.

"Guys, guys," I step in again, patting the air gently with my hands. "This isn't getting us anywhere, is it?" As I talk, I realise that they're both looking at me, but it's more than that, they're looking *to* me. Just like I looked to them when things went wrong at school or I fell out with a friend or did something wrong without realising it. They want an explanation. They want me to have the answers. It's my turn to guide them. Somehow, I've become the Voice of Reason.

Unfortunately, the Voice of Reason is a bit pissed.

"Look," I continue. "I think the problem here is that you've both got things to say, but you've also got to listen to each other."

"When am I going to see Bex?" Dad pretty much ignores me and fires this one straight at mum. "I want to see her."

"I don't know," mum replies. "I haven't thought that far."

"Well maybe you should. This can't be good for her."

There's that twisty snake again.

"Guys, guys," I say again, trying not to take sides, but already doing it. "Here's the thing: what's good about this is you're actually talking. I'm going to suggest that we stop it here and maybe do it again in a few days' time. Give yourselves a chance to think things over. Dad, maybe you could think about what mum's asking – "

"I'm not going to a counsellor."

"Just think about it, that's all I'm saying. Mum, maybe you could think about dad seeing Becky."

"And you, son."

"And me. If we do this again, things might be a bit – I don't know – clearer. Everyone's tempers are up and I don't think we're going to solve everything right now, but maybe we could give it another shot in a few days? Mum?"

Mum looks at dad, then back at me and nods, almost imperceptibly – but it's a nod.

"Dad?"

Dad sighs, long and deep.

"OK," he breathes.

"Great," I say, sagely. "Well, look . . . Dad, you've got to get back to work. Mum, you've got to get everything ready for Becky and I've got to get back to school. Shall we just leave things here and try again another time?"

"Yep. OK," dad grunts, heaving himself out of the chair. He stands for a moment, looking at mum who avoids his gaze. "I hope we can sort this out," he says. His lips go to say something else, but don't quite get there and he leaves, heading for the front door. I get up and follow him.

"OK, then," he shrugs, standing in the open doorway. "I guess I'll wait to hear from you."

"Yeah. I'll keep you posted."

"OK." There's an awkward moment that's usually set aside for the traditional parting hug, but it passes. We both register it.

"OK, then. I'll be off." He turns and walks to his car. I stay in the doorway, to watch him get in, start the engine and drive off. Just to make sure he goes.

The front door shuts with a click and, for a moment, I lean my head against it, feeling the cool wood against my skin. It's all been a bit anticlimactic.

No great resolve.

No film montage of everyone falling into each other's arms.

No return to normality.

Mum's head appears in the lounge doorway.

"Has he gone?" she whispers, her eyes darting to the door.

"He's gone," I announce, reassuringly.

Relief escapes from her like air from a puncture. Her eyes close and her shoulders drop slightly. She looks old and tired.

The hug I give her is meant to be a cheery thing but instead, it sets off some sort of emotional tripwire and she suddenly holds me tightly, as a sob shudders its way along her back and out of her mouth.

"I'm sorry," she sniffs into my shoulder.

"Hey, it's OK. It's all OK." I find myself rocking side to side, like she used to do to me when I was little and upset. After a few seconds, she pats me on the back and pulls away.

"Bloody hell," she puffs, wiping her eyes. "Bloody hell, that was tough!"

"You did good, mum. You said your bit."

"I couldn't have done it without you there." Her smile is

crinkly and crumpled.

"Yes, you could."

"No, Jamie. I couldn't. I don't know what would've happened if you hadn't been there. I'm sorry, you don't need to hear me saying things like that about your dad, but — "

"But it's true. I know."

Mum looks at me, her eyes suddenly piercing, as if she's trying to look right inside me.

"I'm sorry, Jamie."

"I'm not."

"Really?"

"Mum, I'm your son."

"You're his son, too."

"That doesn't mean I have to like what he's done, does it?" The words flow out of my mouth, coated in a carefree honesty that tastes a bit like Christmas.

Mum comes in for another hug.

"God, I'm lucky to have you," she says, squeezing me tight.

"Well, it works both ways," I grin, squeezing back. "But I ought to get to school."

"Yes, yes you should. Go on, get changed and off you go."

"Will you be alright?"

"I'll be fine. Get yourself ready."

As I head upstairs, still dreamy from the drink, a thought sploshes into my head. Dad didn't get me anything for my birthday. For the first time ever, he didn't get me anything. Not even a card.

Maybe it's the Baileys, maybe it's relief that the first meeting is over or maybe I'm just more childish than I thought, but it seems really funny and, as I change into my school clothes, I can't seem to stop laughing.

Nineteen

Mrs Beattie's a Tw*t

It takes me longer than usual to get to school but I put that down to the booze. I'm not staggering or weaving like they do in the films, but I'm noticing things a bit differently. The sunshine seems brighter, colours seem strangely stronger and I keep noticing details in walls or houses or the road or in passers-by that wouldn't have registered on my radar before.

I stop and stare at my school. Even from here, I can hear voices, shouts, laughter. If I go through those gates, what's going to be waiting for me?

Nadia. Nadia's going to be waiting for me.

If I know her, she's going to want more answers. Those pathetic offerings I gave her on Saturday night were never going to be enough. It's going to mean more talking, more tension, more tears.

You know what? I've had enough of that for one day.

I ought to cross the road in front of me, turn right, take the second left up School Lane, go into the office, sign myself in and go to English. Any other day I would, but not today. Because, I note, pivoting on my heels and turning smartly to the left, today I don't feel like it and, today, I've had Baileys Irish Cream Liqueur for breakfast. The Fear of Consequences Department in my brain seems to have gone on strike. The decision is made.

With a smirk of self-congratulation, I shrug my backpack further up my back and head towards town.

Walking past the shops and cafes and people doing their daily thing when I know I ought to be at school is insanely liberating. I can't believe I've never done it before.

Strike that, of course I can believe I've never done it before. My fear of authority is such that it wouldn't take much to persuade me that teachers can actually hear a treasonous thought. The reality is very different. No one seems to care. Nobody's looking at me and all the teachers are locked up in their classrooms and all the police are probably off arresting real criminals. I'm free. Anonymous. Just a face in a crowd that's got better things to worry about.

Right now, I want to find somewhere nice to just sit, stare and be.

By the time I get to the park, I'm starting to wish I'd bought a bottle of water. I'm feeling a bit sluggish and very thirsty. I also really need a pee. It's not that gentle warning you usually get, which means you've probably got about fifteen minutes bargaining time before things get serious; it's a sudden, insistent pressure that says waiting's not an option.

Luckily, the park is fairly empty, apart from an old lady, sitting on a bench, tossing bits of bread into a sea of pigeons. With a quick look around, I slip into some bushes and spatter the contents of my bladder onto the ground, catching an unfortunate beetle in the expanding, frothy puddle. This is also something I've never done before either and the physical relief aside, it feels great. Like I'm sticking the finger up to anyone who ever made a rule.

This must be worth a few Man Points. I giggle to myself. With this widdle, I am Manning Up.

I zip up and step back into the park. No one's noticed my little indiscretion. The sea of pigeons is still bobbing and cooing and the old lady is still launching lumps of bread into their midst. Now to deal with the thirst. Across the grass in front of me, there's a kiosk, selling lollies, ice cream and coffee. They've probably got water. I walk over to it, buy a bottle and find an empty bench.

The water tastes fantastic. It tastes better, cleaner and colder than any water I can ever remember drinking. As I glug greedily away, a column of cold travels down my throat, cooling my stomach. It's as though I can feel the cells in my body rejoicing and soaking it up. I'm an oversized sponge. I pull the bottle from my lips and gasp, dragging air into my lungs.

Air and cigarette smoke.

Without meaning to, I turn my head sharply to the right, to see who is polluting this hallowed moment between me and my holy water.

Wreathed in a cloud of swirling smoke is a girl. A girl from my year. Like me, she's wearing her uniform. Unlike me, she's smoking a cigarette.

I know her. Of course I know her. Not 'know her' know her, but I know who she is. Probably every guy in my year knows who she is. I'm sitting next to Lauren Edwards and Lauren Edwards is hotter than the fires of hell.

Lauren Edwards is so strikingly pretty, it's hard to look at her, but she's also got this permanent look of contempt on her face that makes you feel unworthy to be breathing the same air as her. Or cigarette fumes.

Lauren Edwards doesn't do lessons or teachers or homework. Lauren Edwards certainly won't have a clue who I am; I'm just another male, slobbering incoherently in her wake.

I must be staring because she slowly looks me dead in the eyes, smoke curling from her nostrils.

"Alright? Got a problem?"

"No," I jabber. "No, no, no. No problem. I was just . . . I . . ."

"How come you're not at school?"

"Oh. I just . . . I didn't go. I didn't feel like it."

She turns her body towards me, taking another puff on her fag. I can't help but notice the sun reflecting off the surface of her legs.

"'Didn't feel like it'," she repeats slowly, as if she's sounding me out.

"No. Today was just . . . one of those days, I guess." I chuck in a buffoonish grin and shrug, as if that somehow explains everything.

"What's so special about today?"

Apparently, it doesn't.

"Just . . . just stuff. Stuff at home. Parents stuff." As the words leave my mouth, I'm already questioning why I'm telling her the things I couldn't even tell Nadia. Or anyone for that matter. I don't even know Lauren Edwards. I just know the legend of Lauren Edwards. Is that reason enough to be sharing this stuff with her? I'd make a useless spy.

Lauren Edwards: Tell me your name, rank and number.

Me: No.

Lauren Edwards: Then I'm just going to have to leave and talk to someone more interesting.

Me: James Chapman, Private, Number 6502. Gemini.

Meanwhile in Real Life, Lauren Edwards takes another pull

on her cigarette and blasts out a cone of smoke from between pursed lips.

"Parents," she grunts. "Parents are such shitheads."

Whatever I had been expecting her to say, it wasn't that. Maybe I was hoping she'd clutch me to her ample bosom and caress my head. Maybe I was expecting her to look all concerned and probe further but, in a way, her answer is perfect. A smidgen of sympathy and the sweary acknowledgement that she gets it; that she's probably been through something similar.

"You haven't done this before, have you?" she asks.

"What?"

"Bunked off."

"No," I admit, suddenly feeling ashamed about it.

"Didn't think so."

"How come?"

"I can just tell. You're one of the good kids."

The word 'kid' gets under my skin and itches nastily. I'm a man, for crying out loud! I peed in a bush!

"What d'you mean?"

"You go to school every day, get your stupid homework done, 'yes, sir', 'no, miss'." She waves a hand at my backpack, on the floor at my feet. "Bet you don't even swear."

"I do!" Why am I sounding indignant about this?

"No, you don't," she smiles lazily. "It's written all over you. You don't put a foot wrong."

"I do!"

"Go on then."

"What?"

"Swear."

This takes me aback for a moment. It seems Lauren Edwards has clairvoyant abilities as well as amazing breasts. She's right. I don't swear, as a rule. Not where other people can hear me anyway. It's just not something that registers as a need, but I'm blimming well going to do it.

"OK. I will." My brain empties at the crucial moment. "What shall I say?"

Lauren Edwards snorts a laugh and flicks her cigarette onto the grass.

"School's shit," she squints slyly at me. "Say that."

"OK then."

"Go on then."

"I will!"

"Go on, then."

"OK! You're putting me off! School's shit! There!"

Lauren Edwards erupts into laughter, which isn't unpleasant to listen to, but it's not entirely pleasant either.

"What?"

"It's just the way you said it!" she laughs. "It doesn't sound like swearing! It sounds like you're really old or something!"

I feel my face crinkle up in confusion, which seems to make

her laugh even more. I like this.

"Say, 'Mrs Beattie's a twat'," Lauren Edwards smiles, her eyes full of fire and mischief. "I hate Mrs Beattie."

I'm about to say that I quite like her actually but swallow it. Instead, I hear myself say it.

"Mrs Beattie's a twat!"

Lauren Edwards collapses again. My face crinkles again. Lauren Edwards laughs harder.

"It just doesn't sound right," she gasps. "Not coming out of your mouth." She laughs again and suddenly I'm caught on the crest of a wave. I'm entertaining the myth that is Lauren Edwards and all I'm doing is swearing.

"Balls!" I announce.

Lauren Edwards laughs like it's the funniest thing she's ever heard.

"Fart and tits!" I add enthusiastically.

Lauren Edwards is beside herself.

"Giant cock!" I declaim, Caesar-like. "Fanny!" I roar.

I'm not sure Lauren Edward can take much more of this, so I go for broke.

"Bollocks, bastard, arse and wank!"

Lauren Edwards is now slapping the park bench in her hysteria, her non-uniform-regulation rings making noises like miniature gunshots with each mirth-induced whack. There are genuine tears running down her face, so I give it my best parting shot.

I take in a deep lungful of air and suddenly shout, "VAGINA!"

Lauren Edwards is laughing so hard, I'm worried she might die. From across the grass, there's a sudden sound of flapping, like a ripple of heavy-handed applause. I look to where the sound is coming from and see the old lady pointedly standing up and, fixing us both with a look of disgust, as she starts to walk away. For no reason at all, and despite the instinctive guilt that rushes through my chest, this is unreasonably funny to me. As I collapse into giggles, I point a shaky arm in the old lady's direction. Lauren Edwards sees it and suddenly twists to her right, clutching the arm of the park bench for support as we both howl with laughter.

Slowly, interspersed with lots of hoo-ing and hee-ing, we calm down.

"You – are – funny," Lauren Edwards breathes.

"Am I?" I chuckle. "Why?"

"I don't know. You just are. Maybe it's because a kid like you doesn't say that sort of thing."

"Because I'm a 'good kid'?"

"Yeah, because of that."

Buoyed by my foray into the world of sit-down comedy. I decide to let her know just a little bit more about the man behind the mask.

"I got drunk this morning." That ought to surprise her.

"Oh, yeah? What on?"

Again, not quite the response I was anticipating, but it suggests that she has some experience in this department.

"Baileys."

Lauren Edwards starts to giggle once more.

"Baileys?" she snorts.

"I had wine yesterday!" I protest. I don't think I'm going to earn any extra Man Points by confessing to drinking sherry the night before.

"Woo," she answers, rolling her eyes.

"Alright, babe?"

A new voice has entered the conversation. Slightly affronted to have it interrupted, I look up to see a man in his twenties, with military-short hair. He's wearing a t-shirt and jogging trousers. There's a thick, gold chain round his neck and something similar hanging off his right wrist. Fag smoke travels up his right arm from the cigarette dangling between his fingers.

Lauren Edwards gets up and wraps her arms around him, pulling him in tight for the type of kiss that I can only dream about. His hand, still adorned by his cigarette, snakes around her waist and crawls its way down to one of her bum cheeks.

A moment's slurping later, their lips part and Lauren Edwards turns to face me, her arm still around this shaven-headed stranger.

"Liam," she says, "this is . . ."

Despite our swear-a-thon, it seems Lauren Edwards and

I haven't been formally introduced.

"Jamie," I say, trying to keep it casual enough to mask the immediate fear I have of this Liam character. "Hi there." For some inexplicable reason, I give him a little wave.

As chance might have it, this is the right thing to do. Lauren Edwards laughs again.

"Jamie's having a bit of a rough time," she says. "But he's so funny and he likes a party. Can we get him along on Friday?"

"Up to you, babe," Liam shrugs, looking at me as though he's just trodden in me and his pristine Jordans are now starting to smell.

"Liam's having a party on Friday night at his flat," Lauren Edwards smiles, tucking herself into his chest. "You up for it?"

"Absolutely!" I hear myself saying, as though it's something I say all the time.

Despite my apparent enthusiasm, the idea immediately fills me with terror, but this is outweighed by the fact that I've been invited by the hottest girl in the school. Nay, the universe.

"Should I bring something?" I add, thinking of crisps or those party-food platters you see on the Iceland adverts.

"Bring a bottle," Liam grunts.

"Absolutely!" I say again.

"But not Baileys," Lauren Edwards laughs. "Or wine."

"Right," I nod. "What . . . What sort of thing then?" Surely not lemonade?

"Vodka," she replies. "Something like that."

"Sure," I nod again. "Vodka it is."

I'm going to a party. This has never happened before. It's with Lauren Edwards, and I need vodka.

Shit.

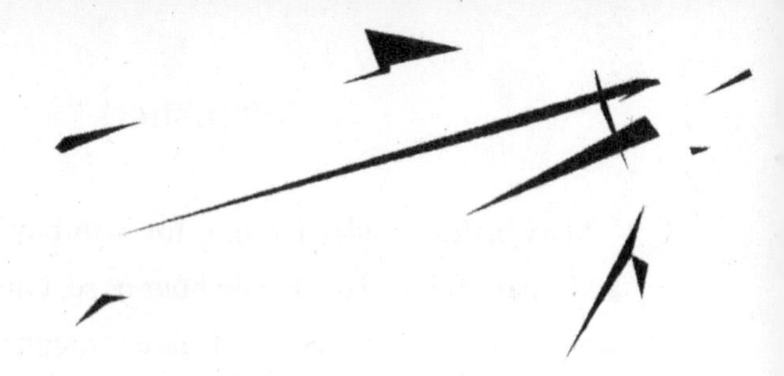

Twenty

007

After I've put Liam's address into my phone and he and Lauren have left, I sit alone for a while. Despite the bright sunshine and the vibrant green of the park, my eyes feel tired and there's this constant feeling of dry in my mouth. There's also an underlying sense of unease. Everything I've done this morning, from mediating my parents to agreeing to go to a party, has been done without any of my usual care or consideration and I'm starting to worry. In the heady heat of the moment, it all seemed like a good idea – liberating almost – but now, as the last of the Baileys slips away from my brain, I'm riddled with fear that I haven't done the right thing. I haven't really solved any problems at all; just put a plaster on and made all the right noises. In fact, when it comes to problems, I might just have added a few more to the list.

My worries wander me into town to buy some more water and a bar of chocolate. For an hour or so, I mooch in and out of shops, browse magazines and stare through windows at things I couldn't possibly afford. The glorious sense of anonymity I felt earlier has now become something more akin to loneliness. I wish Nadia was here to give me a hug and tell me everything's going to be alright. Adil's gangly shrugging wouldn't go amiss either. Even Lauren Edwards and Liam would do. I'm alone with my problems hanging off me, like leeches, silently sucking at any happiness I might have left.

A quick look at my watch tells me that it's half an hour until school finishes. I ought to head home. If I'm spotted by anyone who knows me, the game's up, so I wearily point my legs out of town and back the way I came.

Eventually, after a little meandering to get the just-back-from-school-timing right, home is on the horizon. I stop, stand and stare, my heart beating hard. It's just like school. I don't want to go there. I don't want to go in. Home isn't really home anymore. Home is a battleground; a suburban coliseum where my parents hack away at each other, and me and Bex are forced to watch from the sidelines. Home used to be a place where you could take your problems and somebody would have something useful to say. Since The Night Everything Went Weird, it's the place where problems are created. It's a problem factory.

I don't want to go in, but there's nowhere else to go.

007

Mum wrenches the front door open before I've even turned the handle.

"Jamie!" Her voice is quick and urgent and she looks over my shoulder. "Get in, get in! I need to show you something!"

She half-pulls me in, closing the door behind us.

"What is it? What's up?"

"Hi, Jay-meee!" Becky's voice rings loud from the kitchen.

"Hiya!" I answer back. "Good day?"

"It was OK."

"I'll be in in a minute, love!" mum calls to her, rooting around in her handbag, which is hung on the bannister at the bottom of the stairs. "You learn your spellings and I'll come and test you!"

"Mum?" I haven't seen her this excited in a long time and, to be honest, it's a bit unnerving. She seems almost manic.

Suddenly, mum pulls something from her handbag, keeping it hidden in her hand. She casts a look towards the kitchen, checking to see that Bex is where she ought to be.

"Look!" she whispers and unclenches her fist. In her hand is probably the biggest sum of money I've ever seen in real life; a bundle of crisp fifty-pound notes, rendered in some sort of mad pink, with the Queen grinning back at me over and over again.

I ought to check her handbag for balaclavas or shotguns.

"What the . . .?" I splutter, as quietly as I can. "How did you . . .?"

"I went to the bank," she gabbles, keeping her voice to a minimum. "I saw the bank manager and I told her everything!"

"Everything?"

"Well, most of it. Anyway, I told her that your dad had frozen the account, but that I needed money and all that. She said that he really shouldn't be doing this, but she's just been through a divorce and let me take out this money in cash. Just the once. Never again. I've got to open an account somewhere else, just so I don't drop her in it."

"How much is it?"

"Two and a half thousand!" mum beams, looking about Becky's age.

"What . . . What's it for?"

"Look," she says. "All my money is in that joint account. It's not just your dad's; it's mine too. At the moment, we've got nothing and he's relying on that to bring me back to him. This buys us food and time, but I need you to hide it."

"What?"

"He's going to find out soon enough, Jamie, and he's going to come looking for it. The one place he won't look is your room. In case he does, I need you to hide it somewhere safe. When the time's right, I'll get it off you and open a new account."

"OK," I nod, despite suddenly feeling unworthy of my father's love. Then again, there hasn't been much of that on show lately. I take the wad, smelling the coppery, cottony smell of money.

"Don't tell me where you put it. That way, I won't be lying if he asks where it is."

"OK."

Jesus, this is sad. Is this what 'I do' comes to?

"And this," mum says, reaching back into her handbag, "is for you." She pulls out two slightly-less-impressive-looking tenners and hands them to me. "Happy Birthday. Again."

For a moment, they're not two ten-pound notes. They're a bottle of vodka and my passport to a party.

"Thanks, mum."

"No, thank *you.* I know this is awful, Jamie – I know it is – but you and Becky are all I've got."

"Mum!" Becky's voice shatters the furtive silence. "I've learned them!"

"Coming!" mum yells back. "Go on, Jamie, off you go."

Off I go, up the stairs, with two thousand, five hundred and twenty pounds in my hands; two thousand, five hundred of which I've got to hide from my father. While I can't deny there's a certain James-Bond-style excitement involved, even as I step into my bedroom and scour it for secret hidey-holes, I feel an icicle of guilt, cold and sharp in my chest.

Where in God's name am I going to hide this money?

Dropping my backpack, I try out a few places; in between the pages of books, inside computer game boxes, under my mattress. It all seems too obvious, too discoverable. Then I spy an old Lucozade bottle on my bedside desk; one that hasn't made it to the bin, but really should have a long time ago.

Mum's got a thing about fizzy drinks, says they're almost as bad as smoking, but she lets it slide, now and again; something about me being old enough to make my own choices. Becky isn't accorded the same flexibility. Not yet. For her, it's water or squash, so anything fizzy gets sneaked into my room and drunk there.

I look at the bottle. The bottle looks back at me.

Could it be that simple? At a first glance, it looks like it could. Whatever I put inside there would be hidden by the garish label that stretches from cap to base and wreathes the bottle, in its entirety. I unscrew the cap and look in. There are a few dribbles left which I empty into the bin.

Here it is: the perfect hiding place. I roll the money up as tight as I can, and jam it inside, before screwing the lid back into place and putting it back on my desk. The only worry I've got is that mum might throw it away if she goes into one of her cleaning frenzies, so I park it slightly behind my bedside lamp. It looks just like a bottle of fizzy drink, instead of a bottle of two and a half grand. Hiding in plain sight, the best camouflage of all.

I'm just about to head downstairs, when my phone pings a WhatsApp message from my bed. It's Adil.

Sup? Saw u not @ school hope ur ok fancy doing sum voicework on fri eve?

Two problems present themselves:

I'm supposed to be going to a party on Friday night

What if Nadia's at Adil's? That wouldn't be good for her.

As if he's read my mind, Adil sends another message through:

only be u & me until about 6 zat OK?

I wonder how much he knows about me and Nadia, but I can find out in the week. Until then, he's about the only friend I've got and I'm not going to let him down.

I'm up for it mate. See you tomorrow.

Voiceovers and vodka.

Because that's how I roll apparently.

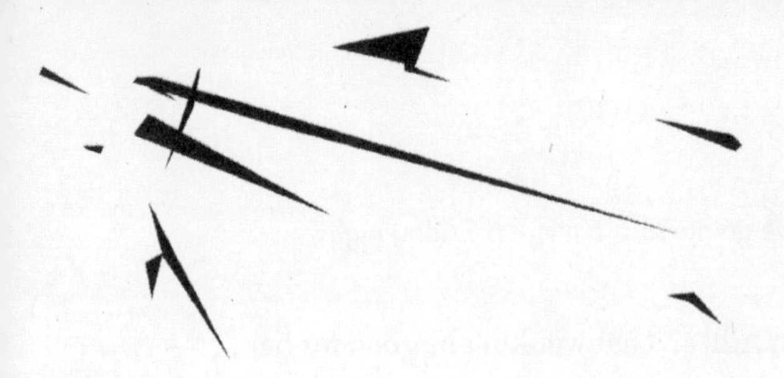

Twenty-One

Morally Weak

As I walk through the doors to the main school building the following morning, my heart gives an uncomfortable leap and it's all I can do to persuade myself to go in.

"Alright, Jim?"

The unexpected hand on my shoulder sends me into a pirouette that would shame the world's finest ballerina. It's only Adil, who starts to shudder with laughter at my open-mouthed panic.

"Sorry, mate," he grins, pulling his earphones out.

"No, that's OK," I pant, trying to regain control of my pulse.

"You OK? You weren't in, yesterday."

"No. No, I wasn't." There's a momentary urge to tell him exactly what's going on at home, but I crush it and instead go with, "But I'm fine". I leave it there. I ought to back it up with some fictional flu or imaginary stomach upset, but I don't. Maybe I want him to ask, so that, if I tell him, the responsibility isn't mine.

"That's good then," Adil shrugs, cheerily. "And you're good for Friday night?"

"Yes. Yes, I am. Just you and me, is it? Not Nadia or anything like that . . .?" The question doesn't sound quite as nonchalant as I'd like.

"Just you and me. Nadia told me what happened, so I thought we'd record separately."

"How is she?"

Adil ruffles his mop and searches the ceiling for guidelines on how to answer this question.

"She's OK," he says, eventually.

"How OK? Crying OK? Angry OK? Hates me OK? What sort of OK are we talking about?"

Adil's eyes go ceiling-ward once more.

"I'd say she was probably a bit angry. Probably confused, I reckon."

"Oh. Did she . . . you know . . . tell you what happened?"

"Just the basics. I didn't want to ask too much. You know me . . ."

"No. Sure. Fair enough."

"I was a bit surprised though, if I'm honest. I thought you two were pretty solid."

"Well . . ." I sigh. "These things happen, I guess."

"True," Adil shrugs.

That's about as intimate as a conversation between him and I ever gets. Which I like. It's easier that way. There's less at risk, like my sanity.

We part company and saunter off to our respective classrooms.

For the best part of the morning, everything goes as well as can be expected, but I know it's only a matter of time before I bump into Nadia. The next lesson, in fact.

According to my teacher, Mr Morgan, physics is "relevant to us all and has plenty of applications to solve everyday problems". So, why am I sat here trying to calculate the weight of a car with a mass of fifteen hundred kilograms, while it's somehow ended up parked on the Moon?

How does that hold any relevance to my everyday problems?

This a waste of time. I sit back, silently hissing my frustration. There's a very real urge to throw my book across the room, but I don't. Instead, I sit, staring at this stupid, irrelevant question. That's the problem with physics, it thinks it's so clever. It thinks it's got all the answers.

Without realising it, I'm getting angry at an entire science.

Alright then, Physics. If you know so much, then let's see if you can work this one out: what's the actual Weight of Manhood? Tell me just how a fully, paid up member of the Man Club is supposed to deal with all the stuff that's going on my life.

Let's see just how relevant this physics thing is.

Fizzing with sudden fury, I set about my calculations with the sort of single-mindedness you'd expect from Dr Frankenstein.

According to Mr Morgan, you calculate the weight of something by multiplying it by its mass, which you've multiplied by the acceleration of gravity. According to my textbook, the standard acceleration of gravity for a freefalling object is $9.8m/s^2$.

Maybe there is some relevance in this. I feel like I'm in freefall so, emotionally, that's how fast I must be plummeting. $9.8m/s^2$. That's pretty fast. With a feverish sweat breaking on my brow, I throw myself further into the calculations.

What about mass? Using my own mass isn't going to tell me anything I don't already know. It ought to be the mass of my problems. Mass is the amount of matter in an object and a lot of what's going on in my life really does matter, so that's got to be a fair amount. I reckon each of my problems feels like about a ton, so now I just need to see how many there are:

Mum. Dad. Bex. That's three.

Nadia. Four.

Hiding money in a Lucozade bottle. Five.

General feelings of inadequacy: I'll make that two tonnes, which brings us up to seven.

Buying vodka. That's eight.

In the end, I round it up to ten.

If I'm reading this right, the mass part has to be converted into kilogrammes and the textbook says that one UK ton comes in at 1,000kg. Multiply that by 10 and the mass of my problems tips the scales at 10,000kg.

So, the formula to calculate the Actual Weight of Manhood reads as:

Weight = Problems x Force of Gravity

This works out as:

Weight = 10,000kg x 9.8m/s^2

Now, for the moment of truth. According to my theory, the Actual Weight of Manhood is . . . (gets out his calculator) . . .

Drum roll, please . . .

98,000 Newtons.

I stare at the numbers, blankly.

I think I might be losing my mind.

The bell goes. Unlike the rest of my fellow physicists, I remain seated, staring at my pointless workings and my even more pointless answer.

"Chapman," Mr Morgan intones, "off you go, lad. Don't make yourself late for your next class."

"Yes, sir. Sorry, sir."

I slowly gather my books and put them into my backpack, which I then sling limply over my shoulder before walking into the corridor.

For the second time this day, Adil nearly induces my first cardiac arrest, placing his hand on my shoulder.

"Jim."

"Are you stalking me or something?"

"In your dreams," Adil grins, his shoulders jiggling. "Where you off to now?"

"English."

"Oh, yeah?" he says, like he wasn't really interested in the first place. "Mate, can we make it a bit later on Friday? Something's come up."

"What time are you thinking?"

"Well, I know I said come and do five 'til six, but could you do – say – six-thirty 'til about seven-thirty?"

Thinking about it, this works for me. Although the idea of going to a party where real-live girls with real-live breasts seemed like the best thing in the world yesterday, today the appeal is slowly being replaced with fear. If I'm at Adil's – which was organised in advance – then I've got a legitimate reason not to go.

"Whatever you like, mate," I shrug. "I can stay on longer if it helps. You know, help out with the filming or prop-making or whatever."

If I was anyone else, I'd be expecting Adil to react with some outward display of gratitude, but I'm not. I'm his friend and I know that, inside he's probably feeling thankful, but those feelings never really make it to his face. Instead, he responds with a shrug and a grin.

"Cool," he nods. "I'll rack up a list of what needs doing."

Our paths part at this point, mine continuing straight ahead and his turning right, towards the Maths Block. In the absence of anyone to talk to, my thoughts implode once more, coalescing into one single word: Nadia.

In a matter of metres, I'll be looking at her and trying not to. The queue outside the English Room is where it'll all happen; the disapproving looks, the muttered comments and the merciless judgement from anyone remotely connected to her. For her, it'll be an equal nightmare. Nadia wasn't made for the spotlight but every tear, every tremble of her lip is going to be scrutinised by the resident tragedy tourists in our class. The ones that get involved for the sake of it. The ones who've got little else going on in their own lives, so like to get firmly entrenched in others, invited or otherwise.

My pace slows. Maybe I need to be a little bit late.

I can't stand being late, but this might be the right thing to do for both of us.

If I delay getting there, I can go and sit in whichever seat's been left for the leper of the day. Given that Nadia's not going to want to sit next to me, which is perfectly reasonable, it'll probably be at the back of the class. I can keep my head down, get on with the lesson and spare both of us any unnecessary dramas. I don't have to enjoy it. I just have to do it.

Decision made, I head for the tiled sanctuary of the boys' toilets and force a wee.

Empty of urine and full of trepidation, I step back into the silent corridor and retrace my steps.

The queue outside the English Room has filed inside and the door is shut. It looks back at me, daring me to open it.

There's no turning back.

I knock on the glass pane, turn the handle and, trying to ignore the flurry of anxiety in my chest, step in.

"Ah, Mr Chapman," Mrs Beattie drones, wryly. "So nice of you to join us."

"Sorry, Miss. I was . . . ah . . . caught short." My flustering produces a soft ripple of snorts and giggles around the room, but I keep my eyes fixed on my teacher.

"Sit down then," she snaps.

Breaking her gaze, I scan the class, looking instinctively to the desks at the back which are all filled. The same for the ones in the middle. Panicking, I look again – just in case I've missed something – but my fearful searches are only met with rows of accusatory eyes, staring back at me.

"Chapman?" Mrs Beattie breathes, her face hardening. "Take. Your. Seat."

My seat is the only one available, two rows back from the front.

The one next to Nadia.

With nowhere left to hide, I make my way between desks, smiling weakly as I make my approach. Nadia doesn't look at me. Her eyes are fixed firmly on her textbook.

"Since you were late, I'm afraid your part has been recast," Mrs Beattie smiles, with all the warmth of an Arctic winter. "But perhaps you'd be so kind as to give us your Second Murderer."

I'm beginning to think that Lauren Edwards might've had a point about Mrs Beattie.

After a nod from Mrs Beattie, Chris Lowe picks up the Thane of Cawdor and reads out loud.

"Upon my head they placed a fruitless crown, and put a barren sceptre in my grip . . ."

"Where are we?" I whisper to Nadia, pulling out my copy of *Macbeth* and opening it.

Nadia's finger slides from where she's following the text and points to the corner of the page.

I find my place and follow on.

"Aye, in the catalogue ye go for men," Chris Lowe drones on. "As hounds and greyhounds . . ."

I risk a fevered hiss under the monotonous iambic beats that he's reeling off.

"Are you OK?"

Nadia doesn't respond, doesn't even acknowledge my existence.

"Nadia," I murmur, a bit louder. "Are you OK?"

She lets out a barely audible sigh and her face sets into a frown.

"I'm sorry," I mutter. "I really am sorry."

"Not now," she finally whispers back.

"OK."

"Chapman?" Mrs Beattie's voice snaps my eyes front and forward.

"Miss?"

"I am one, my liege . . ." she says, wielding a warning look.

"Yes," I cough, finding the right place with my finger. "I am one, my liege, whom the vile blows and buffets of the world have so incensed . . ."

The lesson goes on until we get to the end of Act Three, Scene One and Mrs Beattie embarks on a lengthy discussion about why Macbeth is morally weak. I can't help but feel that she's talking about me. I'm pretty sure that everyone else in the room thinks she is as well.

Finally, the bell rings.

"I will expect your essays to contain quotes," Mrs Beattie bellows over the cacophony, "and I'd like to see a plan at the beginning. Chapman, could you stay behind a moment?"

There goes my chance to see Nadia.

"Will you wait for me?" I ask, knowing full well that I don't have the right to.

Nadia doesn't answer, just slings her back over her shoulder and leaves the room. So much for my powers of negotiation.

Once the class has emptied, Mrs Beattie stands and closes the door.

"Is everything alright, James?" she asks, settling back behind her desk.

"Miss?"

"Well, after your fainting fit last week, your lateness today and your noticeable lack of focus, I do feel compelled to ask."

I like Mrs Beattie, although she can be a little hard-edged. If I was going to confide in a teacher, it'd probably be her. Her stoic logicality appeals to me. It's not invested in emotion, but even that's not enough to persuade me to part with my personal life.

"Everything's fine."

Mrs Beattie seems unconvinced, peering at me through glasses that magnify her eyes to the point where she would make a passable owl.

"If something *is* bothering you," she continues, "might I suggest that you book an appointment with the school counsellor?"

And have the entire school know that there's something wrong with me? No, thank you. Not going to happen.

"Everything's fine," I repeat. I can't think of anything else to say.

Mrs Beattie's lips purse and she looks me over with her saucer eyes.

"In that case, I expect you to turn up to my lessons on time and for you to give them your complete attention. Am I understood?"

"Yes, Miss."

"Off you go then."

I stand, grab my backpack and head for the door.

"James," Mrs Beattie calls after me.

"Yes, Miss?"

"You're a good student. Whatever's going on, you should take control of it and not let it interfere with your school life."

"Yes, Miss."

As I leave, I close the door behind me and sag for a moment. When I look up, I see Nadia at the end of the corridor, her weight on one leg, a bored scowl on her face.

At least she waited. At least I can try and check she's OK.

I walk towards her, trying not to stare at her and trying not to notice just how beautiful she is. Directly behind her, all crossed arms and condemnation, are three of her friends. There's enough distance between them and Nadia that we might be able to have something like a private conversation, but they're close enough to launch an SAS-style rescue mission if they feel the need.

This isn't going to be easy.

"Oi! Vagina!"

Breaking away from a passing group of girls, Lauren Edwards suddenly appears and fills the space between me and Nadia. She stops and shouts again.

"I said, 'Oi! Vagina!'"

I stop and wave feebly.

"Hi, there," I croak. "Hallo."

"You coming down the park again?"

Ordinarily, this level of interest from a girl would make this episode into one of the best moments of my life. Given the circumstances, it's vying for pole-position as one of the worst.

"Sorry, no. Not today . . . I . . . I can't."

"I knew it. One of the good kids." There's a taunt in there, but I'm not going to rise to it. I just want her to go away.

"Yeah," I shrug. "Sorry."

Lauren Edwards rolls her eyes, spins on a non-regulation heel and marches towards her gaggle of friends. Suddenly, she turns back.

"You *are* coming Friday night though, aren't you? You'd better not let me down."

There's no time for me to get into an argument with her about why I'm not going, so I do the manly thing and lie.

"Yes. Yes, I'll be there."

"Good. Seven-thirty." Lauren Edwards' eyes slide sideways,

as if she's just noticed Nadia. "Who's this? This your girlfriend?"

"No," Nadia snaps back at her. "I'm not. You're welcome to him." With that, she walks smartly back to her friends, who fall into some defence formation, like bodyguards, locking down a potential target. With a clack of hard heels, they march her off, down the corridor.

"Looks like someone's in trouble!" Lauren Edwards' smirks. "You are a dark horse."

Then, she too, is gone, escorted off by her entourage. Probably to the park.

Yes, I am in trouble.

98,000 Newtons' worth.

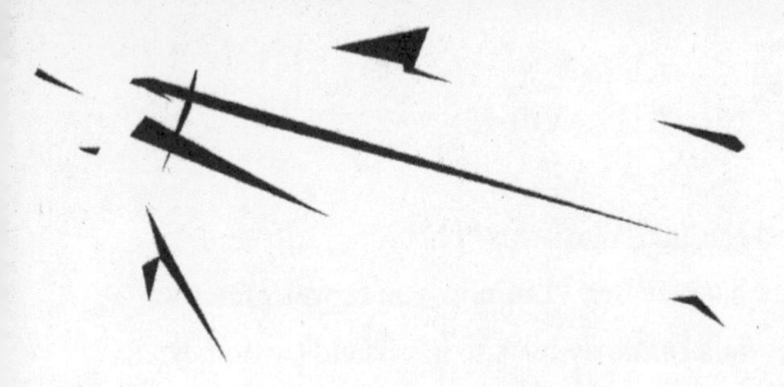

Twenty-Two

Hashtag

The next two days are Absolute Hell. Not the dramatic, fire-and-brimstone inferno religion would have us fear; more a slow and tortuous crawl through silence and ice. It turns out this version of Purgatory is manned by girls.

If guys were in charge of the torments, they would be quick and fast. There might be some insults, some pushing around, maybe even a pitchfork or two, but it would all be done in a flash. It would soon be forgotten about and everyone could just get on with the job of being eternally damned.

Girls seem to know how to drag out the suffering and really make it count.

It begins on Tuesday with the first weapon in their infernal arsenal: The Cold Shoulder. Usually it lasts an hour or two. Girls I would ordinarily exchange a smile and wave with or nod and a quick 'alright' are refusing to catch my eye. I am the Basilisk; a creature so foul that none can bear to look at me. Word seems to spread that there is a beast in their midst. By mid-afternoon, I can't find a girl I know who will engage with me on any level. Even the normally chatty Nicola Baines silently refuses my requests to borrow her pencil sharpener in Miss Rani's art class.

Wednesday is when I discover that Hell isn't run by Lucifer. Hell is run by Megan Jacobs.

Fiercely loyal, but with a fondness for the dramatic, I'm not sure she's ever liked me and now she's making sure that I know it. Wherever Nadia goes, so does Megan Jacobs and she hath written the Men Commandments:

Thou shalt not talk to James Chapman.

Thou shalt not let him anywhere near Nadia.

Thou shalt tut loudly as he walketh by.

Thou shalt whisper in his presence, just loudly enough to let him hear words like 'arsehole' and 'idiot'.

Thou shalt laugh at him for no reason whatsoever.

Unfortunately for me, I need to talk to Nadia.

It's not until lunchtime that the opportunity presents itself. While Adil is in the lunch queue, raking through the vegetarian offerings, I bag us a table and set my meal in front of me: fish fingers and beans. I'm not really hungry. I haven't been hungry since last Friday night. At home, I've gone through the motions; putting food into my mouth, chewing, swallowing and letting my stomach do the rest, but I haven't really enjoyed it. I just do it out of habit rather than hunger. As I cut a fish finger with the edge of my fork, raise it up and stare at it, my peripheral vison zooms in on a lone figure settling down at an empty table. Nadia.

A few furtive glances and my eyes report back that her current coterie of counsellors is also stuck in the queue. Even Megan Jacobs seems to have clocked off and is involved in some intense discussion with the girl behind her.

It's now or never.

Alright?" Adil smiles, nodding at the empty seat, something green and steaming on his plate.

"Yeah," I blink, getting up, "back in a minute."

"Where you going?"

I don't answer him. It's too late. I've committed to pushing and apologising my way towards the one girl who was foolish enough to go out with me.

My stomach starts to flip as I get closer. I wish I didn't notice the way her hair hangs over the nape of her neck. I wish things were different.

"Nadia," I pant breathlessly, sitting down beside her.

Nadia's eyes widen for a moment and shock straightens her spine. With a deep breath, she decides to focus on her food.

"Go away, Jamie," she mutters. "I don't want to talk to you. You had your chance."

"But I really need to talk to you!" I plead.

"And I really don't need to talk to you!" Her jaw clenches and her teeth grind.

This is too important to me. I need to make some sort of peace with her.

"Please, Nadia," I start. "Just listen for a minute . . ."

"Are you deaf?" a voice intones. "She said she doesn't want to talk to you."

This voice doesn't seem to care too much about consonants or volume. I'd been hoping for a quiet, snatched and probably urgent conversation. Until the would-be town crier that is Megan Jacobs waded in.

"No . . . look . . . Megan . . ."

"No, *you* look!" she roars, jabbing a vicious finger mere millimetres from my eyes. "She. Doesn't. Want. To. Talk. To. You. What part of that don't you understand?"

My face burns hot with shame and embarrassment. Out of instinct, I appeal to my recently dumped ex-girlfriend for some sort of moral support.

"Nadia . . ."

"Please go," she murmurs, staring at the table.

"OK, OK." I raise my hands in surrender but, for Megan Jacobs, that's not enough. This one takes scalps.

"*And*," she sneers as I stand up, "for your information, she's fine!" She spits the last word like acid and, to do her justice, it burns. "Nadia is absolutely fine! And? D'you know what? She's always had loads of blokes that want to ask her out! Better blokes than you!"

"Megan..." Nadia protests weakly, but Megan is like a woman possessed. It's as if I've suddenly been elected as responsible for the wrongdoings of any and every man she's ever encountered. I'm the poster boy for bad guys across the world.

"No!" Megan half-shouts. "I don't see why I shouldn't tell him!" She's back to me, her brown eyes red with vengeance. "I'll make it easy for you!" Making it easy for me appears to involve turning the volume up as far as it'll go. "NO ONE WANTS YOU HERE!" she bellows. "JUST! FUCK! OFF!"

"Yes," I mumble apologetically, my hands still raised. "Yes. I'm sorry. I didn't mean to upset anyone."

Megan stands in front of Nadia and stares me down, daring me to say something I'm sure to regret. Her sentence is final. She is judge, jury and potential executioner. Keeping my hands in the air, as though I'm at gunpoint, I stand, cast an apologetic smile at Nadia and slink away.

A mocking cheer goes from one of the tables behind me, the rusty bass of broken voices signifying that I am now a figure of ridicule for both sexes. I'll probably be a hashtag by the end of the day.

Glowing crimson, I return to my seat. Adil looks at me from his.

"Well, that didn't go so well," he shrugs eventually.

"Not quite what I was hoping for," I mutter.

"It'll pass. It'll be someone else tomorrow."

Will it? Or am I doomed to be forever tormented by Megan Jacobs and her pitiless minions?

"I can't eat this." I leave to go and find some small corner of the playground, where I can't do anyone else any harm.

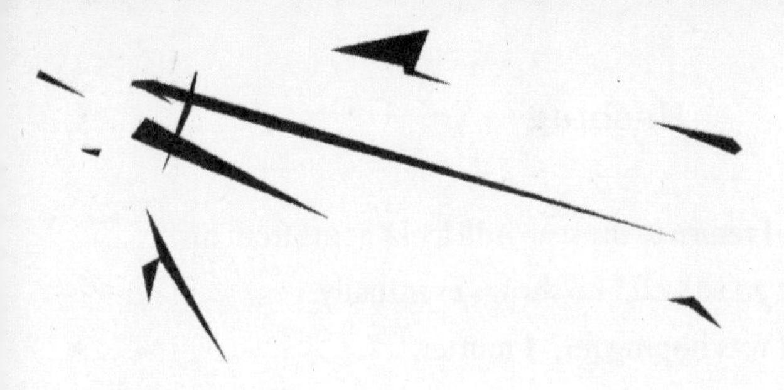

Twenty-Three

Madness

"Jamie! Jamie! Wake up!"

I tumble out of a dream in which I'm falling, falling, falling and land in Thursday morning. Mum's standing over me, her face taut, her voice tight.

Suddenly I'm awake, the now-familiar flurry of fear pumping adrenaline through my chest.

"What is it? What's happened?"

"Nothing, nothing," mum soothes me, although she keeps her voice low. "Where is it? Where's the . . .?" She mouths the word "money".

"Oh. OK." I reach over to the Lucozade bottle that's remained unnoticed on my bedside table and hand it to her. "In there."

Mum frowns at it for a moment, not understanding.

"I put it in there," I explain.

Mum looks at it again, unscrews the cap and peers inside.

"Thank you, Jamie," she breathes, screwing it back up again. "I'm going to open an account today. I just didn't want Bex to see anything. You can go back to sleep for half an hour. I wanted to get it before she woke up."

"It's alright," I groan, stretching. "I might as well get up." A morning adrenaline shot tends not to be conducive to napping.

Mum leans in, plants a kiss on my forehead and ruffles my hair.

"Thank you, Jamie," she says again, before leaving the room, the two-and-half-thousand-pound Lucozade bottle in hand.

I suppose I ought to be pleased. I've helped mum out. At the same time, I've colluded in something that's going to make dad really unhappy, if he ever finds out about it. Actually, it doesn't matter if he doesn't. I'll know I did it. I'll know I took sides.

The shower beckons.

As the seething water scalds my skin, the map of Thursday unfurls before me, charting emotional swamps, scathing forests and X marking the spot which happens to be guarded by a dragon that looks suspiciously like Megan Jacobs. It's going to be a nightmare, unless Adil's lunchtime prophecy that it'll be someone else's turn under the searchlight comes miraculously true. The idea of bunking off again has its appeal, but my inherent cowardice rules that out almost as soon as the thought arrives.

I need something to cling to, something to get me through another day.

Once dried and descending the stairs, it suddenly hits me. What I'm looking for is somewhere to vanish to, somewhere I can leave everything else behind me, even if it's just for a few hours.

What I'm looking for is Lauren Edwards' party.

And a bottle of vodka.

That's my mission for the day. Today, I shall contemplate how one might buy a bottle of vodka without being of legal age. I shall find that formula.

The idea is so illicit and so utterly against my normal code of conduct that something excited and breathless pirouettes through my stomach.

Doing a quick turn on the stairs, I go back into my bedroom and retrieve my birthday money. It would be a shame to have to spend the lot but, even if this is just a distracting, self-imposed pantomime, I want to feel as though I might just go through with it if the opportunity presents itself.

In the kitchen, mum's making tea and toast, with almost-robotic speed and efficiency.

"Mum? Are you OK?"

"I'm fine," she replies, without even turning away from the steaming mugs. "Why?"

"Mum. You've made three teas and a coffee."

The teaspoon in her hand clatters onto the worktop as she

steps smartly back from the counter, a sharp intake of breath signalling her shock.

"Shit," she mutters to herself, as if there's no one else in the room. "Shit."

"It's OK, mum. It's OK."

"He wants to see Becky," she breathes. "He texted me."

"When?"

"Today. I told him no. I said to wait until the weekend."

"When on the weekend? Tomorrow? Saturday?"

She turns around to face me. "I don't know," she sighs. "I just said the weekend."

"You've got to think, mum – and this might sound weird – but you've got to think selfishly, just for once. When's best for you?"

"I don't know." She sniffs and empties the coffee down the sink. As if this action alone somehow gives her a little strength, she says, "Maybe Saturday. He could have her all day and bring her back at teatime. I'm just not really comfortable with him having her in the evening. It might muck her up and I've got to try and give her some sense of normality. Maybe I — "

"Then that's what you tell him," I cut in. "Tell him Saturday. Tell him she needs her routine. Tell him what you like but tell him Saturday."

Mum nods and wipes her eyes.

"You're right," she smiles, breathing in deep. "You're right. I'll text him today, after I've been to the bank. Thanks, love.

Don't know what I'd do without you."

"You don't have to keep saying that, mum. You're not without me, are you? I'm your son. That's what – "

"Sons do," she finishes for me. "I know. You keep telling me, but I just worry that I'm putting too much on your shoulders."

"These are big old shoulders," I grin, patting one, ignoring the Newtons piling up on it. "Oh, I meant to ask you, Adil's making a film and he wants me to record a voice for him. Are you OK if I go over to his tomorrow night? It's fine if you're not. I can rearrange . . ."

"No. That should be fine. I think you could do with some time out of all this . . . madness."

I know what she's just said and I know what she means, but while my ears hear it one way, my brain takes it that I'm somehow showing the strain.

"Really, mum," I sort of argue, "if it's not good for you . . ."

"Jamie," mum says, looking an exaggerated version of stern, "it's fine. Go out. Enjoy yourself. Have fun!"

Lauren Edwards' soiree tiptoes into my mind.

"I might be late," I venture.

"I'll be fine."

"I might even have to stay over at his."

"As long as you text me so that I know what you're doing, it's fine."

"Well, as long as you text me so that I know you're alright,"

I scowl back at her.

"It's a deal." She's wearing that supremely irritating expression that dares me to call her bluff.

"Alright, then," I scowl again. "A deal it is."

I've just secured myself a pass to Lauren Edwards' party, but I don't feel like a triumph has just taken place. Probably because there's been some deception involved.

Who knows if I'll go to the party, anyway, but the option's there.

Now, vodka.

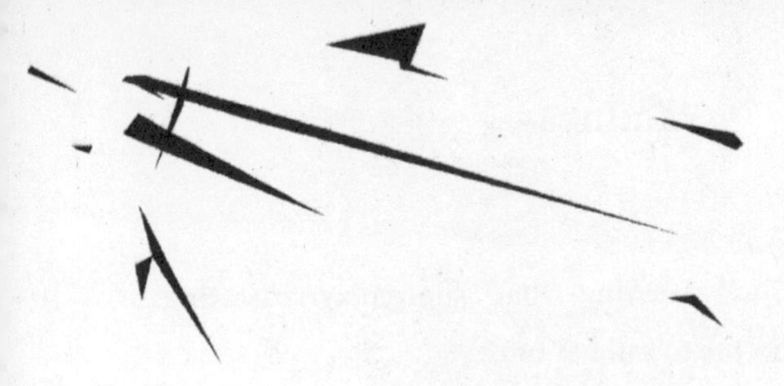

Twenty-Four

Shelf Life

School isn't as bad as I thought it was going to be. Although I'm still studiously ignored by anyone closely associated with Nadia, there seems to be some sort of unofficial ceasefire in operation. I don't want to press my luck so, as the bell rings for morning break, I head for the silence and relative safety of the school library.

As I make my way, I see the lanky, loping figure of Adil coming in the other direction. He's talking to some other kid from IT, but Adil's height gives him a vantage point and he spots me.

"Jim!" he calls, saying a snatched goodbye to the guy he's walking with. "Hold up! Where you going?"

"Oh, I just thought I'd go to the library," I say airily.

"Keeping low, eh?" He gives me an awkward grin.

"Something like that."

"Yeah, I'll come along." He says this like I've asked him to, which I haven't. I'm secretly glad he is anyway; it'd be nice to have some non-judgemental company. I'm not going to ask him about Nadia. I'm not sure how much good it would do me and I'm pretty sure he must be fairly sick of all the drama.

I can't think of anything to say that doesn't involve her. Questions keep rising up in my throat but I swallow them down. Instead, we walk in silence. Adil's good at silence; it doesn't seem to bother him. I, however, find it unbearable. While I'm raking through the sparse selection of topics that don't involve my ex-girlfriend, I'm struck by a thought.

"Adil, have you ever bought any alcohol?"

"No!" Judging by his expression, I've said something funny.

"But you could get away with being eighteen, easily. I mean, how tall are you?"

Adil shrugs. I'm not even sure he knows how tall he is. I'm less sure that he cares.

"No. My dad would go ballistic. Doesn't really interest me anyway."

"Have you ever . . . you know . . .?"

"What? Drunk alcohol?"

"Yeah."

"No, mate."

"What? Never?"

"No. Anyway, why are you so interested in whether I drink or not?"

"Nothing. Just wondered."

As we come to a stop outside the library, Adil squints at me. "Come on, Jim."

"Someone's asked me to get them some." This isn't strictly a lie. Lauren Edwards asked me to bring some to the party, which is much the same as getting it for her.

"Oh, yeah? Who?"

"Doesn't matter," I answer, as nonchalantly as I can, "I said no. It just made me wonder. I mean . . . if someone asked you to get them some . . . you could probably get away with it, I reckon." I cast a line out to see what bites. "Would you do it?"

"Doubt it."

I need to know for sure, but there's a weird sense of something like shame or embarrassment stopping me from asking him outright. So, I put on my best hypothetical voice instead.

"What if it was me? I mean, what if I wanted you to get some for me?"

"Why? Do you want some?"

"No," I lie.

"It doesn't matter then, does it?" he shrugs, putting his hand on the library door.

"No. No, I suppose not."

"Best way is to buy it online, I've heard. The delivery men don't look for ID. They just hand it over."

A feeling of complete stupidity washes through me. Of course that's how you'd do it. Borrow mum's card, enter my details and press 'order'. Too late now though. I need to think of something else. That's *if* I'm going to go ahead with it.

"I know some kids go to Tesco's in town and nick it."

"How? Wouldn't they get caught?"

"What they reckon they do is take in an empty bottle of water, then go to where the vodka is, wait 'til no-one's around and then fill it. Sometimes they stick the vodka in a trolley with loads of other stuff and do the pouring in there."

I am an idiot. It's so simple, it's obvious. Hide it in plain sight. But stealing's way off my moral compass. I don't think the needle even points in that direction.

"Sounds a bit risky."

"Does to me," Adil nods. "Singhsbury's seems to be where it all happens, though. Mr Singh's shop, down the road."

"So, that's where they buy alcohol?"

"Well, he's old, isn't he? And he keeps the hard stuff next to the fizzy drinks. His son works with him, but they can't keep an eye on everything. That's where most people go, I've heard."

"You hear a lot, don't you?"

"I do, I do," Adil grins, tapping the side of his nose with a finger.

"Have you heard anything about Nadia?" I didn't mean to say it. I didn't mean it to come out and certainly not as desperately as it did. Adil's cheery smile droops slightly, softening into something sympathetic.

"Just give her some time."

"Is that what she said?"

Adil shrugs. I take it to be a confirmation.

"Did she say anything else?"

"You know me, Jim. I don't ask these things."

"But you seem to hear an awful lot!" There's an edge of irritation in my voice that I don't mean. Luckily, nothing seems to phase Adil.

"I do, I do!" He grins and taps the side of his nose once more.

"Come on, then," I scowl. "Let's go in." I replace all thoughts of Nadia with vodka and Singhsburys.

It works. It works for the rest of the day. In fact, it works a bit too well. While I ought to be applying myself to quadratic equations in maths and giving the female reproductive system my full attention in biology, I'm weighing up what I might or might not be about to do after school.

It doesn't take long to decide that the Tesco scenario is off my list. Wandering around a supermarket, pouring vodka into empty Volvic bottles, with only a trolley for cover is too frightening a proposition. Mum shops in Tesco and so do her friends. Knowing my luck, the day I decide to apply for five-finger discount will be the day that that particular branch is hosting the National Store Detective Association's Annual Conference. I'll be cuffed and frogmarched past my weeping mother by at least six security guards, just at the moment Nadia walks in. Probably with Megan Jacobs whose dad, in an unforeseen plot twist, will turn out to own the local newspaper. After the resulting headline and centre-page story, complete with accompanying photos, I'll never be able to leave the house again.

"Chapman?"

The store detectives and baying paparazzi are gone. I'm in the biology lab, looking straight into the disappointed eyes of Mr Ross.

"Sir?"

He asks me where we are. Looking at the diagram whiteboard behind him, I make a panicked, but educated guess.

"The vagina, sir."

Judging by the explosions of laughter that detonate around me, my guess isn't that educated.

"I asked you where you were, Chapman," Mr Ross deadpans. "Not where you'd like to be." He gets the requisite sniggers. "Would you care to stay in the present or shall I see you after the lesson is done?"

"Sorry, sir."

Much as I try and stay focused and join the rest of the class on its journey up the fallopian tubes, I'm quickly back in the world of theft and alcohol.

Stealing isn't for me, and while I might be able to conjure some justifiable argument that stealing from a supermarket is somehow balancing the scales, it just doesn't sit right.

Suddenly I'm in Mr Singh's shop. Mr Singh's being targeted by underaged revellers suddenly makes sense. He's very old and, now that I'm approaching things from a criminal point of view, the shop is almost laid out as an invitation to shoplifters. The alcohol is next to the soft drinks, just next to the counter. All it would take is for Mr Singh to be looking the other way and a bottle of booze might inadvertently find itself quickly stashed into a conveniently placed backpack.

But stealing is stealing and stealing is wrong.

What if I were to leave the money on the nearest shelf, tucked away, so that no one else could find it, except Mr Singh, perhaps when he's replenishing the stock? Given I've got two ten-pound notes, I might even pay more than the bottle's worth. I'd be adding to his profit; giving him a little bit extra. He'd probably be quite pleased with that.

While the rest of the class marvels over the passage of an egg from the ovary to the uterus, I'm rehearsing the Great Vodka Heist. After school, Mr Singh's is usually full of kids, using the money they should've spent at lunchtime on something sustaining and nutritious on something either chocolatey or fizzy.

I could loiter by the soft drinks, perhaps scratching my head over which one to buy and wait for Mr Singh to get caught in a tidal wave of transaction and for his son to come to the rescue. Panther-like, I'd drop a bottle of whatever's alcoholic and nearest into my open backpack which I'd cunningly place at my feet and then secrete a note or two on the requisite shelf. I'd have committed the perfect crime. Whichever way I look at it, there are no losers. I get my alcohol and a dignified welcome to Lauren Edwards' party, and Mr Singh gets some extra takings without being an accessory to anything.

Not even Sherlock Holmes could solve this one.

The more I think about it, the more breathless and excited I become. That's all I'm doing, I remind myself. I'm only *considering* it, not *doing* it.

But I have to know.

I have to know just how impossible or possible it is.

That's why I'm swinging by Singhsburys on my way home.

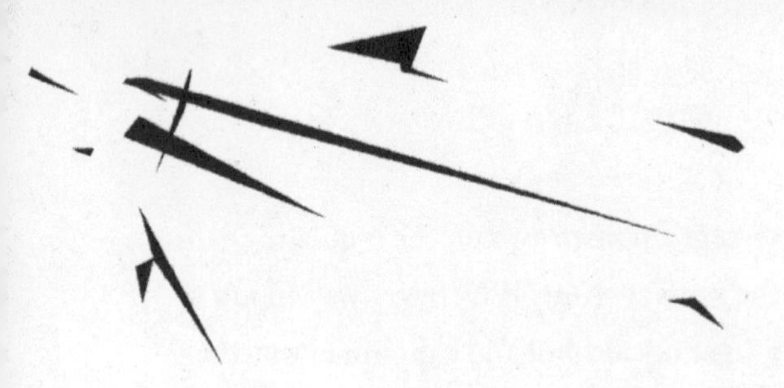

Twenty-Five

Think Like a Criminal

Mr Singh's counter is being stripped clean by sugar-starved school kids.

This was just going to be a reconnaissance mission; I was just going to have a look, frighten myself with the potential consequences and leave, vodka-free, but without a criminal record or potential jail time. Now I'm in here, The Great Vodka Heist seems terrifyingly possible.

As I get closer to the counter, my criminal heart skips a beat. Mr Singh's got help. I wasn't counting on that. A younger guy, probably in his thirties – maybe his son – is manning the till with all the ability of a trained octopus.

Mr Singh sits on his stool, watchful and patient. Occasionally, he points or glares or barks a command.

The drink shelves are about a metre to my left. They're lined with rows of shining bottles, filled with liquids of every imaginable colour – from the watery-tea brown of whisky to the garish greens and brilliant blues of things that I don't even know how to pronounce. It's an alcoholic Aladdin's cave.

Just as Adil said, the soft drinks are next to the booze; their flimsy, plastic containers looking suddenly infantile next to the glistening glass of their grown-up counterparts. I position myself in line with the lemonades, directly next to the final rows of the hard stuff. Trying to look as though I'm deciding which sugar-free beverage is going to quench my thirst, I look left. There's the vodka. At least five different types, each with a tantalising whiff of the Kremlin about them. Just to add a little realism to my pretend heist, I drop my bag at my feet. It waits open-mouthed, vainly waiting for something I know it'll never receive, because this is just pretend. A pantomime. Going through the motions.

I look back to the counter: Mr Singh's maybe-son is still dispensing chocolate and sweets. Mr Singh just sits and looks, hidden behind his frankly impressive beard. If *The Lord of the Rings* were to ever get a Bollywood remake, he'd be first in line for Gandalf. His eyes flick my way, almost as if he knows what's in my mind. I quickly look back to the lemonade and pick one up, as though considering it. Fear kicks up some leaves in my stomach. I look back. Mr Singh is back to surveying the crowd, from under imperious eyebrows.

I look closer, trying to think like a criminal, which is hard. The utter wrongness of stealing is so deeply chiselled into my character that it's like trying to pretend I'm a Martian, but I look anyway. Above the counter, fixed into the wall, is one of those round, convex mirrors. I can see myself in it, as though through a fish-eye lens. If I can see me, then someone else can too.

As this though lands in my brain, relief suddenly relaxes me. I half-smile. Who was I kidding? I was never going to do it anyway. As the tension falls from my arms, my shoulders and my chest, I suddenly start to give real thought as to which fizzy drink might give some life to the desert that is now my mouth. Maybe 7Up.

"Which one?" A voice, untroubled by puberty, is short and low in my ear.

I look right, straight into the eyes of a kid who must be three years younger than me. His eyes are sharp and keen, flicking left and right as he waits for me to answer. This kid's got a touch of the weasel about him; he reads me and all my darkest thoughts. I think know him from somewhere, but I can't place it.

"What?"

"Which one?" he hisses. "It's the vodka, innit?"

"Yes," I hear myself say, almost as if he told me to.

"Get ready. I'll meet you outside. Out the back."

"I . . . I don't . . ."

But he's gone, losing himself with practised expertise into the baying mob of future diabetics.

I stand, my mouth slack and dry. My heart – suddenly overwhelmed – pumps adrenaline through my chest.

Out of nowhere, the kid is at the front of the crowd. His hand works like a piston, grabbing at chocolate bars, sweets, gum – anything. Then he's pushing and barging his way through the masses, shoving his way to the door. As he does so, he flings his stolen goods into the air. Parts of the crowd go down, snatching at the floor for what he's dropped. Mr Singh Jr bolts from behind the counter, like a sprinter after the pistol's fired, but the scrabbling mass of bodies slows him. Mr Singh stands, one arm outstretched and pointing.

Time slows. We're all moving through syrup.

I've been given my opportunity.

This is real.

My hands reach towards the vodka, like I'm hypnotised. Vaguely aware of the cold, smooth feel of glass against my fingers, I seem to be picking the bottle up, but only for a second or two. I drop it. It falls, excruciating slowly, onto the floor. It misses my bag.

Time speeds up. Everything happens at double speed.

I bend down and grab the bottle. I drop it into my bag and zip it up. I notice that it's £6.99. I fumble for a tenner and I pull it out and I try to put it where the bottle was, but my fingers don't work. They can't hold it and it falls onto the floor. I'm already running and there's sweat on my forehead. I'm hot and cold at the same time and I'm running and running, and I'm out the door and whatever that kid said it's all I've got to cling to. I'm running around to the back of the shop, to where he said to meet him.

There he is, freckled, rust-haired and dark-eyed. No grin. No triumph. Just business.

"Did you get it?" he asks. It's more of a challenge than an ask.

I nod, like my head's going to fall off. "Yeah," I manage. "Yeah." It sounds like a surprise the second time I say it. Probably because it is. I'm now a thief.

"Right," he scowls, "your turn."

"My turn? My turn what?"

"Your turn to do me a favour. I done you one; you do me one. That's how it works."

I've seen Mafia movies where that sort of proposition has sounded far less ominous.

"What?" I ask, stupid and sweaty.

"How much you got?"

"How much what?"

"Money."

"Money?"

"Money."

I know exactly how much I've got, but the shock of being complicit in a robbery and his sheer confidence sees my hand go into my pocket and pull out a tenner – brown, crumpled and ordinary.

The kid looks at it and nods. At the same time, my memory starts to piece his face together.

"Go and get me some fags."

"What?"

"Fags. You heard."

"I'm not buying you cigarettes!" I splutter. "You're underage!"

"So are you," he squints, cocking his head to one side. "Plus, you've got some stolen booze in your bag."

I don't reply. I just stand there, appalled and backed into a corner.

"You know my brother?" The implied threat is hidden under a layer of carefree nonchalance.

I know who I'm talking to. I don't know his name, but I know his face. I'm looking at Nathan Douglas' little brother. Nathan Douglas: the guy that Adil rightly describes as "a psycho". Racist, angry and probably with some yet-to-be-discovered murders under his belt.

"I can't go back in there!" I protest.

"You are, mate, whether you like it or not."

"But – "

"I done you a favour. Now you do mine."

The equation is fairly simple when you boil it down.

My eye close in surrender.

"What am I buying?" I murmur.

"Is that all you got? A tenner?"

"Yes."

He presses some pound coins into my hand.

"A packet of Amber Leaf and some king-size skins."

"King size what?"

"Skins." Irritation bubbles dangerously close to the surface of his pale skin. "Rizlas."

"I've never bought tobacco before."

"Yeah, well."

With those words of wisdom ringing in my ears, I trudge back towards Singhsburys and go inside.

The crowd is still as big and still as animated and Mr Singh Jr has resumed his post, but their eyes scan us, harder and deeper than before. I'd sort of forgotten about the booze in my backpack, but now it weighs heavy and obvious on my shoulders. I feel like a criminal Quasimodo.

But nothing happens.

The Singhs' eyes pass through me and over me, as I shuffle forward, inch by inch, getting closer to the counter. As I approach, I can't help but look left, spying the gap in the vodka bottles where mine once was.

"Yes?"

I'm at the front and I suddenly want my mum, even though, given the circumstances. she'd be the worst person to have here. I look into the eyes of Mr Singh Jr and swallow air.

"A packet of Amber Leaf." My voice is as dry and as fragile as parchment. "And some king-size skins. Please."

"Skins."

My mind rewinds my conversation with Nathan Douglas Jr.

"Rizlas. Sorry. Rizlas."

Mr Singh Jr looks me over.

"You're eighteen?"

"Yes."

"Date of birth?"

My heart flips and bumps.

"What?"

"When were you born?"

Even though I can answer this with as much conviction as I can, every digit sounds like a lie. Mr Singh Jr looks me up and down, before opening a sliding door behind him, retrieving what I ask for, before slapping it down on the counter. The till tells me how much it all is and I plonk the money next to the tobacco.

Mr Singh Jr looks into my soul.

"You shouldn't smoke," he frowns.

"I'm . . . I'm giving up," I smile, feebly, putting the tobacco, skins and change into my pocket.

"You."

Mr Singh Sr's voice freezes whatever beat my heart might be about to attempt.

"Yes," he nods, from under his beard.

I'm frozen. I'm dead. I'm a thief and I'm about to be arrested. There are probably SWAT teams gathering outside.

Mr Singh gets up from his stool, opens the till and reaches in. His hand grasps something, which he places in front of me, on the counter.

It's a tenner.

"You drop this." There's a smile somewhere underneath the acres of facial hair.

I just stare at him.

"You drop this," he repeats. "Then you chase the boy. You are a good young man. Your mother is a proud woman."

I look at the money and then back at him.

"It's not mine," I offer limply. I want him to have it. I want to pay for my theft. I don't want to be an actual criminal.

"Is yours," Mr Singh nods. "You are good young man." He pushes the tenner towards me.

"But . . ."

"Your money. You take it."

I do. Like the lowlife, thieving dreg of humanity that I am, I take it, leave and make my way back to Nathan Douglas's little brother.

"You get it?" he sniffs.

I silently nod and pull out the pouch and Rizlas from my pocket, handing them to him.

"Nice one," he pouts, stuffing them into his blazer. "You need anything else, just let me know."

While I know this will never, ever – under any circumstances – ever happen again, I nod.

"Cheers then." Off he goes, slipping down the back roads, off to who-knows-where, to do who-knows-what.

I ought to be pleased. I've got a bottle of vodka in my backpack and guaranteed entry to Lauren Edwards' party.

But I'm not. I feel heavy and low, sad and disgusting.

I'm disgusted at myself.

The journey home is long and slow, and peppered with looks over my shoulder, just in case a Singh or a Douglas is following me.

Because that's what criminals do.

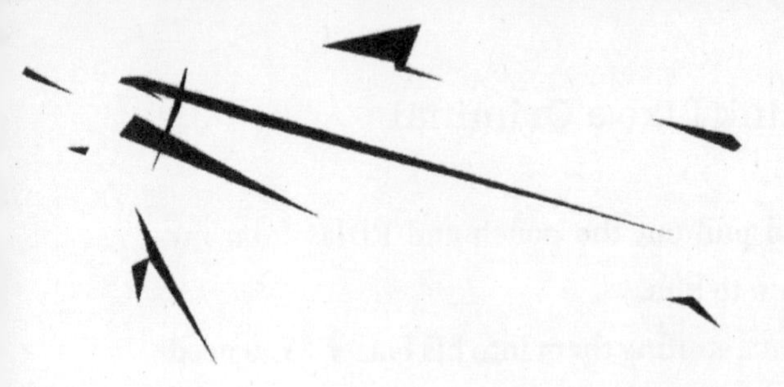

Twenty-Seven

Not a Habit

"And how am I supposed to live then tell? Tell me that. Go on!"

I can hear mum's voice through the front door. I take a deep breath and turn the handle. She's stood in the hallway, her back to me. As the front door opens, she turns my way. Her face is tight with anger. Someone's saying something on the other end of her mobile and I'm not expecting any prizes for guessing that it's dad.

"You OK?" I mouth, closing the door. For a moment, caught up in concern, I go to take my backpack off. I remember what's in it and don't.

Mum closes her eyes and grits her teeth. Whatever dad's saying, it's pressing the right buttons.

"How is it yours?" mum snaps into the handset. "How is it

yours? Have I contributed nothing to this family? You seem to have conveniently forgotten the money that my mother and father gave us. And that I gave up work because you told me we could cope on your salary!"

Money. Of course. How could a row of this size be about anything else?

Dad's garbled voice scratches at the air. I can't hear exactly what he's saying, but there's a very definite tone to it. And it's not a good one.

"Oh, you'd like that, wouldn't you?" mum seethes. "Well, that's never going to happen! And if you ever say anything like that about me to Becky again, it'll be a long time before you see her!"

Dad starts tries to come back with something but mum cuts him off.

"Yet," she states, with laser-beam precision. "We're not divorced *yet*."

A brief pause while dad gets another verbal round in.

"You. Hit me," mum replies, simply. For a moment, the anger leaves her face and leaves her voice, replacing them with something soft and sad, and with more scars than any bruise could ever leave.

The tone in dad's digitised voice changes. I can hear the anger. I can hear the recrimination. It all bleeds together to sound like weakness.

"OK, then," mum says. "I want a divorce. Is that clear enough?

We are getting divorced."

There it goes; umpteen years of marriage brought to a curt end, courtesy of O2's Family Plan Discount Package – except that's not quite true. It was courtesy of the night that dad decided to make a print of his fist on mum's face.

But it's not just about mum and dad.

"Where's Bex?" I mouth. Mum points along the hall.

Part of me just wants to implode and disappear from everything, but I can't.

My little sister needs me. I'm her brother, her dad, her best friend and her counsellor – all rolled into one.

With the sounds of the end of an era ringing in my ears, I go into the kitchen.

Becky is sat on the floor, her back against the dishwasher. Her legs are drawn up to her chest, wrapped tight by her arms, her face on her knees. Not knowing what else to do, I take off my backpack and sit next to her, adopting the same position.

"Hey," I say, softly.

She doesn't say anything. Instead, she holds her position and topples to her left, leaning against me. I put one arm around her and, for some reason, that simple act sends a furnace to my throat and tears to my eyes.

But she doesn't need that. She needs me to be strong. She needs someone she can lean on, safe in the knowledge that they won't fall over.

She needs me to Man Up.

Unfortunately for her, her big brother is becoming more and more like a Jenga tower, with too many people pulling at the pieces.

"What's going on?" I ask, harrumphing down anything that might pass for sadness.

There's a moment or two of silence, before Becky's face peels itself from her knees and her tear-stained school tights.

"I spoke to daddy," she says, in a shaky voice.

"And how was that?"

"He said he misses me."

"I'm sure he does." I give her a reassuring squeeze, which only serves to send a few more tears rolling – fat and hot – down her cheeks.

"And what else?" I ask, wiping the wet from her face.

"I told him about what I did at school . . ."

"And what was that?"

"I got a gold star for my spellings."

"Did you? Well done! Ten out of ten?"

"Yes."

"Well done! That's really good! What did daddy say?"

"He said 'well done'. He said I'm so clever."

"Well, that's because you are."

"I know, but then he said was mummy still cross with him."

"What did you say?"

"I said I don't know." Her face quivers. She feels guilty. Torn.

"And that's the right thing to say," I nod, sagely, a bullshit Buddha on the kitchen floor.

"Then he got cross."

"At you? What for?"

"Not at me. At mummy."

"Why?"

"He said . . . he said . . ." Bex's eyes are wet again, filling up like she's drowning on the inside.

"What did he say?"

"He said that mummy had stolen his money."

As Bex's shoulders start to shake, and her eyes go back to her knees, I think I can feel my heart burning. My teeth grind together and my chest tightens, as though there's not enough room in my lungs for any air at all.

"Is that what he said?" I croak.

Becky's anguished face comes back up and nods.

"Do you think that's true? Do you think mummy did that?"

"I don't know!" she wails into my side. "I don't know what's happening!"

My face gets hot and my vision blurs. Hurriedly, rubbishly, I scrabble at my eyes, smearing tears across my face. My nose suddenly throbs, heavy with liquid that wasn't there before. I can't let Bex see me cry. With a trembling hand, I wipe it away.

I hate this. I hate what's happening. I hate myself.

Squeezing Bex tight into me, I cough again. My lips pout

and churn as I try and swallow whatever might be rising to the surface and, beside me, my little sister weeps and trembles.

I let her. Better out than in. I listen to her tiny, strangled sobs and her voiceless confusion.

"Becky," I manage. "You know I love you, don't you?"

Becky's head nods somewhere in my ribs.

"And you know mummy loves you, don't you?"

"Yes." It's muffled, but it's a reply.

"And you know daddy loves you, don't you?" I clench my jaws as I say it.

"Yes."

"Well, there's something I need to tell you . . ." I'd better think of it quickly because from where I'm sitting, it looks like my sister's sanity might depend on it.

"Are you ready?" I add, trying to buy precious thinking time with insufficient funds.

There's another nod in my ribs.

"It's this," I start, letting my mouth make it up for me. "Whatever happens – what*ever* happens – mummy, daddy and me will always love you. *Always.* I promise you that. I promise you because it's true and no one can take it away or change it. Ever." My stupid eyes start leaking stupid tears again. I paw at them as best I can, without letting Bex know they were ever there. "OK?" I cough. "OK?"

"OK."

I give her a squeeze.

"Whatever happens between mummy and daddy, I'm on your side. Yours. Nobody else's. Just yours. OK?"

"OK."

"Good girl."

We sit in silence, me with my arm wrapped around her, listening to the muffle of mum's words from the hallway. It takes me a moment to realise, but I'm staring at my backpack. I'm staring into it with X-ray eyes, somehow seeing through the black mesh of polyester fibres, past the dog-eared textbooks, to the bottle of stolen vodka.

I can see it, bright and glowing with promise, even in the dark bowels of my holdall. I can see it in microscopic detail; the sheen and glisten of the red cap, helter-skeltered with spirals, just waiting be unscrewed. The communist crimson of the label, highlighting the chunky white letters that spell out its name.

Perfectly clear and perfectly still: the liquid inside; only discernible by a thin line, marking out the angle of a horizon held captive by the bottle.

Right now, more than anything else in this world, I want that feeling of being scooped up and held tight, safe and secure. A liquid embrace. Something that'll lighten the feeling of 98,000 Newtons sitting squarely on my shoulders.

It's just out of reach.

"What's going on here?"

Mum's suddenly in the doorway, her eyes puffy, her nose red and a sketchy smile wavering on her lips. I know she's only trying to make things easier, create a sense of normality, offer some comfort, but I can't help the flash of anger that lights up the hole in my stomach. I can't help the glare that I throw her way.

"I'm looking after my sister," I snap.

It catches her on the back foot and that just-flickering smile almost goes out. Taking a deep breath, she sits on one of the chairs by the kitchen table and looks at the floor.

I feel Becky shift beside me.

"Are you OK, mummy?" she asks, in a tiny voice.

Mum looks up and nods sadly.

"I'm OK."

Becky unfurls, stands up and goes and puts her arm around her. Mum pulls her in tight and buries her face in her shoulder. Her eyes screw up. No one sees it but me.

"OK," mum breathes, sniffing and blinking her way out of Becky's embrace, but still holding her with one arm. "OK. We need to talk."

"Are you sure we need to talk, now?" I ask from the floor, pointedly looking at my little sister. She's been through enough today. I don't know how much more those little shoulders can take.

"Yes, I'm sure. There's no point in dragging this out."

"What is it, mummy?"

Mum drags in a ragged breath and blows it out, her cheeks puffing up as though she's playing an invisible trumpet.

"We're getting divorced," she says. "Me and your dad. We're getting divorced."

Becky's face crumples.

"But why, mummy? Why?"

Mum swaddles her up in her arms once more as they both give in to tears. Fearing I might be the next victim, I haul myself to my feet, resolutely biting the inside of my lip and watch over them.

Mum doesn't say anything. She can't. Her face is lined with pain and grief, sorrow and guilt, all at once. She doesn't say anything, so I do. I have to.

"You know things haven't been good with mummy and daddy for a while, don't you?"

"Yes," Becky nods, turning to look at me.

"What have you noticed? What makes you think things have been a bit bad?"

Becky's eyes flick from me to mum and back again, looking for reinforcements; checking it's OK to say whatever she's going to say.

"What did you notice?" Mum's voice is a whisper, but at least it's there.

"Lots of arguments," Becky mumbles guiltily. "Shouting."

"Yep," I nod. "Arguments and shouting. Anything else?"

There's that shamefaced look on my sister's face again; that look that tells me she's not sure if she should say what she wants to.

"What else did you notice?" I ask gently.

"Well . . . I saw you crying, mummy."

"Did you? When? When was that?"

"You were in the bathroom and I was looking for you. I opened the door but you didn't know I was there and you were sat on the edge of the bath. You were crying and I didn't know what to do."

"What did you do?" mum asks, her eyes little short of a waterfall.

"I went into my room."

"And what then?"

"I cuddled my unicorn."

"Were you upset?" I ask.

"I cried."

Mum's arms are around her again, pulling her in, trying to protect her from everything and anything.

I let them cry for a moment. It gives me some time to try and chew the lining of my mouth off.

"That wasn't a nice feeling, was it?" I manage.

Becky shakes her head.

"Would you like that feeling to go away?"

A nod.

"Then that's why it's a good thing if mummy and daddy get divorced. If they're not together, they won't argue and if they don't argue, daddy won't shout, mummy won't cry and you won't feel bad."

"But I feel bad all the time!"

Then she snaps free from mum and runs out of the kitchen, a tear-sodden moan trailing in her wake. There's the thunder of her feet on the stairs and the slam of her bedroom door.

"Oh, Christ." Mum's head falls into her hands.

"I'll go and see her."

"No . . . No, you've done enough, Jamie. I'll go."

"Are you OK?"

"I don't know," she shrugs. "This is so hard."

All I can do is nod.

"I'll go and chat with her. Talk it through." Mum's hand strokes my cheek, before she leaves the kitchen. "Thanks, love. Thanks for trying."

Then I'm alone.

Just me and the hurting that just won't go away.

And the bottle.

I listen hard. Mum's on the landing. She knocks on Becky's door. She goes in.

Silence.

My legs take me tentatively to my backpack, as though the floor might break if I take a wrong step.

Slowly, quietly, I unzip the back and reach in.

The bottle is cold, hard, dependable.

With one eye on the hallway and one ear on upstairs, I slowly pull it out.

Smirnoff. I'm about to have my first taste of Smirnoff.

The cap clicks as I twist it, shearing at the thin layer of metal that keeps it in place.

It's open. I smell it. There's no real aroma; just a clinical, hospital-style smell. Like wet wipes. Vodka smells like wet wipes.

A conversation happens in my head, in as little time as it takes for my eyes to blink at the alcohol sting from the bottle. It starts with a flash memory of mum handing me a meagre ration of wine and telling me, "We don't want this turning into a habit." I'm asking myself if that's what's happening. Is this turning into a habit? It doesn't feel like a habit. It feels like when you take medicine. I'm answering my own question, reminding myself that no one bats an eyelid when you take cough medicine or headache pills. If you've got a cough, you fix it. If you've got a headache, you fix it. Right now, I've got pain in me. Somewhere deep inside, beyond the reaches of antibiotics and anaesthetic, I'm in agony.

So, I'm going to fix it.

With a furtive glance at the hallway and another quick listen, I bring the bottle to my lips and take a short, sharp swig.

There's an explosion in my mouth and a sudden burn at the back of my throat that makes me splutter and cough. Panicking, I screw the lid back on and drop the bottle back into my bag, making sure to zip it back up.

My mouth is burning, then my nose and then there's the feel

of lava heading down towards my stomach. Another cough sends me to the sink, reaching for a glass and turning the tap on.

Then, as the glass fills, I feel it. That heady hug, all cosy and disconnected.

I stand, holding the glass under the tap, not caring that it's overflowing over my fingers.

This isn't like wine. This is harder, more direct, instant. The fires inside me are suddenly doused, reduced from a raging heat to a warm, comfortable glow.

Instinctively, I look back at the backpack.

This isn't a habit. This is a choice. My choice. I'm choosing to fix myself.

There's time for another quick swip and I choose to do it.

Killing the tap, I retrieve the bottle, take a taste-bud-blasting mouthful, recap it and tuck it back in its hiding place. My choice. My decision.

It's not a very good hiding place, I muse, my mind slowing down to an idle chug. I need something else. I need to ditch the evidence.

A dumb smile creeps across my face.

There's an empty water bottle in my bin. I'll hide it in plain sight, just like the money. I'll fill it with vodka, put it in my backpack and then I'm all set for the party, tomorrow night. I'll lose the empty in the bins outside and no one will know a thing.

No one but me.

Twenty-Seven

Questions

I cannot, for the life of me, fathom how drug smugglers cope with the stress of trying to sneak their contraband past customs officials. All I'm doing is carrying a bottle of loosely disguised vodka through the school corridors and I'm virtually ready to throw myself on the feet of the nearest teacher, confess everything and beg for mercy.

Then there's the constant worry that I'm going to bump into Nathan Douglas's little brother. At that thought, my backpack feels suddenly heavier. I'm going to have to go back into Singhsburys and find a way of returning that ten-pound note. Maybe I'll drop it or put it somewhere that only they'll find it. Maybe I'll ask for change and leave in a hurry. Maybe I could just put it in an envelope and post it to them.

Obviously, I'd have to wear gloves during the whole procedure, just to prevent the sweat from my guilty robber hands from leaving an incriminating drop of DNA on the envelope.

Whatever I do, it'll be the last and only time I go back to Singhsburys.

"Alright, Jim?"

Adil. Thank God. It's only Adil.

"YesyesyesI'mfine," I babble, suddenly beaming with exaggerated joy and rolling out a fear-strangled laugh. I even slap him on the back out of sheer relief. I never slap anyone on the back. "Fine," I add. "I'm good."

"You good for tonight?"

"Tonight?"

"The recording."

"Oh, God, yes. Yes, of course!"

To be honest, given recent events, it had slipped my mind, but I'm suddenly looking forward to it. Just me and my friend, doing something daft for an hour or two.

"Six thirty?"

"Six thirty. I'll be there."

"So will I."

A thought claws its way through the background fuddle of fear in my brain.

"What about Nadia. Is she still . . .?"

"She's still coming, yeah. That's why I wanted to shift the time slots. She's off out, so it's easier if she does her bit, first."

"Off out?" A twitch takes possession of my mouth as I say it.

"Yeah."

"Off out where?"

"A party, I think. I can't really remember."

"A party?" The twitch extends a tremor to my right eye. "Cool. Whose party?"

"You know me, Jim. I don't ask these things."

No, but I really wish he did sometimes. The bottle in my bag now appears to weigh something close to a metric tonne, making the grand total 107,800 Newtons. Could Nadia be going to Lauren Edwards' party? It's highly unlikely. Nadia doesn't go to parties. Unlike me, she did get invites to sleepovers or whatever it is that girls do, but she always said no; said that she liked to be at home. Or with me.

Oh, God. This could be so horribly awkward.

"Jim?"

"What . . . Yes?"

"Alright?"

"Yes, yes. Sorry, I was just wondering whether Nadia's ready to go to a party. She doesn't do parties and what with everything that's happened . . . I was just wondering if it's a good idea. For her."

Adil nods, looking at me as though I've said something terribly profound.

"You broke up with her, mate. It's not your business, is it?"

He makes it sound terribly matter-of-fact and while I know he's trying to make me feel easier in a situation that I've just lied to him about, it makes me angry. Or maybe I'm angry at myself.

"There were reasons!" I scowl. "It wasn't just a case of, 'Oh, I'm bored, let's stop going out!' I had reasons. Good ones!" Even as the words launch themselves from my tongue, I hear the anger and the recrimination.

It all bleeds together to sound like weakness.

I sound just like dad. Is that what Real Men are supposed to sound like?

"Sorry, mate," Adil shrugs. "But . . . you know . . ."

"What?"

"Well, from where I'm standing, it sounds like you still like her. I mean, it's good that you're looking out for her, but that sort of thing can mess you up if you let it."

But I'm not looking out for her. I'm looking out for me.

"I guess," I sigh.

The bell rings.

"You OK?"

"I'm fine," I nod. "You're right, it's none of my business. I need to let it go. I'll catch you later."

"Later."

I can't let it go. I need to know.

The only way I'm going to know is by asking her.

Because life's not hard enough, and I'm an arsehole.

Questions

***

Physics is full of questions.

Is Adil right? Do I still care for her?

Much as I don't want to admit it, the answer is 'yes'. Of course I do. How could I not? She was the first girl to look past the thin veneer of social ability I present to the rest of the world and, for whatever reason, decided she liked what she saw.

My first girlfriend. Probably my only.

Then it comes to me. My problem is that I can't face talking to her about what's going on in my life. I know that what's stopping me is fear; fear that if I had told her and started crying, I wouldn't be able to stop. How would that make me look? That's not what Real Men do. We're supposed to be the silent heroes, who chew down anything that might pass for an emotion and consign it to the depths of our practical, we-can-fix-that hearts. You never saw James Bond or Batman hunched in a corner, covered in snot and tears because their lives got a bit difficult.

They carried the Actual Weight of Manhood in their arms, no matter how heavy it got, and kept walking, no matter how big the odds.

That's what I've got to do. For mum and for Bex.

Is Nadia going to Lauren Edwards' party? If she is, why? Is this merely a dreadful coincidence or is she going for a particular purpose?

While my pencil ought to be tracing the direction of flow between a pump, a condenser and an alternator, my mind is tracing the way the party might flow if Nadia turns up.

There I am, giddy on vodka, mingling with my new-found friends and Nadia comes through the door.

She looks fabulous. She's wearing that blue ballgown we saw in that shop window; the one she said she'd like to wear to the prom. There's someone on her arm; someone tall, wearing a crisp tuxedo.

The image isn't clear in my mind. It's too dark and pixelated. It's got the quality of those dreadful eighties films that mum likes to watch, but dad can't stand. It's a bit fuzzy and poorly lit.

I focus on it and look harder into the shadows. Who is that mystery guy?

The picture hardens and starts to resolve itself. The guy on her arm is tall, much taller than me. He's also leaner than I am.

I force my mental camera, along the perfect white of his shirt and the cheeky wink of his bow tie and focus the imaginary lens on his face.

The soft, shrouded features harden and become unforgivingly clear.

It's Adil.

Adil's on her arm. Of course it's Adil.

An urgent energy shoots along my arm, like I've just put my

finger into a mains socket. There's a shotgun crack across the classroom, as the lead in my pencil gives way to the force put upon it and snaps in half.

I'm suddenly back in physics, looking up and straight into Mr Morgan's quizzical eyes.

Struck dumb by my own imaginings, I don't say anything. I can't. Instead, I lift up my broken pencil and wave it vaguely around, as if that somehow explains everything.

Is this really what I think? Am I scraping so low that I'm now suspecting my best friend of trying to usurp my position with my ex-girlfriend? To my guilt-riddled, self-loathing mind, it makes perfect sense. Adil's been protecting her. He's more or less warned me off her in a way that looks like little more than friendly advice but, now I'm scrupulously dissecting our conversation, I can almost smell the rot concealed in his words.

Then there's Nadia. Nadia can't even look at me.

What was it Megan Jacobs said? That Nadia had loads of blokes waiting to ask her out. Better blokes than me.

What if this has been going on behind my back and my breaking up with her has just provided them with the perfect opportunity to get together? What if I've been nothing more than a convenient cuckold for the last three months?

As much as none of this makes absolute sense to me, there's a greedy, nasty little corner of me that's putting the jigsaw together and – regardless of whether the pieces fit together properly or not – it's created a picture. A disjointed, ill-formed image that, now I've thought of it, I can't help but stare at, over and over again.

This can't go on. After this, it's lunch. Adil will be there and so will Nadia.

I need to find out whether there's something going on or whether I'm madder than I thought.

Twenty-Eight

Seven Days

When the bell finally goes, I'm like Usain Bolt off the starting blocks. I've got to beat Nadia and Adil. If I can get there first, get my fish fingers and beans and then bag a table in the far corner, I'll have ample opportunity to watch from afar.

The canteen's only just starting to fill up. Scouring the tables, I pant my way into the short queue. It looks as though they're not here. So far, so good.

As I grab my tray, gesture wordlessly at the orange baked beans and the even oranger fish fingers, I keep looking over my shoulder, just to check they don't creep in while I'm being served.

Once I've paid, I look over to where I'm going to begin my hiding-in-plain-sight stake-out. I ought to have got a coffee and some doughnuts. That's what they do in the movies.

The table I want has got people sat around it. Only three, but that's three too many. I don't know them either, which would just makes me look weird. Not that by standing in the canteen, clutching a tray and rolling my eyes at every table in sight doesn't make me stand out just a little bit.

There's one at the back; one of the small ones. That'll do. I go and arrange my chair to give the best view possible.

This must be how sharks feel; solitary and forever scanning the shoals, waiting for the tiniest, infinitesimal whiff of blood.

But I'm not waiting for blood. I'm waiting for a drop of treachery to stain the waters.

They're there, framed in the doorway, waiting in the queue: Nadia and Adil.

Nadia is quite animated. Whatever she's saying is punctuated by gestures; her hands keep exploding apart and then moving in random patterns, as though she's casting a spell. Adil, in his usual way, is static, aside from the usual tremors of laughter that pass through his shoulders. Whatever Nadia's saying, he's listening intently, nodding and shrugging and laughing in his silently comedic way.

It's Nadia my eyes keep coming back to. It takes me a moment to work out what it is about her expression and manner that bothers me. Then I get it.

She looks happy.

She doesn't look like a girl whose boyfriend split up with her barely a week ago. She looks like she doesn't have a care in the world.

Is that all I'm worth? Seven days? Is that how long it takes for a broken heart to heal?

Or was it never really broken in the first place?

I suddenly feel very sick.

As they approach the food counter, Adil suddenly looks up at me, as though prompted by some supernatural force. I freeze, caught out, but he nods my way and turns to say something to Nadia. She flicks a quick glance in my general direction, before turning her back entirely on me.

They talk as the cue shuffles along, but Nadia steadfastly refuses to turn around. Adil gets to the till first and pays but, instead of coming over to see his marooned friend, he waits until Nadia has paid and they exchange some short words. With that, Nadia turns away from him, conscious enough of my presence to rotate anticlockwise and present her back to me, one last time. I see her profile as she walks to a table as far away from me as possible; she's smiling again, smiling at a group of girls she knows. She sits and they huddle over their food, before a volley of disapproving looks are fired my way from her lunchtime coven. One of them shouts, "Take a picture, it'll last longer" before they all close ranks, rather like a formation of Roman shields.

"Alright, Jim?" There's Adil, looming over me, tray in hand, trademark benign smile on his face.

"Yes," I mutter, curtly, barely able to meet his eyes. "How's Nadia?"

"Oh . . . you know . . ." he shrugs, sitting. "She's OK."

"Did you ask her about the party?"

"What about it?"

"Whose it is."

"No. That's up to her, isn't it?"

We skydive into silence, but there's something bubbling away inside me. My core temperature rises and suddenly I'm spewing words. I'm a verbal volcano.

"She looks pretty happy to me."

Adil's his head cocks to one side but, instead of replying, he just shrugs again and turns his attention to his mass of gloopy vegetables.

"You looked pretty happy too." My heartrate rockets up and I can feel the flush of anger blotting my cheeks.

Adil looks up at me, blinking. The smile on his face isn't quite so comfortable. It looks awkward.

"I was just talking to her, Jim."

"What about, then?" I spit.

"About her coming over to record tonight."

"Well, that's handy, isn't it?"

"How d'you mean?"

"Convenient."

"Well, I am recording her tonight. It is 'handy' or 'convenient' if she's there."

The mask of innocence and confusion is slipping from Adil's face. I can see it. I push harder.

"And probably 'handier' or more 'convenient' if I'm not!"

"I'm not with you, mate."

"No, because you'll be with her!" Checkmate.

Adil squints at me and slowly puts his cutlery either side of his plate.

"Jim," he shrugs. "What's up? What's going on?"

The nicey-nicey routine. The 'I'm Just Concerned about You' speech. My God, I should've seen all this coming. How could I have been so stupid?

"You like her, don't you?" My words are low and measured.

"Jim, she's my friend. Of course I like her."

"Yes, but you *like* her."

Adil takes a deep breath and rolls his eyes.

"Jim," he says, eventually. "I don't know what's going on here, but you need to get a grip, mate. You haven't been like you for a bit and if you've got stuff you need to deal with, that's fair enough."

"That's rich, coming from you!"

"Jim," he says, again, "whatever's eating you up, you need to get on top of it. Talk to someone. I don't mind listening, but

I get it if it's not something you want me to know about. What about the school counsellor? Something's up – I know it is – but no one can help if you don't tell them what it is."

This is a distraction. A smokescreen. He's trying to put me on the back foot and make me reconsider what I'm saying. I notice he hasn't answered my question, so I lean forward and enunciate it as clearly as I can.

"You *like* her, don't you?"

"OK, mate," Adil shrugs. "Let's leave this one, I reckon. Don't worry about tonight. Another time maybe." He gets up, collects his plate and turns to go.

"Going to sit with your girlfriend, are you?"

"If you mean Nadia, then no, because she's not my girlfriend. I'm just going to go off, eat my lunch and get to my next lesson. I don't think she needs to hear about this. If she does, it won't be from me."

With a final, forlorn shrug, he walks to another table, sits down and starts to eat.

I glare after him but it's wasted energy. All the confirmation I needed was in his inability to answer a straight question.

It's official: I can't trust anyone. Not even my ex-girlfriend and by best mate.

Let's make it 117,600 Newtons.

Twenty-Nine

Wildfire

I'm tired of having no control in my life.

The chatter in the back of my head, which I've fought with since The Night Everything Went Weird is remarkably quiet as I enter Mrs Beattie's classroom. As I briefly make eye contact with Nadia, who's conveniently stashed herself at a desk, next to one of her friends, I understand why.

There is no Happily Ever After.

There is no 'Til Death Do Us Part.

In the instant that I meet Nadia's eyes and suddenly understand that, I'm calm and collected.

I take a seat without caring who I'm sitting next to and I feel no worse for it. I open my textbooks and listen to what Mrs Beattie is tartaning on about. I find the Act and the Scene she wants us to read and I don't flinch when she casts me back in the role of Macbeth.

Perhaps out of some soft-hearted notion of romance, she casts Nadia as Lady Macbeth. I don't care. It doesn't touch me. I am immune to everything.

This is the scene where Macbeth supersedes his wife as the dominant force. He plans to kill his best friend. Maybe Shakespeare is relevant in the modern day after all.

We read. Instead of the fearful revulsion of having to speak out loud, my voice is clear, hard and devoid of emotion. The fearful, shadow-scared, self-hating Jamie is gone, replaced by the human flatline that is James Chapman.

Lady Macbeth blathers on about me being bright and jovial among my guests tonight, which makes me smile. I'm going to be bright and jovial tonight, alright. I've got a bottle of vodka and I'm going to Lauren Edwards' party. It doesn't get brighter or more jovial than that.

But I'm going to talk to Nadia as soon as this class is done. I'll be first to the door and I'll wait and then I'll tell her I know what's been going on. No fireworks; just a series of statements and then I'll walk away.

I'm ready. I'm taking control.

Then, there's a knock at the door. We all look up. Some kid from a couple of years below steps in.

"Yes?" Mrs Beattie asks, a little surprised.

"Sorry, Miss," the kid answers, "but Mr Norris wants to see

James Chapman. He said, 'right now'."

The comfortable Arctic wasteland I've buried myself in starts to melt. The headmaster wants to see me. All eyes swing my way, silently wondering what I've done, which also happens to be playing heavily on my mind too.

I remember the vodka in my backpack.

Someone knows.

Someone's said something.

It has to be Nathan Douglas's little brother, but how does he know?

The kid hands a piece of paper to Mrs Beattie. She unfolds it, puts on her glasses and reads it.

"James," she says, "off you go."

"Yes, Miss."

I stand and put my books into my bag. The incriminating blue of the water-bottle cap flashes back at me.

"Hurry up, Jamie."

"Yes, Miss."

I zip my burden and leave the classroom, faintly aware of Nadia's eyes following me out. I've got bigger things to worry about, like booze on the school grounds.

The awareness that the kid who came in is walking by my side makes me realise that, unless I ditch him, I can't ditch the evidence. Even a passing bin is useless to me, now.

"Which lesson are you supposed to be in?" I grunt, as we

round a corner.

"RE."

"You can go back to it, if you want. I know the way."

"Mr Norris said I had to walk you to his office."

There goes that ruse then.

"Did he say what this is about?" I try and keep my question nonchalant and light. For all I know, this kid could be watching the way I'm acting, ready to report his observations.

"No. He just said to bring you to his office as quickly as possible."

A curtain of cold sweat threatens to drop into my eyes.

This is it.

I'm doomed.

We round more corners and cross the playground. Then we're climbing stairs up, up, up, to the silent corridor that leads to Mr Norris's office. I can see his door at the end of it; grey-painted wood with the suddenly sinister plaque on it that says 'Head Teacher.'

Jesus. If he drags mum into this, it'll send her over the edge.

My guide knocks on the door, efficient to the last moment.

"Come in."

Mr Norris looks like a head teacher. His receding hairline and hollowed cheeks speak of someone who has lost parts of himself to his job. Even his lips seem to have been stolen from him, leaving his mouth no more than a frowning paper cut.

"Chapman?" he asks, looking up as I step into his courtroom. "James Chapman?"

My heart suddenly hammers against my sternum. I'm ready to plead guilty. The game's up.

"Yes, sir."

Mr Norris looks down at what I presume to be his diary and then looks up again.

"I've had a phone call from your mother," he says, easily. "She needs you home this instant. It's to do with your father."

I don't even reply. I spin on my heel and run.

I take the stairs two, three at a time. The corridors flash by and then I'm running through the school gates, the bottle in my backpack jigging and bouncing against my spine.

Fifteen minutes. This should only take me fifteen minutes. I only need to run for quarter of an hour.

Within five, I've slowed to a gasping jog. A bus stop on the other side of the road; maybe I should stop and wait. No. No telling how long I'd be hanging around.

Come on, legs, mum needs me.

Just like she needed me The Night Everything Went Weird, but I let her down.

There it is, the thought that's been skulking around in the shadows. The one that's always been there, but I haven't wanted to listen to it.

I let her down.

I let it happen now, so I can use it. Every time my pace slows, I rake that thought across my mind and use the white-hot eruptions of anger and guilt to push me through the fire in my thighs and the trembling in my calves.

"I let her down." I even chant it in a dry whisper. "I let her down."

My legs start to fail again, so I line up the memories of that night and let them fall like dominoes.

They go out. It's to a party. Whose party? Can't remember. Someone from dad's work. I'm babysitting Bex, for the first time. I'm in charge. I'm the man of the house. I'm going to make sure it's fun.

We watch a DVD. Disney. Frozen. Olaf makes her laugh and that makes me laugh. We eat pizza and I give her some of the lemonade I've got in my room. The snow monster scares her a bit and the buries her face into me, when it comes onto the screen. We eat ice cream. Vanilla. Or was it cookie dough? Cookie dough. It was cookie dough.

I put her to bed and she comes down once or twice with some excuse about being thirsty. The first time, I get her some water. The second time, I get stern. She goes to bed and I'm in the lounge, alone. I watch TV. I text Nadia. I text Adil.

It's midnight and there's still no sign of mum and dad. I'm tired and I go to bed. I lie there, fiddling with my phone.

I fall asleep.

While I'm asleep, mum and dad come home. A taxi drops them off. There's been a row brewing since they left the party.

Something trivial but, with drink loosening their mouths and their minds, it's got bigger than it needs to be.

They come into the house. More drinks. Spirits. It's all there is.

The argument builds, but they seethe at each other in hoarse, strangled whispers, so as not to wake me and Bex.

Bex doesn't wake. But I do.

I wake to hear voices that are suddenly loud and then drop into muffled anger. I know it's mum and dad, but it doesn't sound like them anymore.

They sound like acid, burning and fizzing and eating away at each other.

Mum's angry. She doesn't get angry often, but it's there now, every time I hear the word, 'You'. Her sentences fracture and splinter under the weight of dad's insistent, caustic shushing.

"You . . ."

I can't hear the rest of what she's saying; it's lost in the static of dad's urgent hisses.

"Shhh!"

"You . . ."

"Shhh!"

"You . . ."

"Shhh! For Christ's sake! Shhh!"

"You . . ."

Then, it's dad's voice that's loudest.

"SHUT! UP!"

An odd and sudden stillness follows for the tiniest moment, like when the air eats up all the sound just before a lightning strike.

There's a new noise. Something like a grunt or a growl that can't contain itself and comes out as a roar.

Then, a bump or a thud.

Something falls to the floor.

A new silence floods the house and I'm lying there with my mouth open so I can't hear my breathing. My hand's on my chest to try and stop the thudding of my heart, in case it shakes the house down.

I know what's happened. I know.

I know because mum isn't saying anything.

Dad just hit her.

I should get up. I should be down there. I should be checking to see if she's OK. I should be protecting her. I should bundle her out of the room or call an ambulance or the police or . . . something.

I should be doing something.

Everything is suddenly wrong and, if this was anything else, I'd be calling out for mum or dad, asking them what to do. Fear has dried my voice out and there's no one to call for anyway. Not now.

I lie there, listening. My hand trembles its way to the edge of the duvet, almost as if it's going to pull it back, and I'm going to get out of bed and go downstairs and try and help mum.

But my legs won't move. They're solid and cold, as though someone's just pumped ice into my veins.

I lie there and I fail her.

Because I'm scared. Because there's something new and dark and unfamiliar in the house.

Dad.

Even when I hear mum stumble up the stairs and shut her bedroom door, I stay in my bed.

I don't sleep. Not for ages. Instead I listen to the muted sounds of dad's pacing. He pants, swears and eventually falls into the sofa.

Across the landing, I hear the gentle, shuddering sounds as my mother sobs into her pillow.

I failed her.

I let her down.

I let her down.

"I let her down."

Not today.

My legs fall into a steady rhythm; not quite a run, but more than a walk.

Another five, sweaty minutes and I'm puffed out. My thighs are burning and twitching in protest.

I stop, just to catch my breath, leaning against a lamp post. Christ, come on! A Real Man would've done this in seconds.

A few lungfuls of air and I'm off again, feeling the sun's heat sucking the moisture out of my body, through my forehead, from under my arms and along my back. Suddenly I'm wishing that the bottle in my backpack was actually carrying water.

The end of my road comes into view, just as my legs lose the will to run. I change down a gear into something between a stagger and a trot. I can see the house.

There, sitting on the doorstep, I can see mum.

I give my legs a final push, lurching over to her. I take off my bag as I go, dropping it to the floor as I lumber down the drive.

She looks up at me and puts her arms out. Her face is puffed with tears. There's virtually no white left in her eyes, just a cobweb of crimson veins.

"Jamie!" she blubbers, trying to stand, but falling back onto the doorstep. I gasp my way over to her, almost toppling into her desperate embrace. Dropping to one knee, I wrap my arms around her and hold her tight.

"What? What is it?"

"He took her!" she sobs. "Bex! He took her!"

"Who took her?" I know the answer before the words have even left my mouth.

"Your father! He took her, Jamie! I don't know where she is!"

She's shaking now. I've never seen her like this before and it frightens me. There's too much going on in her head. Too much going on for one head to bear.

"Come on, mum. We need to get inside."

Gently, I pull her to her feet, push the front door open and lead her into the front room. She falls onto the sofa, her hands cupped over her face. I kneel at her feet, my hands on her knees.

"Mum. What happened?" I make my voice as firm and as clear as I can, without going anywhere near a shout. She needs to come out of herself and talk to me.

"He just turned up." Mum sounds like a little girl. "Becky was getting ready for school and he just turned up and said he wanted to see her. I tried to say 'no', but Becky heard him and came out. He just grabbed her. I tried, Jamie, I tried. I hung onto her arm, but he just kept pulling and I wasn't strong enough." Her face falls in on itself once more.

As something ugly and angry fills my body and burns my face, my brain reconstructs the crime scene, playing out her fear, her tears, her confusion as the two people she loves most in the world pull at her in some twisted tug-of-war.

"Mum, have you called him? Have you tried his phone?"

"Yes, yes. He's not answering. What do I do?" Her voice plays in various keys of hopelessness.

"OK. Well, maybe he'll answer me."

I dial dad.

It rings. It rings. It rings. There's dad's voice telling me how he's sorry that he can't make to the phone, but if I'd like to leave a message, he'll get back to me as soon as he can.

A tone sounds; my cue to say something.

"Dad. It's Jamie. Call me back. Bye."

It's all I can manage.

Mum's on me as soon as I get back into the lounge.

"Did you get him? What did he say?"

"Not answering."

"Bastard!" mum hisses, rage suddenly coming out of nowhere. "I'll kill him! If he hurts her . . ."

"Mum!" I put my hands on her shoulders, but it's like trying to contain a tornado. "Mum, he's not going to hurt her. Whatever else he is, he's her dad and he loves her."

Defending my father doesn't make me feel quite like the champion it ought to.

"How long've they been gone?" I need mum to focus, to think.

"Why? D'you think I should go to the police?"

She wants me to decide. She wants me to decide whether or not to have my father arrested. I loathe myself for not having the balls to say 'yes'.

"No. Not yet. This can all be solved. Think: d'you know anyone else you could ring to see where he might be? What about Auntie Hannah? Have you tried her?"

"No."

"You do that and I'll text him."

Mum's in the hallway in an instant, picking up one of the cordless phones and stabbing buttons frantically.

I type a message into my phone.

Give me a call, dad. Or a text. I just need to know everything's OK.

No kiss. I don't leave a kiss.

While mum's babbling in the background, I nip upstairs to the bathroom. I don't need a wee. I don't think there's enough liquid left in my body for a solitary drop.

I look in the mirror. I look like I'm running on fumes, but they're angry fumes and they'll keep me going for now.

I splash my face with water and then realise how thirsty I am. My mouth goes to the tap and I drag in great gobfuls of water, feeling the shock of the cold as it travels down my throat.

Right now, I'd rather be drinking something else, but now's not the time.

Downstairs, mum's still on the phone.

"I know, Pearl," she's saying. "I know and I'm sorry for calling like this, but I don't know what else to do . . ."

She's called grandma. Dad's mum. That's why she sounds so reasonable, but I can hear the grinding tension in her voice.

"OK, Pearl. Thanks, anyway. Not to worry. I'm sure it'll be fine. OK . . . OK . . . Bye."

"What did you tell her?"

"Not everything. Just that I couldn't get hold of him."

"Auntie Hannah?"

"She hasn't seen him since he left for work this morning. Has he texted you?"

"No. I'll try again."

Five o'clock comes and goes, followed by six o'clock. It's just a flurry of phone calls, texts and frustration. Everyone's drawing a blank.

At twenty past six, my phone goes. A text. It's dad.

Hi. Will drop B off in 10 mins. Dad.

No kiss. He doesn't leave a kiss.

"Mum!" I go into the kitchen where she's making yet another cup of tea that she's not going to drink.

I show her the message. Her face sets like concrete.

"Let me deal with it when he turns up," I instruct her. "You stay out here."

Mum chews on her lip and starts pacing the kitchen, having forgotten about the cup of tea that needs some milk. On her return journey, I give her a hug. More for me than her.

"It's all OK," I mutter. "Becky's coming back and it's all good."

"I know," she nods. "But I'll never forgive him for this. Never."

I believe her.

"Mummy!"

Bex's voice is in the hallway.

I leave the kitchen to find that dad's there too, his arms crossed around my little sister's shoulders, walking behind her like he's using her as a shield. There's a smile on his face; not a smile of empathy, sympathy or apology.

It's a smile of triumph.

Something ignites in my chest and travels like wildfire to my right hand. It clenches. I want to hit him and knock that grin right off his face.

Becky takes dad's hand and pulls him towards the lounge.

"Come and sit down, daddy," she beams. "You don't have to go yet, do you?"

Dad looks down at her and smiles again.

"No," he says. "No, I don't."

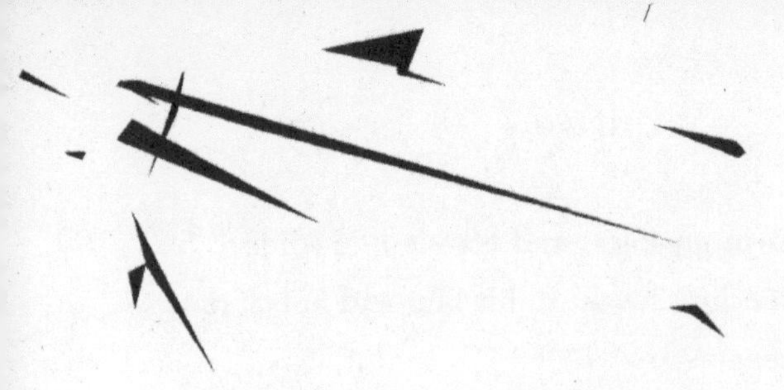

Thirty

Cocktail

It's like I'm seeing my dad with new eyes. As he walks into the lounge, still holding Bex like an unwitting hostage, I notice his shoulders. Although he's not a big man, his shoulders are broad. Somewhere, deep down, I probably thought they were made to bear all the problems that the rest of us couldn't. Shoulders worthy of Atlas, forever holding our little world up and holding our little world together. Shoulders meant to take the strain of money, mortgages, tears and fears; to bear the weight of untold Newtons.

Now I see them just as muscles; muscles that knotted tight one night and changed everything.

Something unfamiliar takes form in my chest. I don't know what it is, but it feels as though my body might not have the space to contain it.

Dad sits on the sofa – in *his* space – and it all looks terribly wrong, like even the thing he's sitting on doesn't really want him there. He lifts Becky onto his lap with hands that were once used to make things in his little workshop in the garage; hands that made things for me like my first catapult and that wooden sword for that time I was in the school play in juniors. It was brilliant, that sword. It had all the detail on the handguard on the hilt and even one of those lines up the centre of the carefully blunted blade. Everyone else was so jealous of that sword and I was so proud of it. When they asked me where I got it, I was able to tell them that my dad made it.

Those hands that used to make things are the same hands that have ripped our little world apart; the one that he was supposed to carry on those big, broad shoulders.

Let's make it 127,400 Newtons.

"Alright, Jamie?" Dad suddenly looks up from my little sister and smiles again. "Want to sit down?" He casually pats the space on the sofa next to him.

"No. I'm fine standing." My words are tight and barely make it out between my clamped teeth.

"OK," he laughs. "You look like you're trying to burn holes in me with your eyes."

I force a taut smile onto my face, my mouth going through the motions, but it doesn't reach my eyes. They continue trying to produce laser beams, just like he said. I keep the smile there –

forced as it is – for Becky's sake because that's what brothers do.

It's all I've got.

Dad looks up as mum comes in. God, she looks frightened. She too, manages to plaster on something like a smile and sits in the armchair in the corner opposite the sofa.

"Alright, Liz?" Dad's behaving as though it's just another ordinary day, but there's something in his eyes that says otherwise; something a bit wild.

Another ingredient is mixed into the cocktail. It tastes bitter.

Mum doesn't answer him.

"Did you have a nice time, Bex?" she says, instead.

"We went into town," Becky replies, completely unaware of the silent gunfire going on all around her. "Daddy bought me a necklace: look!" She reaches around her neck and pulls a pendant – dangling on a chain – from under her top.

"It's your special necklace, isn't it?" dad says, squeezing her again.

"Yes," Bex nods. "Then we went and had something to eat in Frankie and Benny's. I had the spaghetti and it was so delicious, mummy! I ate it all up! I ate all of it!"

"And you had some garlic bread, didn't you?" dad adds, a sly smile sliding across his lips.

"Yes, and daddy says we can go there whenever I want!"

Mum flinches slightly but manages to keep her cheery mask in place. She looks small and scared. I can see what's happening: dad's taking back control through my little sister.

The cocktail starts to fizz.

"We can," dad nods. "Whenever you want."

"Well, that's lovely." Mum's lips move little more than a ventriloquist's, forcing the words out through a rictus grin. "But you've got a spelling test tomorrow and you need to get some learning done."

"Oh, mum!" Becky moans, rolling her eyes with far more effect than any teenager ever could.

"Oh, mum!" dad echoes, chuckling. He knows what he's doing. I wish I did.

"You really should, Bex," I say, airily. "I mean, you got ten out of ten last week and . . ." I'm at a loss for what on Earth could make wanting to learn ten spellings desirable. Then I hit on something: dirty tactics. "I think mummy's going to get you a treat if you get them all right this time." I'm not proud of it, but it's all I can think of. If he wants to play it that way, then I will, too. At least Luke Skywalker and Darth Vader slugged it out with lightsabres. Mum catches the quick glance I give her and throws it to Becky.

"That's right," she nods. "You've worked so hard this term."

"What is it?" Becky gasps, her eyes widening. "Tell me!"

"Nope," mum teases, as best she can. "It's a surprise."

"Can it be Frankie and Benny's? Can I have a pudding this time?"

"We'll just have to see," mum shrugs, trying to keep the

tension out of her voice. "You've got to get ten out of ten first."

"Oh, mummy!" Dad tries to undercut the deal being made with another round of mockery, but whatever it is that's in Frankie and Benny's spaghetti has practically signed the contract.

"OK!" Becky announces importantly. "I'm going to go and learn my spellings!"

"You should go and help her, mummy," I add, suddenly a master strategist. "Just to make extra sure."

"Yes," mum nods, again. "Come on, Bex. Let's do it in your room."

"OK. Where's my bag?" She hops off dad's lap and makes for the door to the hallway. Hating myself for it, I'm suddenly relieved that he's not holding her. His shield has gone.

"On the bottom of the stairs. Say goodbye to daddy."

The spell breaks. Becky stops in her tracks, confusion sending her eyes ping-ponging between her parents.

"But daddy's staying . . ."

Dad looks at her, looks to me and then mum, but he doesn't say anything. He just sits back, waiting to see how we're going to wriggle out of this one.

"I don't think . . ." mum starts, but Becky's back at dad's lap, folded over his knees and hugging his waist. As he hugs her and kisses the back of her head, he shares a look with us. It's full of accusation.

"Actually, Becky," he says, after drenching us in silent

contempt, "I probably should go. I'm going to do some more work tonight, so I can get you a bigger treat next time I see you!" He peppers his words with tickles, making Becky twist and giggle against his legs. "Go on, go and do your spellings with your mother."

"O-kay," she surrenders glumly, before giving him a tight hug. "I miss you."

"I miss you, too." He squeezes her back and, for a split second, I see a flash of the dad I used to know.

"Come on. Up we go." Mum stands and ushers Bex out of the room, unable to look at the man she married. For better or for worse.

It doesn't get much worse than this.

There's a desert-dry moment of silence. Dad sits and looks at me.

"Right then," he says, getting to his feet. "I'd better be off."

"OK."

He walks out into the hallway and opens the front door. I follow him.

"Seeing me out, are you?" he laughs, over his shoulder. "Making sure I go?"

I don't reply. I can't. I don't know why he's being like this; why he's talking to me like this. Everything he says is like being stabbed with something made from ice.

"You dropped this." Dad picks up my backpack from the

drive and hands it to me.

"Thanks."

We stand, just looking at each other, but I can't hold his gaze. It's too full of things I don't want to see.

"Get in the car, son. Let's have a chat." He gets into the driver's seat. I don't move. "Get in the back." It's not quite an order, but it's close enough. "You don't have to sit next to me if you don't want to."

Again, another icy stab, but this one breaks inside me and I can almost hear the pieces plop-plop-plopping into the fizzing, hissing cocktail inside me. Robotically, I open the passenger door behind him and climb in, clutching my backpack tight across my stomach, my fingers blindly feeling out the shape of the bottle inside.

It's still there. Still there. Ready for when I need it.

Looking up, I can see dad's eyes looking at me from the rear-view mirror, sifting through my body language for anything that I might be giving away.

"I'm sorry," he says eventually.

I don't know what to say, so I don't say anything.

He drags a hand the length of his face and sighs.

"Look," he breathes. "I know I look like the bad guy here but it takes two to tango, Jamie . . ."

"It only takes one to throw a punch."

"So, that's it, is it?" He twists in his seat, fixing me with a blazing gaze. "You've made your decision. Already thrown me out with the trash!"

Somewhere in the anger, I can hear something like sorrow, but for who? Mum? Me? Becky?

Or himself.

"*One* mistake!" he begs. "One *stupid, stupid* mistake!"

"And what about last year? The holiday. Mum's *food poisoning*. She told me what happened." The sentence is out of my mouth before I've even thought about it.

Dad's hands suddenly grip the steering wheel tightly and he turns away from me.

"OK," he hisses, almost to himself. "Good. Great. I'm glad you've got all the answers, Jamie. Really happy for you." His eyes meet mine, courtesy of the mirror. "Because, you know why? One day you'll find out what it means to fall in love and have a family. You'll work harder than you've ever worked in your life to provide and protect and keep a roof over their heads. Then you'll make that *one* mistake. All you'll want is a second chance. That's all. When it's your turn, you'll remember this. You'll understand, because it'll be someone else with all the answers. Then, you'll know what it feels like to have the people you love turn their backs on you."

What is he *doing*? What *is* this? Some sort of attempt to justify lamping my mum? Because it's somehow done out care and love? Is that it? Beating people up is OK, as long as you care about them?

The furious buzzing and spitting in my stomach reaches a crescendo.

Then it suddenly dies and goes very, very cold. I can feel it in my arms and in my head and in my eyes. Dad obviously notices a change in me. He turns, twisting in his seat again, fixing me with those blue, wild eyes.

"Go on, then," he mutters, low and level. "Hit me. That's what you want. Hit me. Make yourself feel better. Be a man."

127,400 Newtons.

The cocktail freezes my blood. I see my fist clench. I feel the surge of anger whooshing through my arm, willing me to pull it back and send it to his face.

I'm trembling.

I want to hit him.

I want to punch my father square in the face.

But I don't.

I don't.

I'd love to report that, in the second it takes me to reach that decision, I've come to the profound understanding that if I do, I'll be no better than him. I'll prove him right and he'll have created me in his own image: a fist-swinging, manipulative *man*.

I'd love that to be true, but it isn't.

The truth is, I'm too scared to do it.

Just like The Night Everything Went Weird.

As my eyes film with tears, I taste the cocktail in the back of my throat. It's cold and pure with no flavour at all. I know its name.

It's called hate.

With shuddering fingers, I pull at the door release.

"I've got to go," I blurt.

Dad doesn't say a thing. The minute I've shut the door, the engine starts, and he drives away, leaving me shaking and quaking on the doorstep. I feel old and cold, like I'm the only person on the planet.

The vodka. The vodka.

Rushing, shaking and fumbling, I open the zip, and pull out the bottle, unscrew the cap and take a swig.

A big one.

Big enough. Big enough to separate my head from my shoulders and let it float, balloon-like over myself; watching my stupid, cowardly body putting the bottle away, holding its arms out and looking at them to see just how high on the Richter Scale the tremors are. Big enough to replace the hypothermia of hatred with the fire of booze. Big enough that my breathing starts to slow and the tears in my eyes start to dry. Big enough that I don't have to feel anything anymore.

"Has he gone?" Mum's head pokes nervously around the door.

"Yes," I reply, from somewhere else. "He's gone."

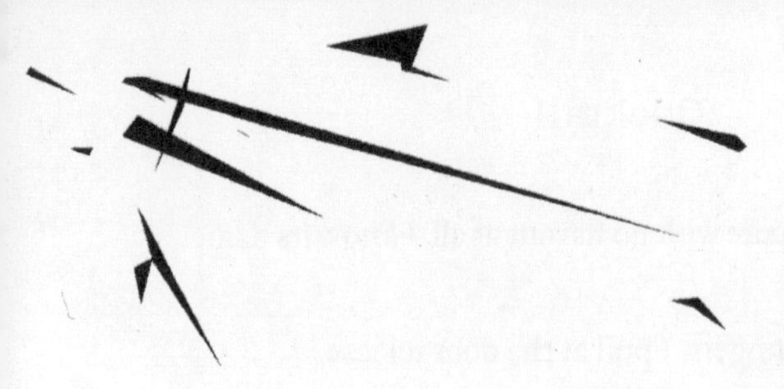

Thirty-One

Super Mario Me

As light-headed and as distant as I'm feeling, there's no way I'm leaving mum and Bex tonight. The party's off.

For the hour or so that it takes for mum to get Becky off to sleep, I sit in the front room, staring at the clock.

Seven thirty comes and seven thirty goes. I ought to be at Lauren Edwards' boyfriend's flat, guzzling booze and spouting profanities like a curse fountain, but I'm not. I'm here in the lounge, listening to the silence of the house.

The weird thing is that I'm quite relieved to be honest. As the alcohol starts to lose its grip on my mind, the idea of the party loses its appeal. I'm exhausted.

The hour hand is creeping up to the eight when mum walks into the room and falls into the sofa. She looks as though she hasn't slept for a week.

"Did she go off alright?" I ask quietly.

Mum shakes her head.

"She's so confused," she answers. "I don't know what your father said to her, but she's all over the place."

"We just need to let her know that we're always here," I hear myself saying. "Whatever she says or does. That we're always here for her."

Mum nods and looks in on herself. Whatever she's wrestling with isn't pleasant.

"D'you want me to get you a drink?" I ask hopefully, nodding towards the drinks cabinet. An evening spent sharing a bottle of something with mum would do my soul good.

"No," she says, distantly. She says it again, more decisively, as though she's just come back into her skin. "No. That wouldn't be good. I'm not in the right headspace. It'd only end in tears."

"Fair enough." I am disappointed, though.

"I forgot to tell you," she says, suddenly sitting upright, a worn out smile lightening her face. "The money."

"What money?"

"The money you hid for me."

"OK."

"I put the bottle into my bag and took it into the bank. When was it? Monday? Or was it Wednesday? Oh, I can't remember. Anyway, I went in and I stood in the queue and I waited for the cashier and then it went 'cashier number six is open' or whatever it says — "

"Ready."

"What?"

"'Cashier number six is ready.'"

"Ready, that's right. Anyway, I went up and I was so nervous. I started telling her I needed to open an account and she said she needed to see my ID. So, I got that out and that was all fine and then it was 'how much do you want to deposit?'"

"So?"

"I'd forgotten the money was still in the bottle! I got it out the bag, opened the top, but the money had sort of unravelled itself and I couldn't get it out!"

I start to chuckle.

"So, what did you do?"

"I just mumbled something about keeping it safe and I just handed it over the counter! They must think I'm mad!"

"What? The whole bottle?"

"Yes!"

"The whole Lucozade bottle?"

"The whole thing!"

I start to laugh; not a belly laugh, more a throat laugh, and more out of fondness for my dopy old mum than at the ridiculousness of the situation. Mum starts to giggle too.

"You great idiot!" I grin, suddenly loving her more than ever.

"I know," she sighs, rolling her eyes. "What a prat!"

"No, you're not," I scold her, very, very gently. I lean over and give her a hug. "No, you're not."

"Thanks, Jamie. Thanks for today. Thanks for being there. I couldn't have done it without you.""

Mum's arms are wrapped around my back and I suddenly want to cry. I just want to bury my face in her and cry until I can't cry any more. I want to tell her that I've split up with Nadia, that I'm feeling like my shoulders are too small to carry the weight of what's going on and that the only way I can feel anything like normal is with alcohol inside me. But I don't. I can't. That's not what she needs. She needs me to prove that at least one of the men in her life is dependable. So, I bite it back, along with a sizeable chunk from the inside of my cheek.

"I didn't do anything," I manage, sitting back down.

"You did, Jamie, you really did."

"Well."

"I need a cup of tea," she declares, slapping her hands on her knees and standing up. "What time is it?" She looks at the clock. "Ten past eight? Aren't you supposed to be somewhere?"

"Oh, yeah. Adil's," I sort of lie.

"Well, why aren't you there?"

"I can't be bothered."

"Why?"

"I just can't."

"Jamie!" There's a scold in there, somewhere amongst the concern.

"What?"

"If I remember rightly, your friend – your *good* friend, Adil – is doing something he needs you for tonight."

"Yeah, but — "

"But nothing."

"But, mum! I can't be . . . I don't want to!"

"Jamie!" That face mum's pulling belongs to my childhood. It's the one that told me to go to so-and-so's birthday, even though I didn't want to. It's the one that made me shake hands with playground traitors who went on to become my friends, even though I didn't want to. It's the one that won't take no for an answer.

"What?"

"Jamie." Her voice is suddenly soft. "I know what this is about and while the thought is very lovely, you've got to get on with your life."

"What?" Parrots have got nothing on me.

"You're being very loyal, but I'm not having you let down your friends because things are difficult here. You've got to have a life. It's been organised for a week and I want you to go and have a good time." Case closed.

"But — " I try, feebly.

"No buts, Jamie. Not this time. If anything happens – which it won't – I'll call you. I promise. Jamie, I want you to go out. I want you to have a good time. Nothing would make me happier."

In the distance, I hear the vodka singing.

"OK," I nod.

Much as I was prepared not to, I'm going to Lauren Edwards' party.

"Well, you'd better go and get changed, hadn't you?"

"Yes, I s'pose I had."

Oh, God. What am I going to wear? What does one wear to social gatherings of this sort?

I jump into the shower and try and boil the fear out of my system, before pulling out almost every item of clothing I own and scowling at it. In the end, I decided to keep it simple: jeans and trainers, with a white t-shirt and a grey, zip-up hoodie. I think the hoodie is important. I imagine all Lauren Edwards' friends wear them. It'll be like being in a monastery that's thrown all the rules out of the window.

Got my phone. Got my backpack. It's time to go.

"OK . . . I'm going," I announce feebly through the lounge doorway.

"Hang on," mum answers, getting off the sofa and scuttling into the kitchen. Two minutes later, she joins me by the front door and presses a tenner into my hand. I start to protest but she raises a warning finger, before tapping me on the end of my nose with it.

"Go. And have. Fun," she tells me, her finger bouncing off my nose with every syllable.

"OK."

"And stop worrying."

"OK."

"Text me if you're staying at Adil's."

"OK."

"Go on, then, you're late!"

"OK. Love you."

"Love you, too."

Then I'm walking in the lazy evening sun towards town, but I feel like a Satnav waiting for a signal, so it can start planning the route. Part of me still isn't enamoured with this party idea. It suddenly seems all a bit real.

Adil's house suddenly seems like a better idea, but that would mean an apology that I don't mean. If I remember rightly, Nadia was going 'round before me. Convenient. Handy. She's probably still there now. I bet there never was any party. They're probably sat on the end of his bed, listening to music and at some point, she'll turn to him and he'll turn to her. She'll look at him in that way that was only meant for me and they'll slowly lean in together. I don't want to think about the rest of it.

The only other option I've got is to head to the park and sit there for the evening, sipping vodka, like the drunks who gather once the shops shut. I've seen them – hunched over cans of cider, circled around whisky – bearded, dirty and lost. The alkies. At least I'm not one of them. It's not like I put the stuff on my cornflakes. It's not like I get the shakes. I don't have a problem with alcohol; I just have a problem with life at the moment, and that's different. It's not the same. I don't have to have a drink. I could not have one anytime I wanted to.

Just not tonight. Tonight, I'm choosing to have one. My choice. Maybe I'll not have one tomorrow.

I stop under the clock tower in the town centre. All around me, people are coming and going, probably to the next pub. Some stagger in groups, laughing and loud. Some are couples, better dressed and quieter, probably heading out for dinner and a bottle of wine. They all look happy. Why shouldn't I have a good time too? Mum wants me to.

I pull my vodka-filled water bottle out of my backpack. It's like I've got one over on the entire world. Clever old me; here I am, with a bottle of booze and no one knows. Giving myself a mental medal for services to subversion, I take a gulp. That hot burn isn't such a shock this time. In fact, I quite like it.

The vodka starts to gently fill my head with helium. Chuckling, I take another mouthful. I feel it blasting its way into my belly. A gentle numbness spreads from my head into my arms and legs. I'm Super Mario when he's had that hundredth star. I'm levelling up. All I need is a moustache and a cap, and I could take on the world.

A high-pitched 'Woohoo!' squeaks unprompted out of my mouth.

My God, I'm funny. I laugh again and take a final, lesser swig, flooding my veins with a few more power stars. They make me light and distant and carefree.

Mum'll be fine tonight.

Whatever happens between Adil and Nadia is fine by me. Whatever.

My father's an idiot.

Each thought is clear and concise, sterilised of any accompanying feelings. Screwing the cap back on and putting the bottle back in my bag, I know exactly where I'm going tonight. I even shrug contentedly to myself as I head off, away from Adil's house and towards Lauren Edwards' party. It'll be fine. I'll have a laugh, have a drink and then I'll probably go home.

Woohoo!

Ordinarily, I'd be more than a little apprehensive at walking into the part of town where Lauren Edwards' boyfriend's flat is. This is the part where the houses start to look a little less well looked after, where the dogs have shorter fur and longer teeth.

There's not even a trickle of the usual trepidation. I even start to walk with a bit of a swagger; nothing too obvious; just enough to communicate to the natives that I am indeed, one of them.

A block of flats tower over me. This is the place. I can hear music coming from somewhere overhead. A row of buttons to my right, each denoting who lives where, with scruffy, fading, handwritten stickers below them.

I'll just have one more swig. Just in case.

Grinning to myself, I imagine just jumping up to the party, Mario style.

With a final 'woohoo', I press the buzzer to Liam's flat.

Nothing.

I give it a minute and try again.

Nothing.

One more press.

After a few seconds, there's the scrape of static through the intercom below.

"Yeah?" It's a male voice.

"Oh. Hi. It's James. I'm here for Liam's party."

"Who?"

"James. James Chapman."

There's another hiss of white noise. I can vaguely make out distorted voices and laughter in the background.

"Lauren invited me," I add, just in case.

There's some more silence and then the voice is back.

"Yeah," it says. "Second floor."

"OK. Thanks." I'm sure it pays to be nice to the gatekeeper.

There's a loud buzz and the metal thunk of something happening in the door in front of me. I push it.

It opens.

I'm going in.

Woohoo?

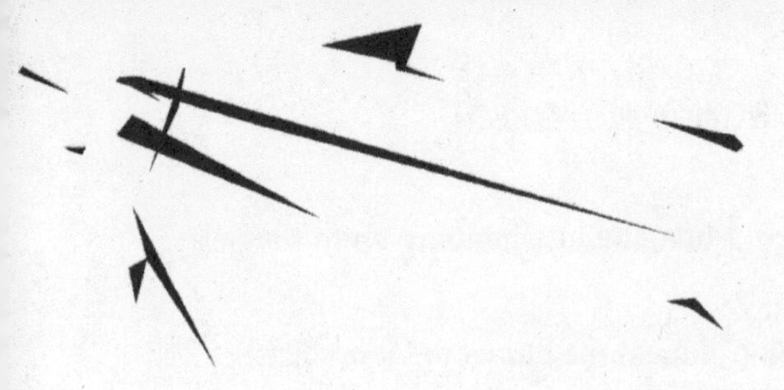

Thirty-Two

The Portal

I make my way up the stairs. Here it is: the portal to Partyland. I knock. As expected, no one comes to answer it. I doubt they can hear much at all over the rib-cage rattling music pulsating away. I knock again. A lot louder.

On the second thump, the door swings open an inch or two.

Do I go in?

Before I'm aware of it, the bottle has found its way, uncapped, to my lips, and I'm taking a small shot. I push the door open and step inside.

The hallway is tiny but is obviously a popular hangout, judging by the number of people leaning up against walls or sat on the floor. I don't recognise any of them.

I ought to find out where the host is and announce my arrival.

This might be harder than I thought.

I step around people, nodding a friendly smile at anyone who looks up at me. It isn't returned. They just look at me before turning back to whatever it is they're talking about.

There's a small kitchen up ahead and a door to my right. A bolstering swig later, I go for the kitchen, briefly sticking my head in. Again, there's no one I recognise; just people sitting on the worktops or leaning against the cooker, talking, drinking and passing cigarettes between themselves. One girl is blowing smoke into a guy's mouth. Another couple look as though they might be trying to actually eat each other. With an apologetic shrug at the few that bother to look my way, I go for the other door.

Another sip will dampen my rapidly escalating levels of anxiety.

This is where the music's coming from and, despite the ear-drum-shattering decibels being pumped out by the sound system, people seem to be engaging in conversations, albeit ones where they have to shout directly into each other's ears. Again, any surface seems to be have been commandeered as a seat: the floor, the sideboard, the coffee table, the sofa, the arms of the sofa . . . If there's enough space for a pair of buttocks, it seems it's fair game.

I scan the room for signs of Lauren Edwards or Liam, my brain ransacking its memory banks for even the faintest glimmer of someone I might know. A guy – older than me – is sat on the floor with his back to me. I sort of know the severe cut of his hair. He turns – in profile – to accept the hand-rolled cigarette that's being passed to him and my brain comes up with an instant match. It's Nathan Douglas. Even through the vodka vacuum that I'm comfortably housed in, a shard of panic makes its way – quickly and efficiently – into my nervous system.

As if he's heard it, he suddenly swings his head my way, two jets of smoke gushing from his nostrils like a mad bull. Somebody shouts something in his left ear; someone I can't see. Whatever they're shouting, it's enough for him to disengage the vice-like look he gives me and turn to them. He leans in to reply. Something else is shouted back and he nods, smiling.

The person who's been shouting into his ear stands up. My brain comes up with another match: it's none other than my self-appointed partner in crime, Nathan Douglas Jr. Great. The only people I seem to know at this tinnitus-inspiring gathering are the school psychopath and his criminally minded little brother.

He gets up and walks over to me, nimbly stepping between people and ashtrays – a vicious version of the Artful Dodger. As he approaches, his eyes dart all over me, no doubt seeing what information he can scavenge about me. Luckily, he can't see quite how tight my sphincter has become.

"What you doing here?" he says, cocking his head to one side.

"I'm looking for Lauren Edwards," I offer meekly. "Or Liam."

"What d'you want them for?"

"They invited me."

This obviously isn't the answer he was expecting; the blink gives it away. He starts to nod slowly, as if seeing me in a new light.

"OK." There's a pause while he looks me over one more time. "My brother says you're a twat."

Given that his brother has a propensity for levels of violence that I can't even consider, who am I to disagree? If Nathan Douglas says I'm a twat, in my eyes, it's as good as established fact. I shrug and smile, as if being a twat's something I can't help, which I can't.

I shrug and grin again. If he's trying to throw me a baited hook, it's going to take an awful lot more to get a reaction out of me.

"D'you know what I told him?"

"No," I tremble. "What?"

"I told him you were alright. Told him about the fags and the booze."

"Thanks."

"He doesn't like you though."

"OK."

"But nothing's going to happen so don't worry about it." In effect, he's just told me that I owe him, because he's put his pit bull of a sibling on a shorter leash. I'm sure he'll be wanting me to settle up, probably on another shopping trip to Singhsburys.

"Thanks. D'you know where Lauren Edwards is? I ought to say hello . . ."

"Try the bedroom." He nods over my shoulder.

"Great. Will do. Thanks again."

"Here. Give us a go on that."

It takes me a second to work out that he's talking about the vodka, so I hand him the bottle. He unscrews the cap and takes a mouthful and then offers it back to me, gesturing with it, as though he wants me to have some. Fighting the urge to wipe the top, I take a swip, assuming that the alcohol will kill any germs he's left there. Nathan Douglas Jr nods something like approval and goes back to his brother.

The bedroom is a similar story to the rest of the flat: smoke, people and drink everywhere. People sitting on the floor, sitting on the edge of the bed. One guy's lucky enough to have secured the only chair in the room. Even luckier for him, a girl in a very tight top has secured his lap as her resting place. There, sitting at the head of the bed and leaning against her boyfriend, is Lauren Edwards. She sees me, standing in the doorway, smiling awkwardly, like a priest in a brothel.

"Vagina!" she shouts, pointing.

All heads turn my way, wondering at who I might be. All the women in the room start mentally dressing me.

"I told you he'd come!" she roars at Liam. "Here, Vagina! Come and sit over here!" She slaps the mattress and shifts to make room. Somebody else I don't know gets up, whether to go to the toilet or what I don't know, but it leaves a spot right next to Lauren Edwards and Liam.

Despite the awkwardness of sitting next to Lauren Edwards on the bed that I assume she and her boyfriend use as a sex trampoline, I have no choice but to obey.

Vagina has entered the building.

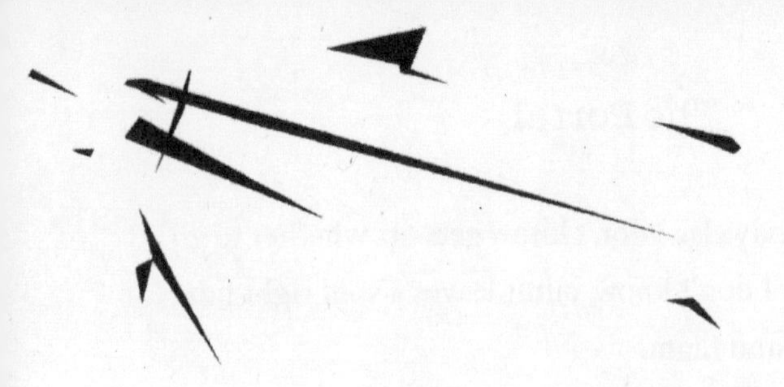

Thirty-Three

SuperJim

Sip.

Meanwhile, James Chapman has left the building unnoticed.

Sitting in his place, wearing exactly the same clothes, is SuperJim. SuperJim is brilliant. SuperJim is funny. He's already done the swearing thing, much to Lauren Edwards' cackling delight. Even Liam joined in, giving SuperJim new words to try out. SuperJim enunciated those words, rolling them around in his mouth with relish. He even did them in some comedy voices that sent anyone in earshot into uncontrollable laughter. SuperJim is a born comedian.

SuperJim doesn't even feel the Actual Weight of Manhood. It is a feather in his grip. It is a speck on his hugely masculine boulders for shoulders.

Unlike James, SuperJim makes friends, quickly and easily. Already he's been shooting the breeze with a guy called Josh, as though he's known him for years and years and years. It's like they grew up together, but they didn't. SuperJim knows that this is a Special Moment, where a true connection has been created between strangers and allows them to see each other for what they really are. Because SuperJim knows this, he feels compelled to tell Josh. He tells him twice, three times, four times, just so Josh can share in the magic. Not even Josh's multitude of piercings fazes him. If James was here, he would be alarmed by someone who looks like they've been attacked by a rivet gun, but James isn't here. SuperJim is. SuperJim can see past the studs and the hoops and the jewellery and laugh at Josh's risqué jokes, and even high-five him when the rest of the bed joins in with the mirth.

Even more unlike James, SuperJim likes the music that's blasting dust off any surface that isn't occupied by a bum or two. In fact, SuperJim isn't even afraid to get up and dance when Lauren Edwards tells him to. SuperJim has enough insight to recognise the fact that he's no Justin Timberlake, but he doesn't care. Instead, SuperJim makes his dancing even more stupid. SuperJim has the audience in the palm of his hand, because he was born to entertain.

SuperJim knows things, because one of SuperJim's superpowers is to know things. He sees those stray looks that the girls flick his way; the ones that their boyfriends don't see; the ones that they don't even want SuperJim to notice. SuperJim does notice because another one of SuperJim's superpowers is to notice things. Beneath the laughter and the camera flashes, SuperJim can see that these girls are attracted to him. He knows that it's that unicorn combination of wit, intelligence, humour and his just-don't-care attitude that elevates him above the rank and file specimens of menfolk that litter the flat. Those girls find SuperJim sexy, especially that one in the corner with the short, dyed-red hair and the nipples. SuperJim even angles some of his dancing towards her, just so she can get a look at what's on offer. Not in her face, like a lap dancer; just a glimpse, a coy spin, a saucy high kick. SuperJim knows he's right when she demands that he twerks. SuperJim can twerk, so SuperJim does. Even though the twerking makes him stagger forward and fall onto the bed, SuperJim knows that this is funny and he laughs along with all of the other voices that laugh into the vivid, brightly lit room.

Timeslip

SuperJim is talking and the girl with the nipples is listening. SuperJim understands how hard it must be to be a girl because men are all the same. SuperJim isn't the same and he tells her that, because she needs to know it, because it's important that she does and he tells her twice, three times, four times, just so she can know it.

Timeslip

Liam is shouting something, getting up off the bed and shouting something and everyone's got to have their drinks ready because this party's getting started. Nipples was here a minute ago, I'm sure she was. SuperJim has decided to call her Nipples even though he knows it's wrong, but he doesn't know her name and that's all that he can think of. The music stops and SuperJim looks into his bottle. A lot of the vodka isn't there. Where did it go? People's faces are a bit blurry, but SuperJim doesn't care because these are his friends; everyone's lovely and we're all the same. SuperJim has never been so happy.

Then there's music. On the curt, opening rap of drums and the sultry, pouting vocals about a party girl – how her phone's blowing up and her doorbell's ringing – a huge cheer rolls like a wave throughout the flat, sending arms skyward, caps off bottles, rings off cans and liquid into plastic glasses. The song gets louder. There's a chorus and everyone sings it, the voices all haphazard and connected and one, like the wind in trees.

"Onetwothreeonetwothree drink!"

"Onetwothreeonetwothree drink!"

The wind in the trees sings out the numbers and the wind in the trees shouts out the word "DRINK!". Every time they shout that word, they drink, they laugh and they cough. They onetwothree drink and this party's on. SuperJim's back on his feet, onetwothree drinking but the ground keeps veering away from under his feet and he keeps lurching, having to meet the wall with his hand and tripping over people. It doesn't matter because SuperJim doesn't have any relatives because he doesn't need them. Onetwothree drink and onetwothreedrink.

Outside. How did I get outside? So cold. Cold and shaking.

Dark. Streetlight.

My hands. Those are mine. All four of them.

On the pavement.

Music.

Music far away.

My body rolls again, my spine like rope, undulating like a whip crack.

A noise. Coughing. Choking.

Eyes open wide. Too wide.

Water with lumps. Carrots. So many carrots. I didn't eat carrots. Did I?

My back hunches up again. An accordion in the hands of a maniac.

That noise.

Coughing.

Choking.

Snot. Snot looping in strings from nose to hands.

Footsteps. Laughter.

My eyes hurt.

A cough from my soul, threatening to force my eyes out of my head.

Tears. Tears, Tears.

Cough.

I can't.

I can't.

Please.

Walkingwalkingwalkinginthedardarkdark.

Myheadistooheavy.

Itleansforward.

Mylegshavetofollow.

Intowallsintolamposts.

Ontothefloor.

CryingI'mcryingI'mcrying.

Morebrownoutofmymouth.

Splatteringontothepavement.

Butthere'snothingleft.

I heave and heave hard, hacking, my throat burning, my eyes forced open to look at the meagre mess I'm making.

Walkingwalkingwalkinginthedarkdarkdark.

Myfeetaretoofast.

Itripandstagger.

Home. I need home.

But I can't go there. Not home.

WhereamIwhereamI?

Smashed

Iknowthisroad.Iknowthis road.

I know this road. I know this road.

Lurchandstaggerandtumbleandweep.

There'sadoorIknowthisdoor.

Iknowthis door. Iknow this door.

I know this door.

Knockingandringingandcrying.

I'msorryI'msorryI'msorry.

Ican'tcarryitanymore.Ican'tcarryit anymore.

Ican'tcarry it anymore.

I can't carry it anymore.

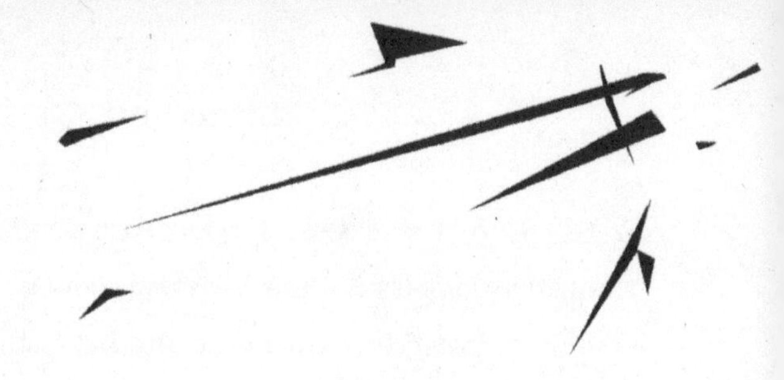

Thirty-Four

No Words

Oh, Jesus.

Jesus Christ.

My head.

My head hurts.

Someone forced a red-hot, iron bar through my temples in my sleep. I can feel it burning, baking my head. God, it hurts.

I'm cold. Shivering cold.

Where am I?

My eyes slowly creak open as dry as crisps.

Pillow. My head's on a pillow.

I'm on a bed. I'm on the edge of the bed. On the floor, by the bed, there's a washing-up bowl. There's something in it. The stink of bleach punches my nose. There's another smell, fighting for dominance. Vomit. Bleach and vomit."

Oh, God. I was sick. I remember vomiting in the street. I must've done it here, too. Wherever here is.

Slowly, gingerly, I turn onto my back and sit up. My head hurts. It feels too heavy and the world lurches with it. Nausea rolls up from my gut to my throat but stops there. My throat. God, it feels like someone went at it with some sandpaper.

I know this room.

This is Adil's room.

How did I get here? I don't remember getting here. I don't remember getting into this bed.

I don't remember my trousers coming off, but there they are, on the floor. Did I take them off? Please, no – did somebody else?

Something rustles on the floor at the end of the bed. I look forward as far as my wretched head will let me, and then a face appears, groggy and rubbing its eyes. It's Adil. He's in a sleeping bag. On the floor. In his bedroom.

Blinking, he looks over to me and smiles wearily.

"Morning, Jim," he croaks, coughing his voice into gear. "How you feeling?"

"Terrible," I manage. "Like death." I do. My body feels weak. My eyes are exhausted and gritty. My throat's so sore it stings at every swallow. My head echoes with a sharp, burning pain. Sickness lurks in my stomach. An anvil of depression sits in my brain.

Adil nods and rubs his eyes again.

"You were in a bit of a state," he nods, grimly. "A bit of a mess."

"I guess . . . What . . . what happened?"

"Don't you remember?"

"No, not really . . . bits."

There's a knock at the door. Slowly and stupidly, I look at it.

"Come in!" Adil calls. It's not a shout; it doesn't sound like he's got the energy for that.

The door opens and there, in a dressing gown, is Nadia. She comes in, quietly closes the door behind her and looks at me.

"How are you feeling?"

So, I was right. They have got together, but I feel too ill to get angry or upset. There's nothing left in the tanks; I'm just a James-shaped vessel for pain, sickness and exhausted sadness.

"Not very good."

There's something off about the way she's looking at me, like she wants to say something, but doesn't know if she should.

"What happened?" I ask again. "And can I have some water?" My tongue feels like one of those dried dates that my Nan likes at Christmas.

"There's some by your bed, mate," Adil answers, sitting up in his sleeping bag and stretching. "Some paracetamol too. You'll be needing them."

There it is: a glass of water. Pure, clear and cold, and if my throat didn't hurt so much with each gulp, perfect. I can feel it travelling down my oesophagus, cooling and calming as it hits my belly. I can almost feel my parched cells trying to soak it up.

Panting, I take a breath, before putting the pills in my mouth and glugging again.

As I put the near-empty glass down on Adil's bedside table, Nadia sits on the end of the bed, pulling her dressing gown tighter.

"How much do you remember?" she asks, gently.

"Nothing," I rasp. "I don't remember anything."

"You don't remember knocking on the door?"

"Vaguely . . . but nothing after that. I don't even remember it opening."

Nadia looks at Adil and he raises his eyebrows.

"What?" Despite the fatigue, I'm starting to feel a bit panicky.

"So, you don't remember my dad opening the door?" Adil shrugs.

"No . . . What did I do?"

Again, they look at each other.

"Well, you practically fell on him for a start," Adil continues. "And then . . ."

"What?"

"You were sick on him," he finishes. "You threw up on his feet, while he was trying to hold you up."

My head is in my hands.

"You don't remember me coming over?" Nadia looks at the floor, as if she can't look at me.

"No . . ."

"I rang her," Adil chips in. "You kept demanding to see her.

So, I rang her."

"But you were at a party . . . weren't you?"

"I *was*," Nadia nods. "But then I came over."

"I was worried, mate," Adil adds. "I've never seen you like that."

"Like what?"

"You were just . . . really angry. It was like you'd gone mad. You wouldn't sit down. You kept getting up and falling down, and just going on about Nadia."

"What was I saying?"

"Just stuff."

"Like what?" I don't really want to know, but I've got to ask.

"Like how we were seeing each other behind your back, how you knew she was here somewhere and how you needed to talk to her."

"Oh, Jesus." I don't think I've ever experienced shame of this level – pure, distilled shame.

"My dad wanted to call your mum, but I managed to get him not to. Took a lot of persuading, though . . ."

"Oh, Christ. Mum! I was supposed to text her . . ."

"I did it, mate. She sent one about half eleven and I just replied. Said you were staying the night."

I have no words. None.

"So, you don't remember me turning up?" Nadia asks, again.

"No," I groan.

"You don't remember accusing us of going behind your back?"

"No." I want to put my hands over my ears or hide under the bed sheet. Anything to make this not be true.

"You don't remember falling over?" she asks, throwing another look at Adil.

"No . . ."

Adil gives her a slight shake of his head. Whatever she's about to say, he doesn't want her to.

"What?" I wince. "What did I do?"

In reply, Nadia turns her head towards the small table at the end of the room. The small table with Adil's set on it.

Or what's left of it.

The miniature front room looks as though it's been hit by a full-size bomb. Two of the walls are just gone, reduced to something that might pass for matches. The third is more or less intact, apart from the chunk missing out of the top-left corner. The tiny sofa is flattened. The tiny pictures are crushed and snapped. The tiny TV is in pieces. There, in the middle of the devastation, is the figure that was going to represent Nadia's character, its plasticine face smeared to one side, its limbs twisted and mangled.

"Oh!" My voice is a dry whisper. I can feel the last flecks of precious colour draining from my face.

"It's OK, Jim," Adil shrugs. "I can sort it."

"But the competition . . ."

"It doesn't matter."

"I am so sorry. So sorry. I'll pay for it. Whatever you need, I'll pay for it . . ."

"It's OK, Jim. Don't worry about it. It probably wouldn't've won anyway."

"Jesus, mate, I am so sorry!"

"Jim. It's OK. You've got enough on your plate."

"What d'you mean?"

This time it's Adil who throws the look and Nadia who catches it. For the first time since she came into the room, she looks me in the eyes.

"After you fell onto the set, you started crying but, like, really crying. You just sat there and cried."

I can't bear this. It's like someone's playing dot-to-dot with my memory and I can't even see the picture it's supposed to be making. The more dots that are joined, the more horrendous it looks and if I look really hard, which I don't want to, I can see that it's me. All the worst aspects of myself put together to make one hideous image. A mosaic of anger, jealousy, stupidity and self-pity.

"Did I say anything?" Please say I lost the ability to speak.

Adil and Nadia play another round of look-tennis before she carries on.

"Well, we managed to get you on the end of the bed. You told us about what's been going on at home, about your dad . . . hitting your mum."

My head's back in my hands.

"What else?"

"About how your mum's coping. And your sister. About hating your dad. About the money in the Lucozade bottle. The Rainbow Eye."

"Oh, God."

Nadia leans in, fixing me with an intense stare.

"About how you can't talk to anyone about it."

"Christ. Did I say anything else?"

Nadia sits back, pulling her gown tight, once more. She doesn't want to say it. So, Adil does it for her.

"You told us you were a criminal. You just kept saying it."

I just groan. My mouth's too worn out to form actual vowels and consonants.

"What did you mean?" Nadia asks softly.

"It doesn't matter," I sigh mournfully. "Just something I've got to sort out. Did I say anything else?"

"About what?"

"About anything."

"No." She looks at Adil who shrugs and shakes his head.

So, I didn't mention the drinking, but that's OK because there's really nothing to mention. It's not a problem. It's just how I'm coping. It's fine.

"Is there anything else?" Adil throws down a gauntlet without realising or meaning to. I could use this moment to tell them absolutely everything, to tell them that I haven't got what it takes to carry the Weight of Manhood and the only way to lighten the load is to soak it in sherry, wine or vodka. Even thinking those things sounds ridiculous. It sounds stupid and if those words came out of my mouth, that's how I'd feel.

"No." Even as I say the word, I know I don't believe it. There's a part of me that wants to let them know I'm a bit worried about how I'm dealing with things, but I suck that thought down, with quicksand strength, burying it deep.

"Jim," Adil says. "We can help you, mate. We're your friends. If there's something else, we might be able to sort something out."

'How?' I want to ask him, but I don't. They don't really know how screwed up everything is. No matter what I've told them, they're not living it. They don't breathe it or see it or hear it or feel it every single day. I do.

Instead, I nod and make apologetic noises.

My phone bleeps an incoming message from the floor. Adil picks it up and tosses it to me. It's mum.

Hey, J! Hope you had a good time. Are you coming home for lunch? Love you. Xxx

"I've got to go," I mutter.

"Is everything OK?" Nadia's face is the picture of concern that I never wanted it to be.

"Yeah . . . Just lunch. I ought to be there, after what happened yesterday with dad and that."

Not really caring that Nadia's in the room, I gingerly swing my legs out from under the covers. They're covered in scratches and bruises that I don't remember getting. I place my feet on the floor, not really trusting that it's not going to try and escape from under me again. Walking like a pensioner, I take sore, rusty steps to my trousers and put them on.

I feel dreadful; not just the head, the nausea and the fatigue, but the shame, the humiliation and the embarrassment.

"I'm really sorry about the . . ." I gesture limply at Adil's broken set.

"Let it go, Jim. I have. Maybe I'll use it for something else."

"And I'm sorry if I had a go at you guys," I add, looking at the floor.

In response, Nadia gets up and comes and gives me a hug. A tight squeeze. Nothing has ever felt this good, this welcome, this needed. She's soft, warm and full of care. There's still a faint smell of the shampoo she uses. It's hard not to cry at how it feels, like a solid object in a world of holograms. A hot tear escapes my right eye. I bite the others back and hope she won't see it, but she does. As she pulls away, she sees it and wipes it away.

"It'll be OK," she murmurs.

"Yeah," I gasp, trying to get myself together. "Trainers. Where . . .?"

"Downstairs," Adil answers, climbing out of his sleeping bag and putting some trackies on. "With your backpack. By the front door."

"Right. I'd better go. Sorry, guys."

"Give me a minute," Nadia says. "I'll get dressed and I'll walk with you."

"You don't have to."

"I know. I'll see you downstairs."

She leaves. Adil and I go down the stairs, me taking them very, very slowly. As I'm putting my trainers on, I hear a new set of feet behind me. It's Mr Khan.

He looks at me and shakes his head sorrowfully.

"M-Mr Khan . . ." I stutter. "I'm so, so sorry. I can't tell you how sorry I am. I've been a complete idiot and I just hope you can forgive me. I'm so sorry."

Mr Khan looks at me again, disappointment in his face and in the way he's standing. Even his clothes look disappointed in me.

"The only person you've let down," he says eventually, "is yourself, Jamie, but your actions compromise other people. You are lucky to have such good friends."

"I know. I'm so sorry."

"This time, I'll let it go, but if you ever turn up in that state again, the door will remain closed. You won't be welcome. I will call your mother. I should have last night." He directs a stern scowl towards his son. "That's what I should have done. Next time, I will."

"I know. I'm sorry. Thank you."

"Then we understand each other."

"Yes. Yes, we do."

With a curt nod and another scowl at Adil, Mr Khan returns to the living room.

He never once said to call him Sid.

"OK?" Nadia asks, trotting down the stairs. She looks beautiful. I guess her clothes are what she wore to the party. She looks stunning.

"Yeah," I nod.

"Let's go then," she says, cancelling out the rest of the world with a smile. "Let's get you home."

Thirty-Five

Nice Guy

We walk the first ten minutes in silence, the lava in my head sloshing around. Once or twice, I feel that numbness in my lips that sets off the I-might-vomit alarms, but I don't. Which is good, because my stomach is so empty that the next things to appear would probably be major organs.

My skin tries to sweat, making me cold and hot at the same time, but I don't think there's an ounce of water in my body, so my pores just open and scream silently.

The only real sign that I'm alive is that fact that my heart's still beating and that's going like a pneumatic drill.

I feel awful and angsty, as though each arthritic step I take is hobbling me closer to some unknown horror. The only thing that stops me from stopping and curling up into a ball is walking beside me, worry scratched into her face.

"How are you feeling?" she asks.

My tacky tongue stickily tries to make some words but fails. Instead, I nod as much as the molten ball bearing in my head will allow.

"I was really worried about you."

"I'm really sorry."

"It's OK."

"No. It's not. I've treated you like dirt." Deep breath. My heart flip-flops in my chest like a gasping fish, but I keep pushing the gluey words out. "But it wasn't because I don't want to be with you or anything. I just didn't know what to do. I just thought that you might . . . I don't know. I don't know what I was thinking. It all made sense at the time."

"It always does when you keep it to yourself." Nadia nods and I wonder what she means.

She breathes deeply.

"You know that going out and getting drunk doesn't . . . help." Whatever she's trying to say, she's digging deep.

"I'm starting to get the idea."

"But, seriously, it doesn't."

A silence separates us for a few seconds.

"Did you ever really wonder why I don't go to parties, Jamie?"

I rub my aching head which only makes it hurt some more.

"I just thought . . . well, you knew I didn't go to them and . . .

well, I thought you didn't like them."

"You know my uncle? Ajay?"

"Yeah . . . I think so. Wasn't he there at that barbeque? Your folks' house?"

"Yes."

"Yeah . . . he was a nice guy. I think he thought I was a bit of an idiot. He was funny though.

"Uncle Ajay is funny. One of the funniest people I know. But, when I was little, he wasn't like that. He wasn't funny. Not funny at all."

"What d'you mean?"

"Uncle Ajay used to drink too much. He wasn't drunk all the time, but when he got drunk, he used to get really drunk, and that's when he'd get nasty with my aunt and my cousins . . ." Judging by the look on her face, it's either still a sore memory or she's realised that what she's saying is a bit close to home. My home.

"It's OK," I shrug and look her in the eyes. "I would never, ever do that. Ever."

"I know, I know," she protests, shrinking slightly. "That's not where I was going. When we were little, our cousins – his kids – and our auntie used to have to come and stay with us, because he used to . . . do what he did. Mum used to tell us they'd been in a car crash and, for years, I believed them. For years, I used to think that uncle Ajay was the worst driver in the world."

"Ha." It's almost a laugh, parched as it is.

"But it was alcohol. He talks about it, if you ask him. He's sober now, but I did ask him and he said it all started when his father died. His father died when he was young, and he said it was like there was a part of him missing that ought to be there. The only thing that stopped him hurting so much was alcohol."

Ajay. I remember the first time I met him. I was stood by the barbeque, a bit awkward and reeking of outsider. He came and said hello, all jokes and laughter. I'd never have guessed.

"But it didn't help at all," Nadia continues. "It just made things worse. That's what alcohol means to me. I know that for other people, it means fun and silliness and good times, but I've seen something else: bruises and tears and . . . ugliness."

"Are they still together? Your aunt and uncle?"

For a moment, Nadia looks surprised by my question. Then, her face lights up with that glow of wholehearted optimism that I managed to convince myself was something to be loathed; back when I didn't know what I had.

"Yes," she smiles, "he got help. He hasn't drunk for years."

"So, he's OK?"

"He still goes to AA. Every week. He says it's what keeps him on the right path."

"But he doesn't drink."

"No. He's in recovery and he always will be. 'One drink is too many and a hundred isn't enough.' That's what he says.

Auntie Manjali won't leave him. They're a team. It's an illness. They've beaten it together."

"So, there's hope for you and me then?" Oh, God it's clumsy. It's so blunt, so workmanlike, but I can feel the delicate wings of hope fluttering above the nausea in my belly.

"What d'you mean?"

Mentally, I'm scurrying like an ant under a magnifying glass on a hot, summer's day. Did I really say that? Judging by the confusion on her perfect face, I did. Now I have no option but to see it through.

"I know I dumped you," I mutter. "But now, you know why I did. I'm sorry. What you said in the card . . . I think you might be right . . . Maybe I have taken on a bit more than I should, but I didn't mean to. It just sort of happened that way. All I can say is that if I could go back in time and not dump you, I would." For the first time in a long time, I'm being frighteningly, heart-stoppingly, unfamiliarly honest. "Can we get back together?" There it is: I've said it.

Nadia blinks. In that blink, I see it all: the hurt, the confusion and the sadness.

She steps forward.

My legs mutiny and it's me who takes the step back.

She doesn't say anything; she doesn't need to.

"OK," I nod, even though it hurts physically, mentally and emotionally.

"Jamie. You chose to cut me off when we could have talked. I was supposed to be there for you, but you wouldn't let me."

She's right; I can't hide from the truth.

"No," I agree. My voice is gone, worn out and sore, like the rest of me.

"My friends hate you," she frowns. "They tell me what a dick you are, but I know different. I always did. I don't want to have to join in with them. I don't want them to be right. I want to be able fight your corner, but that can't happen if you're still hurting me. I have to be what I was before we started seeing each other. I have to be your friend."

Mr Khan was right; everything I've done has compromised everyone else. Trying to keep everything locked inside has just been like shaking a can of Coke and opening it in a crowd. All that you're guaranteed is mess and stains.

I could really use a drink right now. Something soft and fizzy.

Another pause. Another hopeless silence. My tongue cracks against the roof of my mouth, too dry and sad to make anything but parchment sounds.

"I'm going to walk you to where we usually go," Nadia smiles, failing to hide the hurt and loss. "Then I'm going home."

"OK."

And she does. She takes my hand in hers and it burns. It burns with all the nervousness and excitement I felt when I held it for the first time and with all the fear and dread that it might be the last time it happens. It burns hotter than the sun.

Then we're at the corner of the road and we're silent. She looks at me and her eyes are wet, but they don't cry.

"Friends?" she says, timid and hopeful.

"Friends."

She leans in and kisses my cheek and for the fraction of a second, everything stops – as still as stone – and there is order in the world.

Then, it's just her back as she's walking away, and there's a horrible lurch as the world starts to spin once more.

I feel so ill.

I need a drink.

I know where I'm going to get it from.

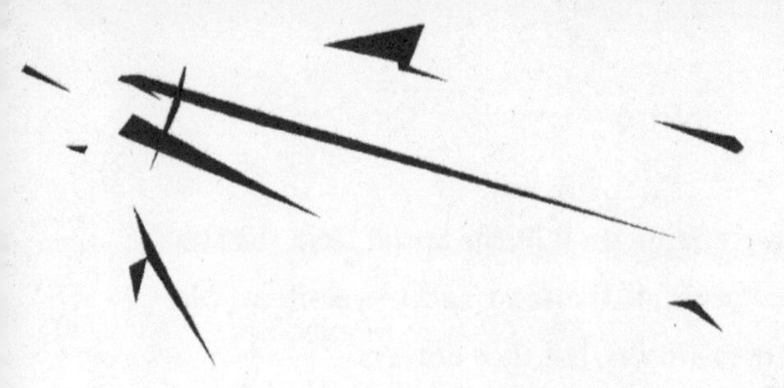

Thirty-Six

I Am a Tw*t

For a Saturday morning, Singhsburys is remarkably empty: just a couple of pensioners browsing the glossy pages of grinning celebrities getting married and a woman pushing a pram, stuffing a lottery ticket into her handbag as she turns to leave.

My Singh is perched on his stool, his blue turban like a cloth minaret, his beard seemingly bigger since our last encounter. His eyes – magnified behind glasses – fix on me, making my empty bag of a stomach turn over. The skin around his eyes crinkles and he sends me an almost-imperceptible nod. I think, buried behind the ever-expanding carpet of whiskers, there's a smile. Feebly, I return it, before going over to the wall of drinks.

The vodka I stole has been replaced with another bottle. It's as though nothing ever happened. They're all lined up like soldiers, sleek and gleaming and ready for action. My heart stutters as I look at Mr Singh who crinkles another smile in my direction, before turning back to the rest of the shop. He approves of me. He trusts me.

It takes my hungover brain a moment to work out what's different about the picture. Then I spot it. His son isn't about.

This is good.

I'm relying on Mr Singh's advancing years and the fact that English isn't his first language to get me through this. Having Mr Singh's maybe-son around would only make it more complicated. He might be out back, he might be in the toilet; wherever he is, I need to move fast, because he could be back any second.

As if my hand knows what I want more than I do, it opens the chiller cabinet door and retrieves a bottle of 7Up. Screw what the experts say: cold, liquid sugar feels like the best idea in the world right now.

"Hello," Mr Singh nods. "What are you buying?"

With a trembling hand, I hold up the bottle.

"Nothing, for you. Free. A reward," he nods, again.

This isn't quite what I was hoping for.

"No, I must pay for it . . ."

"Another time. Not today. Today, it's yours." He gently pushes the bottle across the countertop towards me.

"But, Mr Singh . . ."

"No. I remember you. You chased the thief out of my shop. Good things for good people."

Oh, great. Now I'm one of the 'good people'. I don't think I've ever felt less good or less plural. Then my brain lances a reluctant thought from its depths.

"Well . . . OK," I swallow. "But the thing is . . . a bottle of vodka was stolen, too." Mr Singh's eyes suddenly become a bit more piercing, so I start babbling. "The boy who stole the vodka, well, I know him and he told me that he's really sorry and that he wanted me to give you this." I hold up the tenner mum gave me last night and put it in front of Mr Singh. He looks at it and then at me.

"The boy who did this, he is your friend?"

"Not really . . . Not a *friend.* Just sort of someone I know."

Mr Singh's spectacular eyebrows knot over his glasses.

"You shouldn't have a friend like this," he frowns. "You are a good boy. You don't want this friend in your life."

"No. No, I don't," I say, truthfully. I'm not sure if I'm talking about Nathan Douglas's little brother or the me who goes out, gets drunk and hurts the people close to him. Getting rid of either of them would be a bonus.

Mr Singh nods again and then drags the tenner across the countertop. The ching of the till sounds his acceptance. He's bought my story and I've belatedly bought some booze.

"I cannot judge your friend, this boy. My son would like to, but he is wrong. Only God can judge. If you have no God, only you can judge. Stealing is wrong, but I think your friend must feel bad about who he is, if he feels he must steal. I will not be happy to see your friend here, but I will not judge him. He will not be welcome here if he steals again. Do you understand?"

I nod, not quite sure what to say.

"You are a good person," he says, again, making me feel even worse.

"Thanks."

I slink out of the shop, into the far too bright sunshine and scrabble at the screw-top cap. There's that short, sharp shushing sound, as all the bubbles race to the top. I put the bottle to my lips and drink.

Oh, God, it's fantastic. It's like I never fully appreciated just how delicious this carbonated mixture of sugar, sodium citrate and natural lemon and lime flavourings was before. The cold bubbles trail a happy little path down my throat, fizzing and popping, the sugary goodness hitting my stomach. Flying in the face of the burp that's already boiling in the depths, I take another belt from the bottle. My stomach starts to tighten and bloat, straining against the increase in pressure. A huge bubble of gas it rolls up my throat, exploding out through my mouth in a loud, guttural belch.

It feels so good to be able to do that, without it being followed by a stream of partially digested food.

"Oi!"

Before I even have a chance to turn, a pair of meaty hands have grabbed me. I'm dragged around the side of Singhsbury's, off the street and out of the way, still clutching my 7Up.

Nathan Douglas. Senior.

He slams me against the unforgiving brickwork, battering my breath out of my lungs.

"What's your game, then?" His face is so close that I have to turn my head and look at him out of the corner of one bulging eye.

"What?" I gasp. "What is it?"

"Fink you're hard, do yer?" he barks, pulling me from the wall, just so he can ram me back into it. I'm so frightened I don't even think to correct his pronunciation.

"God, no! I'm not hard! Look at me! I'm soft! A wimp! I'm jelly!"

"Different story last night though, weren't it?"

"What? What d'you mean?" My voice is so high it's like puberty never happened.

Nathan pushes his face forward to the point that our eyeballs are almost touching, like he's trying to see into my head.

"Don't play 'I can't remember' with me," he spits.

"But I can't!" I squeal. "Remember what? What am I supposed to remember?"

My brain pulls some deleted files out of the Recycle Bin. It's fuzzy, like it's filmed underwater, but I'm talking to that girl with the red hair and the nipples under the t-shirt and she's laughing and then someone grabs her hand and tries to pull her up and she doesn't want to go. I don't want her to have to go. I grab her other hand and stand up. It's Nathan Douglas's little brother and he's shouting at me over the music to fuck off. We're pulling at her and suddenly something snaps.

It's not me and Nathan Douglas's little brother and the girl with the red hair, it's me and dad, with Bex in the middle.

Everything that I thought I'd put a cork in comes boiling and sputtering to the surface and the cork fires out like a bullet.

I go for him, kicking, flailing and punching with every ounce of anger I've got. He's got me in a headlock and he's spinning me round. There are more people, but I'm fighting them too and lashing out and suddenly, I'm out on the pavement, puking my life onto the pavement.

"Oh, God," I groan.

"Yeah," Nathan hisses.

"But I thought he was hassling her."

"That was his girlfriend."

"But it was like she didn't want . . ."

"They'd split up, hadn't they? He was trying to get back with her."

"Oh, God."

Nathan Douglas readjusts his grip on my hoodie and lifts

me further up the wall, staring at me with unblinking eyes.

"You're lucky," he breathes. "Shall I tell you why?"

"Yes, please." Pathetically polite, even in the face of certain death.

"Any other time, I'd give you a slap. Any other time, the police would be ringing your dentist to find out who you were, you get me?"

I nod. I get him.

"But Lauren doesn't want me to hurt you. And Liam's my mate, so you're lucky."

"Lauren? Lauren Edwards?" I squeak.

Nathan Douglas nods slowly, never breaking his murderous gaze.

"Lauren Edwards. She says you've got stuff going on at home. The way I see it, we've all got stuff going on at home, but she reckons you're alright. I reckon you're a twat and I reckon that if you ever go near my brother again . . ." He lets the threat swing in the air like a corpse in a gibbet.

"I won't! I promise!"

"I know you won't."

"Yes."

"I don't care how pissed you were. If you can't hack it, don't do it. Next time . . ."

"There won't be a next time!"

"*Next* time, she won't be there to save you. Doesn't matter that my brother's a dick, does it? That's the way it goes. You hurt him, I hurt you. Got it?"

"Got it."

"Good. Then, piss off and don't let me see you again."

With a final, spine-straightening shove against the wall, Nathan Douglas lets me go, turns and walks away, like nothing ever happened.

But something has. Something that shakes me hard. Even worse than the fear of being reduced to a smear of raspberry jam at the significant hands of Nathan Douglas.

I lost control.

I completely lost it.

I made a mistake.

One stupid mistake.

Was dad right?

Am I like him?

Oh, my God.

Am I?

My phone buzzes a text. Mum.

What time are you coming back? Xxx

On my way. Be about 20 minutes. X

Xxx

X

Smashed

Swigging and burping, shuffling and shivering, I gingerly make my way home.

127,400 Newtons' worth of idiot.

My father's son.

Thirty-Seven

Falling

By the time I'm turning the key in the front door, the paracetamol's starting to take effect.

"Hello, love," mum smiles, coming down the stairs. "Did you have a good time?"

"Yeah, thanks. It was . . . nice." I feel as though I might fall apart in a light breeze.

We walk into the kitchen.

"Tea?"

"No thanks. Have we got any cold drinks? Anything fizzy?"

"Come on, Jamie. You know better than that. It's water or squash."

Of course it is. Wishing there was at least a Coke or something in the fridge, I fill a glass with water. It'll do.

"So . . . what did you get up to?" mum asks, putting the kettle on.

I got drunk on booze that I stole, attacked a kid younger than me who was trying to get back together with his girlfriend, got thrown out of a party, accused my best friends of having an affair and nearly got killed by a vengeful thug. Plus, I discovered I might have more in common with my father than I thought.

"We recorded the voices and that was it really."

Mum rolls her eyes; she hates it when I don't give her enough detail, but I hate it when she asks for more. I hate it especially when I'm lying because it means I've got to think of some details that might not crumble under further questioning and, given that the inside of my head is like a seized engine, trying to think up anything at all requires a Herculean strength that I just don't have to hand. Instead, I opt for the tried-and-trusted distraction technique.

"Where's Bex?" I sip the water and sit down at the table.

A flicker of something crosses mum's face. She breathes out a mixture of frustration and weariness.

"With your dad."

"When's she back?"

There's another angry sigh.

"Tomorrow afternoon, I hope. He'd better not do anything stupid . . ."

"He won't." I try and sound reassuring, but nothing's going to settle mum's nerves. Nothing except getting her baby girl back home.

"He'd better not."

"How was it when he picked her up?"

"It was ridiculous really. He rang the bell, got back in the car and left the door open for Becky. Didn't say anything at all. Didn't even look at me. I suppose I should be grateful."

"He's an idiot," I mutter, sipping more water

We sit in silence for a while, the ticking of the kitchen clock and my pulse the only music in the house, thudding in my ears. I look up from my life-giving ice cubes. Mum's looking into the middle distance, chewing something over, her eyes seeing things that I can't.

"I couldn't very well stop him from seeing her, could I?" she says, suddenly. "She's been missing him so badly." There's a plea in her voice; she wants someone to tell her that she's done the right thing and that everything will be alright.

"It'll be good for her," I nod gently. "It's what she needs."

"I just wish I was there, wish I knew what he was saying to her," she hisses, desperate and afraid.

"I can do it." The words are out before I've even had a chance to think them through.

"Do what?"

"I can check everything's OK."

"How?"

"I'll text him and say I want to see him."

"Do you want to?"

"Not really."

"But would you?"

"Of course I would." Because that's what loving, devoted sons do with their fathers; they spy on them.

"Really?"

"Yes," I say, with as much finality as my worn-out body can muster. "But not now. We stayed up late last night and I'm really tired."

Mum peers closer at me.

"You have got black circles under your eyes," she agrees.

My eyes do feel tired and gritty. I feel the skin under them, heavy with shadow and toxins. To be honest, I'm amazed I've got eyes at all. The way things went last night, I'm surprised I didn't vomit them out of their sockets.

"So," I continue, "what I'm going to do is go to bed for an hour or so, and just get some sleep. I'll text him after that."

"Are you sure?"

"Mum," I snap, getting up from the table, "I'm sure. In an hour or so."

"Sorry, love. Sorry. It's just . . . thank you."

"Give us a knock in a couple of hours if I don't appear."

I'm telling mum what to do again. She's existing moment to moment and it's up to me to organise the itinerary for the next few hours.

"OK." She sounds relieved and sad at the same time.

Clutching my glass, I shuffle into the hallway, climb arthritically up the stairs, creak into my room, put the water on my bedside desk and flop onto the bed, groaning.

My mattress has never felt so good and comfortable. I'll have a shower later.

I shut my eyes, but sleep takes a little longer to claim me than I'd like it to. Although I feel as though I've been recently exhumed, all I can think of are the stupid things I've done and said over the last few days.

And that I lost control.

I blundered in, trying to defend a girl who probably didn't need it, from a kid who – by his own brother's admission – is a dick.

I did it out of care; some misguided sense of right.

Just like dad said in the back of the car.

Lying back on the bed, I look at my hands: the scratches on my knuckles.

I think of mum and The Rainbow Eye, and I cry.

I don't want to be like him.

I don't want to be like my dad.

***

I'm in class: Mrs Beattie's class. We're reading Macbeth. Nadia's next to me, looking so beautiful, so pretty, so happy. She's reading her lines out; she's Lady Macbeth. It's my turn and I look at the page, but there's nothing written there; just blank pages and no matter how hard I look at them, I can't see any words. Mrs Beattie's looking at me and for some reason mum's there with her Rainbow Eye all shiny and coloured.

My chair tilts sideways and I start to slide off it. I stick out a hand for Nadia to grab me, but she's too busy reading to notice and my chair's tilting more and more. I look at the floor and there's a hole next to my chair. It's huge and vast and black and endless. Somewhere from deep, deep down, I can hear voices laughing at me; laughing, laughing, laughing; calling at me to be a man. I'm scared and frightened. I try and pull myself along the chair, but it keeps tilting until it's on its side. I fall into the hole and I'm falling, falling, falling.

I wake up, moaning something incoherent and kicking at the air with my legs. It takes a second for that freefall feeling to pass, and for my senses to come together and work out where I am. My heart's hammering and I'm wet with sweat.

Slowly, I sit up and reach for the water. The ice has long since melted, but it's still cold. I can feel my cells sucking it up as I drink it down in greedy, gasping gulps. I'm so tired; biblically tired.

There's a tentative knock at the door and mum's voice through the wood.

"Jamie, time to wake up."

"Yep," I call back a bit too loudly. "Awake. Going to have a shower."

"OK, love. See you downstairs."

"OK."

God, I still feel rough. How long is this going to last? Am I doomed to feel fossilised and fearful for the rest of my life?

OK: to business. I pull out my phone and look at the blank screen, wearily dreading what I'm about to do. The last time I saw dad, he tried to get me to punch him.

Is this what this is all leading up to? Was last night a dress rehearsal?

I try three or four clumsy, hangover-fogged versions of the same text before settling.

Hey dad. Thought it might be nice for you, me and B to hang out together. Am around today if you're up for it. x

I camouflage it with a kiss.

A minute or two passes and there's nothing, so I leave the phone on the bed and head to the shower.

The thought of boiling myself into something like normality is too much; the heat might kill me outright. Instead, I leave the temperature dial on the setting set by whoever showered last and gently wash myself.

Showered and feeling slightly more on the up, I go back to my room and change into some fresh, clean clothes that don't have the lingering tang of smoke and my pancreas on them.

I check the phone. Dad must've messaged while I was scrubbing myself clean.

Mum getting you to check up on me? Lol. X

Lol or not, anger lights up in my chest and face. Even in his texts, there's something twisty and turny; something snaky about the whole thing. I can't rise to it. I need to crank my brain into life and find the right way to see this through – for mum and for Becky.

No. Lol. mum's out for the day. At home and bored. Lol.
Maybe we could hang out? X

Fight lols with lols.

The phone buzzes his reply.

Out at the moment. Maybe dinner? We could go out.
Pick you up at 6. X

Great. See you then. X

I pocket the phone and head downstairs.

"Mum?"

"In the lounge!"

I go in. She's sat in her reading chair, not reading.

"What're you doing?" I ask, sitting on the sofa.

"Nothing, really. Just thinking."

"Oh, yeah?"

"Am I doing the right thing, Jamie? Splitting the family up."

This is an awful lot to cope with on the spot.

"Mum, dad split the family up the moment he did what he did."

There it is, I've staked my claim, drawn my line in the ground.

This time, I'm not trying to please anyone else or make mum feel better. I'm saying it because it's true.

"I know what you mean, but . . . it's a big thing, Jamie. Our lives are going to be really different . . . It's not going to be easy, is it?"

"Maybe, but what's the alternative? Living with a man you're scared of?"

"But maybe I had something to do with it. He does work hard, your father. Maybe I pushed him too far, maybe I said the wrong thing, maybe it was just the wrong night. I had had a bit to drink . . ."

"Why?"

"Why, what?"

"Why were you drinking, mum? Think about it."

"I don't know . . . I was . . . I don't know."

"Because you were sad, mum. Because you didn't know what

else to do to make that sadness go away." Uncle Ajay, trying to put me at ease over the barbeque, appears in my mind. Now that I think of it, he's holding a can of Coke.

"Maybe."

"Maybe this and maybe that, but the one absolute is that dad hit you. There's no 'maybe' in the world that makes that right. You've got to be a bit selfish, mum. Think about yourself and what you want. Me and Bex will always be there, whether you like it or not!"

Mum laughs. It's a bit teary, but it's a laugh.

"And I'll help you. Mum." It feels like we're setting off on a voyage, like the explorers of old, leaving everything we know behind us and setting sail for the unknown.

"You already have, Jamie. I don't think you know how much."

"That's what I'm for," I shrug theatrically, already fearing that the Earth might be flat after all and I'm charting a course over the edge. "Anyway, here's the latest: dad's picking me up at six and we're going out. I'll see how things are with Bex. It might be better if you're out when he gets here."

"Where should I go?"

Her question is so plaintive and so little, it makes me hurt. Think, brain, think.

"How's your new bank account?"

"The card arrived this morning. Why?"

"Then here's what you're going to do: you're going to go to

Tesco's and you're going to buy some nice food for tomorrow, and maybe a good DVD and when I get back, We'll watch it and then when Bex gets back tomorrow, we'll have a really nice, family dinner. That's why. Because we're still a family and you're still the most important person in it."

"Thank you, Jamie." She starts to well up, so I go to her, sitting on the arm of the chair, my arms awkwardly around her, my head resting on hers.

"Shut up with the crying, mum," I say, gently. She cries because she needs to. I sit there and hold her until she's all cried out.

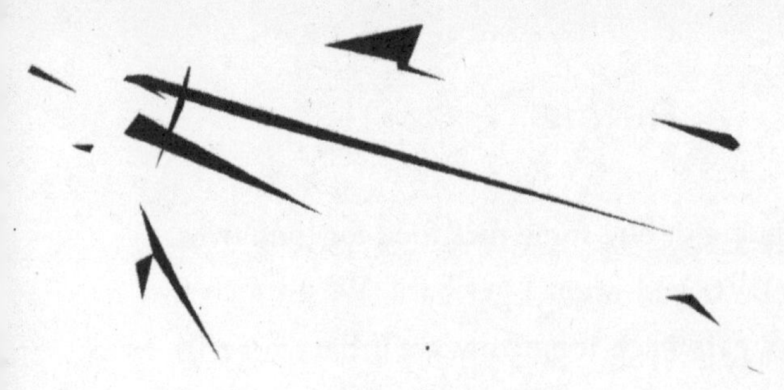

Thirty-Eight

Something Missing

Five thirty-six and I'm alone. Mum's gone to the supermarket and I'm pacing the lounge: twelve steps forward, twelve steps back.

The last remains of the hangover have been usurped by something else: nervousness.

I'm nervous.

But why? It's only dad.

But the dad I've got to know since The Night Everything Went Weird isn't the dad I knew as kid; the dad I knew when I was Becky's age. That dad was huge; he was enormous. That dad held the world above his head and did it because he loved us. No other reason.

It's like *that* dad shed his skin, writhed out of it and

metamorphosed into something different; something made of sinews and twists and turns, and something else that I can't quite identify.

I look at the clock on the wall. Twenty minutes to go.

The pacing stops. I'm beside the drinks cabinet.

My hand strays to the cabinet handle and my nose is filled with the heady perfume of alcohol spills embedded into wood. I stand, looking at the bottles: some half-drunk, some untouched and some with sugar-encrusted growths below the caps.

Would my stomach take it? Just a quick slug? Just something to get me through tonight and that's it? Never again?

My stomach and throat don't like the idea.

I sit, cross-legged on the floor, staring at the various boozes as though waiting instruction.

What am I doing?

I'm waiting for my dad.

Why do I need a drink to do that?

I need it because things might not go according to plan, because there might be confrontation. There might be raised voices. He might want me to put my boxing gloves on again. Because Bex'll be there.

Because I'm scared that I might turn out to be like him.

The doorbell rings and the blood drains from my face.

He's here.

Trembling, I get up and open the front door. I look into the face of one of my possible futures.

"Hallo, son."

He looks different somehow. It's not the smile; I've seen that a million times in my life. It's something to do with his eyes. He looks for it over my shoulder in the hallway; probably to see if mum's there. He looks at me but it's like he's probing, testing for weakness and looking for a way in.

This is what I'm scared of, that he'll get inside my head and that everything I think I know about right and wrong won't make sense anymore. That there'll be reasons for why he did what he did; reasons that will slink, snake and coil around my brain and make things muddy.

Am I like him?

He hit mum. That's wrong. There are no reasons that make that right.

As if he hears that thought or sees something change in my face, the probing stops. The smile's still there, as if nothing's happened, but his eyes back off in a flutter of blinks. I know that the testing isn't over. Somewhere in the back of his head, he's collating whatever information he's just picked up, getting it ready to try again from a different angle.

"Shall we?" Dad nods to the still-running car. Instinctively, I go to the front passenger side and open the door. Bex grins back at me.

Something Missing

"I'm in the front, today!" she laughs. "You've got to go in the back!"

"But mum says you ought to go in the back, Bex," I say. "It's safer."

"Well, not today!" dad chips in, from behind the steering wheel. He looks at me, but I know he's talking to my little sister. "This is Daddy Time, isn't it? And if daddy says it's OK, then it's OK."

Those eyes are so blue, flaring and daring me to challenge him. I don't. I get in the back like a good little boy.

"Good lad," dad says, pulling the handbrake off. "How do you fancy a curry?"

Becky's favourite. I can't decide if he's being nice or if there's a ploy buried in there somewhere.

"Fine by me." I inject my words with a hefty dose of cheeriness and hope it sounds authentic.

We drive to the restaurant and, although he talks to Becky in his soft, familiar daddy voice, he doesn't say a word to me. I can see him looking in the rear-view mirror, flicking glances my way; glances full of masked frustration, second guesses and that thing I haven't got a name for yet – that something I'm missing. I see that in there too.

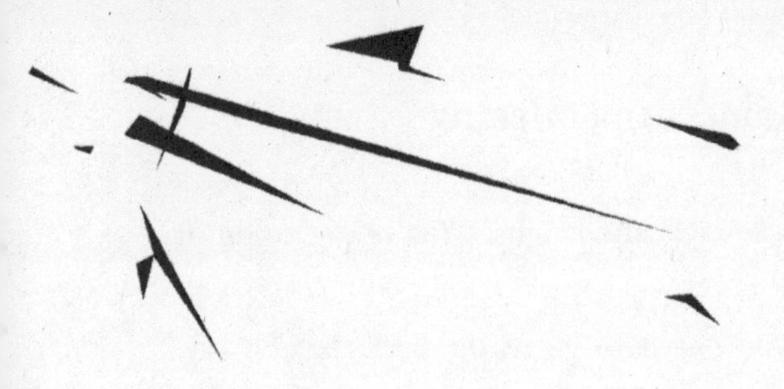

Forty-Nine

Not a Game

The restaurant is far from full. It's ten past six. I suppose it's a bit early yet, but the coward in me is silently glad for the three couples eating at their tables. If there are people around, there won't be any shouting.

We squeeze between empty chairs and sit at a small, round table. Various Hindu gods smile down at me, from picture frames on the walls. A flute and a sitar play through discreet speakers.

"Good evening." A waiter appears – suited and booted – three menus cradled against his chest. He puts them on the table, in front of us and produces a small notebook and pencil. "Would you like some drinks while you make up your minds?"

"I think so," dad nods. "What beers have you got?"

"Singha, Tiger and Kingfisher by the bottle. We have Heineken on tap."

"I'll have a Heineken."

"A pint, sir?"

"Please."

"Excellent. And what about the young lady?"

"What would you like to drink, Bex?" dad asks. "Lemonade? Coke?"

My heart starts racing. There's too much blood in my face. Too hot, I'm too hot. My heart's in my throat; thumping, thumping, thumping and then it thumps words out of my mouth. They're too loud and too fast and I can't quite catch my breath, but I say them. I say them and I look dad in the eyes.

"She can't have lemonade, dad. Or Coke. Mum says."

A smile slides across his face, unblinking. Snakes don't blink. He sits back in his seat and turns to my sister.

"What would *you* like, Becky?" he asks her. His voice is pleasant and deliberate, but he can't help himself. A quick look flashes my way and, in an instant, I know he's testing me again.

Becky looks at me, then at dad, unsure of what to say or do.

"She should have water," I say, taking the decision from her.

Then, I take it from dad. I don't mean to, it just happens. In slow motion, I turn to the waiter.

"A glass of water for my little sister, please."

"Very good, sir."

Dad's smile broadens, showing teeth. He nods a nod that's below anyone else's radar but mine.

"And what about you, Jamie? You're sixteen, now. You can have a glass with your meal. What about a belated birthday drink with your old dad?"

There's so much challenge in his voice, it almost knocks me back.

"A beer?" he continues. "A glass of wine? Come on, Jamie: what does the Man of the House want to drink for his birthday?"

I'm so light-headed. The adrenaline makes everything too real. I want some distance. I want to be away from here. I want to leave it all behind.

I don't want to be like him.

"Water," I croak. "I'll have a glass of water. With ice, please."

"Certainly, sir. Water with ice."

"He really knows how to enjoy himself," dad jokes with the waiter as he goes.

No one says anything. Dad looks at me and then Becky, that sideways smile sliding around his face. Still hanging onto the table, just to feel attached to something, I break the awkwardness.

"So, Bex . . . Had a good day?"

"We've had a great day, haven't we, Becky?" He's off again, taking control, steering the conversation just the way he wants it to be.

Bex nods, her head toing and froing between us like she's watching a tennis match.

"And what have you been doing? I ask airily. It's all very well dad answering for her, but I want to know that she's OK.

"We went to a pet shop," she announces, suddenly. "Daddy's going to buy me two rabbits!"

"That's nice." I throw in a cheery nod, just to keep things light.

"A boy one and a girl one. Then there'll be little, tiny babies!"

"Wow!" I gasp, theatrically. "D'you think that Aunty Hannah's dogs are going to be OK with that?"

"We're not buying them *yet*," she replies. "We're getting them when daddy gets his new house and I go and live with him."

All other sound in the room is suddenly gone: the sitar, the flute, the chatter from other tables. All I can hear are my little sister's words ricocheting around my ear drums. There's a split-second flash of jealousy that I'm not included in these plans; that I'm not considered worthy enough of rabbits or being asked to live in a new house, but then I spot what this is. Drive a wedge into the herd and pick them off as individuals – bite-sized chunks.

Dad's still smiling, but the smile is slipping a little, revealing what's hiding behind it. Now I can see what it is, that little something that I keep missing – it's fear.

Fear of not being in charge.

Fear of losing everything.

Fear of failure.

Fear of not being able to bear the Weight of Manhood.

Like father, like son.

Adil and Mr Khan, Mr Singh and Nadia: they were all absolutely right. You can keep those things hidden away for so long but eventually, they'll start to eat away at you. They'll get bigger and louder and put down roots, until they spread through your system like a weed.

The Weight of Manhood isn't 127,400 Newtons at all.

It's as heavy or as light as you make it.

It's not even about being a man or a woman or anything in between; it's about being alive, about being who you are and about trying to be the best person you can be. Part of that is sharing the load and letting people know when you're down and when they can help.

All you've got to do is talk to someone.

It's that simple. So simple, it makes me laugh. Out loud. In a restaurant.

Now I've started, I can't stop. Bex is looking at me, eyes wide with bewilderment, and then she starts laughing too.

"Your drinks. Are you ready to order?"

The waiter's there, putting our drinks on the table and it's the funniest thing I've ever seen. The more I try to keep a lid on it, the funnier it gets, so I don't. I just laugh, not caring who's looking or listening or about the tears rolling down my cheeks or the pain in my stomach. I'm letting it all out, taking the lid off and popping the cork.

"Jamie. Jamie."

Dad doesn't get it. Through the blur of hysteria, I can see he just doesn't get it. He's scared of it. He doesn't know what it means. Everything he says, thinks and does is guided by 127,400 Newtons of unshared fears and bottled-up emotions, which he just can't carry but is too scared to admit it. He's more scared than I am. He's the scaredest man in the world!

"Jamie!" He's angry, now, but I don't care. "Jamie! What do you want to eat?"

Wiping my eyes, I turn to the waiter, who's doing his best to ignore me.

"Nothing," I gasp. "Nothing. I'm fine. We're going. Come on, Bex."

I stagger to my feet and put out a hand for my little sister.

Without a second thought, she takes it and stands up.

I lead her between the empty tables and the silent outrage of the other diners, and on and out through the front door.

"Why are you laughing?" Becky beams.

"Because . . ." I try to catch my breath. "Because it's all going to be OK. We're all going to be OK."

"Does that mean mummy and daddy will stay married?"

No." I crouch down to her level. "No, they'll get divorced,

but that's OK. They'll still love us."

"I don't really want to live with daddy," she says, suddenly looking afraid, as though she's done the wrong thing. "I just said it because he kept saying it. I always want to live with you and mummy."

"I know." I take her in my arms and hold her tight. "I know, and it's OK."

"Jamie! What the hell are you doing?"

Dad's in the street, his face a map of all the places between Angry and Furious.

"I told you," I answer, standing. "We're going home."

"You can go home all you like," he hisses, "but that's my daughter and she's coming with me. Isn't that right Becky?" His question sidewinds across the pavement, heading for my little sister, but I gently push her behind me and deflect it.

"We're going home, dad."

He steps forward: one step, two steps and then a third. My peripheral vision sees his hands twitch into fists.

So does mine.

"She's coming with me." His voice is low and level. "She's still my daughter."

Everything is silent and perfectly still.

My fist tightens.

This is it.

This is the chance to channel all my anger and loathing

into one final, deliberate act, and show him that I won't take any more.

That I can stand up for myself.

Do it for mum.

Do it for Bex.

Do it for myself.

I drop my voice to match his, just low enough that Bex can't hear me, but he can.

"And she's still my little sister. I don't need to bribe her with bunnies because this isn't a game. You don't win it. She's not a prize, dad. She's a little girl who needs you to start acting like her father, which is going to mean doing things you don't want to and won't like, but if she's as important to you as you seem to be telling her, you'll do them. Because that's what dads do."

The fists open and close, balled tight and shaking.

There's a moment.

My fist relaxes, opens.

Not through fear, but because I make a choice.

My choice.

My choice to let 127,400 Newtons go.

"You could," I murmur, nodding to his hands. "You could. I'd fall over and that would be that, except it wouldn't. You'd stop being her dad. Instead you'd be the man who punched her brother. That's all you'd be remembered as. And I know that because you hit mum. And I can't forget that. Maybe I'll learn to forgive it but, until that day comes, you're the man who hit my mother. That's going to hurt me more than anything you can do with your hands. It already does, but I'm going to sort that out."

My father's eyes tighten and his nose wrinkles, as though he's just smelt something bad.

"You don't know what you're talking about," he sneers. But he doesn't reach for Bex and he doesn't try and persuade her to go with him. Instead, he turns and walks back to the car and relief takes hold of my body, sending trembles through every part.

A little hand squeezes mine because that's what hands are for.

"Where's daddy going?"

"He's going back to Auntie Hannah's, Bex. He's going to try and think how he can try and make things better for all of us."

Because that's what I would do.

"Are we going home?"

"Yup."

"But it's a long way and I'm tired."

"What about a piggyback?"

"All the way?"

"As far as I can anyway."

I squat down and she climbs onto my back. Groaning, I haul myself to my feet.

"God, you're heavy!"

"Why don't you ring mummy and she can come and get us?"

"You know what? That's a good idea. But, before I ring mum, I need to send a message."

"Who to? Your girlfriend?"

"Something like that."

As I walk, I manage to pull out my mobile phone.

Nadia or Adil?

Nadia.

I'm going to tell her everything, in proper, sober detail, from The Night Everything Went Weird until right now. I'm not going to dump it on her shoulders, all at once; that wouldn't be right.

Same goes for Adil. I owe him honesty, if nothing else, but I don't think he needs 127,400 Newtons' worth of it. One Newton at a time.

I put my phone back in my pocket. I'm not going to send a text yet. I'll see them at school on Monday. We can talk then, if they're willing. I'll give them the rest of weekend off; they could probably use it.

Something dad said suddenly pinballs out of nowhere and bounces around my head. Something he said when mum suggested they saw a counsellor. What was it?

"I don't need to talk about my problems." That was it.

I thought something similar when Mrs Beattie suggested I go and see the school counsellor.

Mrs Beattie was never a twat.

She was right and Adil was right. It's that simple. All I need to do is start talking about my problems.

Even that thought makes me feel a bit lighter. Maybe I just took a few Newtons off the Weight of Manhood. Deep down, I know that the Weight of Manhood doesn't really exist. It's just the Weight of Being and it's different for all of us.

I don't have to be 'a man' or 'manly' or whatever; I just have to get on with the job of being me, whatever that turns out to be.

So, what's the Weight of Being Jamie?

At this moment, it's roughly 19.9kg of six-year-old sister, squealing and giggling on my back.

That much, I can carry.

THE END

ACKNOWLEDGEMENTS

I'd like to say a huge and heartfelt thanks to my agent, Jenny, for always steering me in the right direction. I'd also like to thank Hazel and the talented bunch at UCLan Publishing, for making this book the best version of itself.

AUTHOR BIOGRAPHY

Andy Robb is the author of the *Geekhood* books, the first of which was shortlisted for the *Waterstones Children's Book Award.* He's had many jobs over the years, most notably as an actor working on stage and screen but now spends his time writing on his house boat on the Thames; occasionally stopping to feed the ducks.

HAVE YOU EVER WONDERED HOW BOOKS ARE MADE?

UCLan Publishing are based in the North of England and involve BA Publishing and MA Publishing students from the University of Central Lancashire at every stage of the publishing process.

BA Publishing and MA Publishing students are based within our company and work on producing books as part of their course – some of which are selected to be published and printed by UCLan Publishing. Students also gain first-hand experience of negotiating with buyers, conceiving and running innovative high-level events to leverage sales, as well as running content creation business enterprises.

Our approach to business and teaching has been recognised academically and within the publishing industry. We have been awarded Best Newcomer at the Independent Publishing Guild Awards (2019) and a *Times* Higher Education Award for Excellence and Innovation in the Arts (2018).

As our business continues to grow, so too does the experience our students have upon entering UCLan Publishing.

To find out more, please visit
www.uclanpublishing.com/courses/

RESOURCES

If you or someone you know is facing some of the issues that Jim has faced, you might find you need someone to talk to. Below are a list of charities and organisations in the UK where you can find out more. Please note that contact information is correct at time of publication.

Refuge. For women and children. Against domestic violence.
www.refuge.org.uk/ 0800 2000 247

NSPCC (National Society for the Prevention of Cruelty to Children)
www.nspcc.org.uk/keeping-children-safe/talking-drugs-alcohol/underage-drinking/ 0808 800 5000

drinkaware
www.drinkaware.co.uk/advice/support-services/alcohol-support-services/ 0300 123 1110
(weekdays 9am -8pm, weekends 11am -4pm)

AL-ANON FAMILY GROUPS UK & EIRE
www.al-anonuk.org.uk/ 0800 0086 811